I0719885

RUINED

SPARROW AND THE MAFIA KINGS

BOOK 2

MAGGIE ALABASTER

TRIGGER WARNINGS

Hi lovely reader. This book contains darker themes.

Assault
> Abuse
>
> Violence
>
> Mentions of sexual assault
>
> Mentions of child death

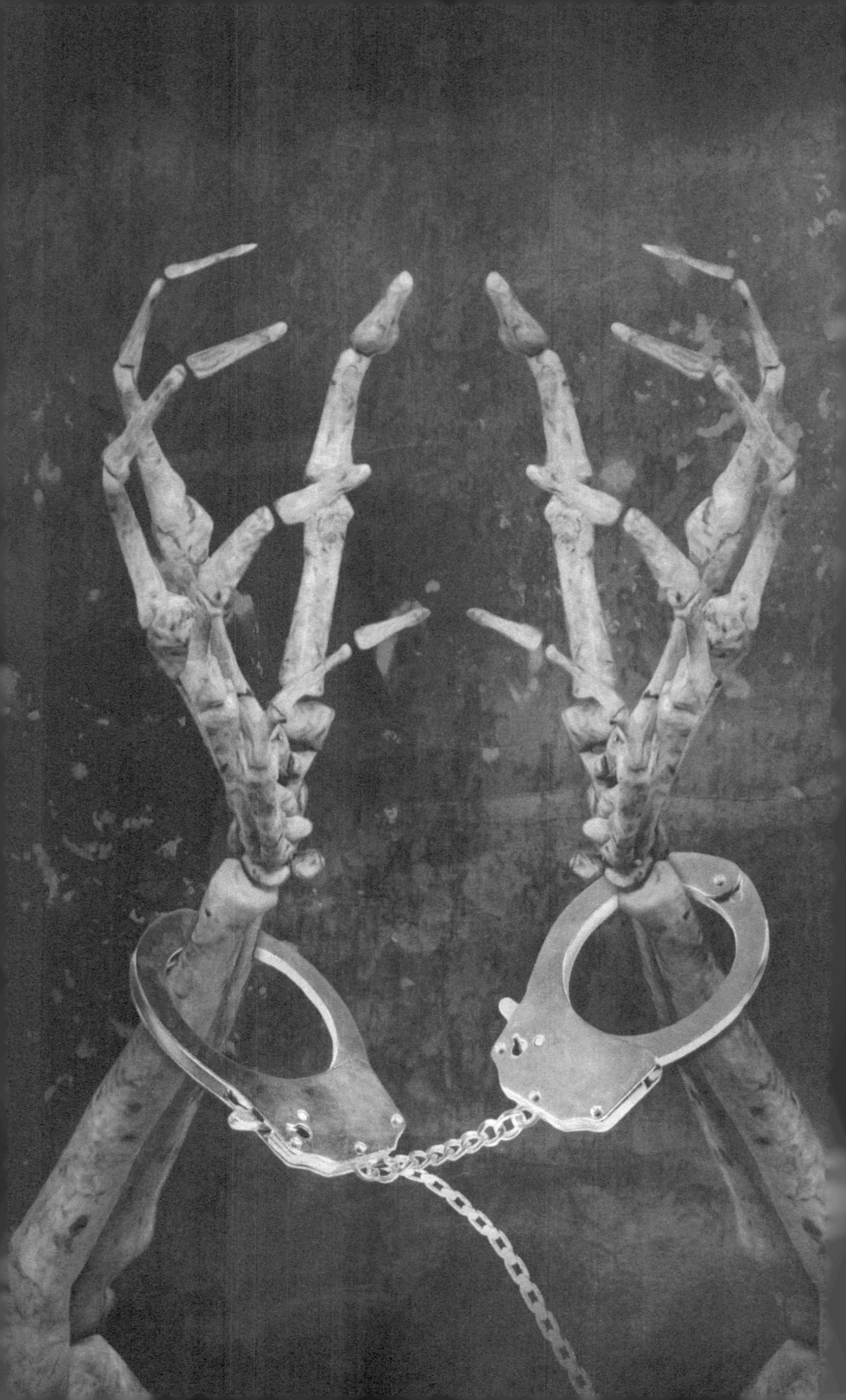

CHAPTER 1

MINA

The dream was always the same.

I stepped through the darkness, silent as a ghost.

The layout of the house was seared into my memory. I'd gone over the map more times than I could count, making sure it was embedded tight. Every room, every door, every corridor.

The only variable was the placement of furniture, and that was predictable. The couch under the window, dining table near the kitchen. 'Standard for today's living,' as those home design shows on TV called it.

The room where my target should be sleeping was at the other end of the house.

Some people in my line of work like to wake up their targets before they kill them. I didn't. It was a waste of time, and added another unknown variable to the situation. The target might wake quickly and set off some kind of alarm. Worse than that, they might offer more money than the hit out on them. That created conflict and uncertainty I had no time for.

Once I took a job, I saw it through until the end.

No, they'd never know I was coming.

I placed my gloved hand on the doorknob and started to turn it.

"Who are you?" a voice said behind me.

I turned.

What happened next was always a blur. I don't remember the knife going in, or… much of anything. I went from standing beside the door, to finding myself on the floor, holding the girl until long after she died.

"You shouldn't still be here."

Even in my dream, hearing Kurt's voice, looking up to see him, gave me chills. He loomed over me, dressed like I was, all in black.

"What did you do?" he demanded.

I had no answer. This was not what I'd come here for.

"Mina," he hissed. He grabbed my arm and tugged me to my feet. "We need to get the fuck out of here."

I let him pull me to the door and out into the night. The moment the cold air hit my face, I stopped.

"I need to finish what I started." I turned to go back in but froze at the sound of a scream from inside the house.

Kurt's grip tightened on my arm. "Too late." He huffed out a frustrated breath. "You fucked this up. Hell, Mina, you were trained better than this."

"It was an accident." But he was right. I had fucked it up. Badly. I was better than this. I'd never been sloppy before. Never killed anyone who wasn't my target. Especially not…

"Cry about it later," he snapped. "We need to go."

I nodded vaguely and followed him through the dark, to our waiting car. We just got inside when the front of the house lit up. Sirens wouldn't be long.

Kurt started the engine and drove away like we weren't in a hurry. Even if we were seen, we'd soon ditch the car and use another. We'd have to, to be sure we weren't caught.

"What the hell, Mina?" He glanced over at me.

"I don't know," I said, vague and numb. "I don't know what happened." I ran through it in my head, over and over, but all I found was a blank space between her seeing me, and her dying. I didn't remember moving toward her, but obviously I had. Her death was evidence for that.

"I'll tell you what's going to happen next," he said. "The Sparrow is going to have to disappear for a while. We'll put it out there that someone else was behind this tonight. With any luck, they'll buy it. Fortunately, at least one of us did the job they were there for tonight." He lifted a hand from the steering wheel and rubbed his chin.

I pressed myself down, smaller against the seat. I'd had a bad feeling about this job from the start. I was used to working alone. Kurt was there to hack into the computer system and get some information. I was there to take out my target.

I'd failed.

"We'll get past this," he said. His voice was a fraction milder now, his attempt to soothe me after what I'd done. Him and me against the world. That was what he wanted.

We were never going to happen. Not like that. He was too short-tempered and aggressive for my taste. Too much of a hothead. I preferred men who weren't rash and snappy. Sooner or later, he'd realise I meant it when I said I wasn't interested. Not in him.

Not in anyone except the one man who was completely out of my league. There was no way he'd look twice at me, but my heart ignored my attempts to tell it that. Either way, Kurt Lasalle wasn't my future.

"Are you listening?" Kurt snapped, reminding me again why I should keep my distance from him.

"Yeah," I lied. I'd tuned him out for the last couple of minutes.

"Good, then we understand each other. You know why I need to do what I need to do next."

———

"Mina?"

I awoke so violently, I almost threw myself off the side of the bed. The covers were tangled around my legs. My body was slick with sweat. I wasn't in the car with Kurt, and I wasn't chained in a filthy cage in a dank basement.

The mattress underneath me was comfortable, the room clean and tidy. Like everything else in Reuben Brantley's house.

It took a moment to register that someone else spoke. I wasn't alone.

As if he knew he occupied a place on the edge of my dream, Reuben sat on the side of the bed. He was dressed only in a pair of black, silk pyjama pants. The early morning light that slipped between the curtains illuminated the frown etched on his brow.

"You were dreaming," he said. "Or having a nightmare."

I pushed myself up to sit back against the pillows. "I'm sorry if I woke you."

"You didn't." He rested his weight on the palm of his hand, and made no move to touch me.

He seemed to know when I'd be more likely to freak out. Clearly uncomfortable at the prospect, he held himself back, more tightly controlled than usual. Which was saying something, given how controlled he generally was.

"I was already awake," he added.

I glanced at the clock on the bedside table. One of those old-fashioned ones with an analog face and little feet.

"It's not even six o'clock in the morning yet." My eyes lingered on the grooves of his abs and the light sprinkling of hair on his chest. Unless he had one hidden under his pants, he had no tattoos. That didn't surprise me. There weren't too many people he'd trust to go anywhere near him with a needle. Besides, his body was a work of art without one.

"Is it?" he asked. "The day is half over then."

I snorted softly. He wasn't given to joking overtly, but he had a sense of humour, even if he wouldn't admit to it.

"Do you want to talk about it?" he asked quietly. Like everything else about him, his voice was under-stated and controlled. I wasn't sure if he knew how to shout, even if he was inclined to. He didn't need to. If Reuben Brantley spoke, people listened.

"I don't remember it," I lied.

Parts of it were vague, like they always were. The bits that lingered in my memory… I couldn't explain. Not yet. I wanted to. I *needed* to. But I needed to find Kurt first and kill him. Before that, I couldn't risk Reuben not understanding what happened that night.

Then there was the additional concern that he might not want an assassin living under his roof. No, his response was a variable I couldn't control, even though he made it clear how he felt about me. That I was his.

I was sure he must see right through me, into my thoughts, but he nodded.

"I can have a therapist come to the house," he offered. "A discreet one."

I appreciated his offer. I even considered it. Five

years of being chained up, tortured and used, would fuck anyone up. Five years of dwelling on what happened that night and being so sure I deserved everything Kurt did to me.

I fought him at first, or at least, I tried to. Between the chain, the cage, the lack of food and guilt, fighting was difficult. Once I realised it got him going, I stopped. All he got from me were occasional bouts of anger or frustration. Most of the time, all I really wanted was to die so it could end.

"I'll think about it," I said.

He rolled his lips a couple of times. "You can talk to me anytime. There's nothing you could say that would shock me." A hint of a smile played around the corners of his mouth. "Bear in mind, I've had nineteen years of listening to the twins. I'm desensitised to shock value."

That got a smile from me.

"I'll bet. They seem to get great pleasure from trying to push the buttons of everyone around them."

"Especially mine," Reuben agreed. "Lucky for them they're both useful. Otherwise, I wouldn't keep them around."

"They would say otherwise," I said. "They'd probably say you keep them around because you love them or something." I couldn't resist the gentle tease.

"They *would* say that," he said. "I'll neither confirm nor deny the accusation."

He wouldn't, but I was certain he loved his brothers, and that was reciprocated. It was hard not to like

Hunter and Parker. They could charm the pants off almost anyone. Anyone but me. They were also too wild and hotheaded for my taste.

Reuben placed a hand on mine and laced our fingers together. "I understand how difficult it is for you to trust anyone. Between our lifestyle and what that asshole did to you, I don't blame you for being guarded. Anyone would be. I hope someday you can come to trust me."

"I want that too," I said softly.

I knew what he was asking. It wasn't just about trust. He knew I was keeping secrets and he'd prefer I tell him before he found out some other way.

I'd do whatever I could to make sure he didn't find out from anyone else. As far as I knew, the only person alive who knew what I was, was Kurt. That was another on a long list of reasons why he needed to die. Not only because he might tell Reuben, but because he might reveal my identity to the world.

How many people would believe sweet Mina DiMarco was really an assassin?

Perhaps more than I'd like. Once everyone knew, I'd never get another job.

I was anxious to get back to work. I needed the money to help fund the search for Kurt. For that, I'd take on anything.

Almost anything. I'd never take a job that meant killing anyone who lived under this roof. Or any of my family members. Anyone else was fair game.

"Would you care to join me in the gym?" he offered. "I was headed down there when I heard you cry out." He squeezed my hand lightly.

"I'd like that," I said. "I need to build my muscles back up."

After so many years of disuse, I was weaker than I liked to be, my reflexes slightly slower.

I knew from the two people I killed a few weeks ago that I still possessed the ability to take a life, but I wanted my body to be quicker and sharper, like a knife. I had to be able to rely on it as well as any tool. I could not, *would not* screw up again. I needed to be even better than I was five years ago. If they thought the Sparrow was daunting then, they'd seen nothing yet.

"I'll see you down there." He leaned in to swipe his lips over mine.

Electricity crackled between us, so tangible I could almost see it. It could have set the whole city on fire.

He wanted more. If I let him, he'd press me down on the mattress and slide his cock into my pussy. He'd fuck me long and slow and thoroughly. When I was ready, that's what he'd do. As long as it took, he'd wait for me.

If I wasn't careful, I might just fall for him the way he'd already fallen for me.

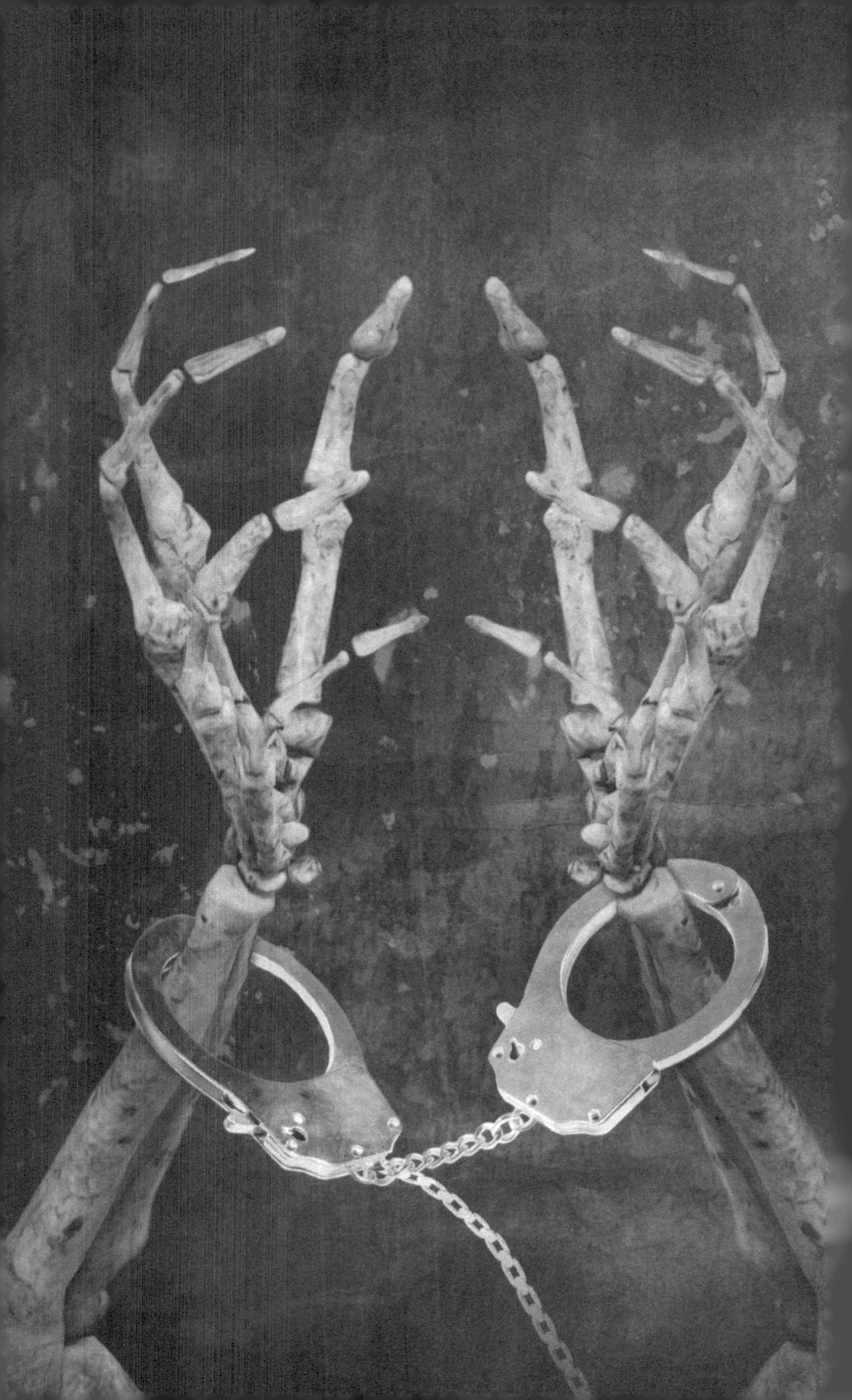

CHAPTER 2

MINA

Damon entered the kitchen, his eyes on his phone. He managed to navigate his way around the chairs and over to the electric kettle, without looking up.

"I know that face," Gianni remarked. He sat beside me, eating fruit loops and sipping coffee.

Damon glanced at him and frowned. "Yeah, it's the same handsome-as-fuck face I've always had."

Gianni grinned. "I meant the expression on your face, but that's true too."

"That he's a fuck face?" I said, deadpan.

Damon scowled at me, but looked over to where Reuben sat watching us while chewing on toast. "You're not going to believe this, boss."

Reuben lowered his toast. "You'd be surprised what I might believe."

Damon shrugged one shoulder to concede the point.

"This might be an exception. The Sparrow is active again."

My heart skipped a beat. I'd expected this conversation. Anticipated it. I was ready with my mask in place.

Sweat still broke out on my hands.

Reuben placed his toast back on his plate. "I believe you, but you're right, I'm not surprised. Just like that?"

"Just like that," Damon agreed. "The notification popped up on my phone sometime in the middle of the night. I've spent the last hour confirming that it's legit. As far as anyone can tell, it is. The Sparrow is operating again."

"Cool," Gianni said around a mouthful of cereal. "Maybe I can meet them this time."

Damon looked over at me, slightly smug. "The Sparrow is—"

"An assassin," I interrupted. Clearly he'd expected I wouldn't know that. "I've heard of them from before."

"Not just any assassin," Gianni said. "One of the best. They could get in anywhere, anytime. If anyone could get in here and take out Reuben, it would be them."

Reuben arched an eyebrow. "You might be over-stating slightly. However, that's reasonably accurate. The Sparrow had impressive skills." He turned to Damon. "Is there any chance it's someone else stepping into the role?"

Damon placed his phone down on the kitchen island and poured himself a coffee.

"After all this time? Why now? It's been years. If someone was going to take on their persona, wouldn't they have done it by now?"

"They might have been honing their skills," Gianni suggested. "It would take a lot of work and practice to be that good."

"I'm still not convinced it's one person." Damon leaned back against the kitchen counter top, his long fingers curled around his mug.

"What makes you think that?" I asked. "Maybe they were just that good." I was, apart from that one major fuck up, but I was interested in his theory.

"It would take more than one person to break in here," he reasoned. "They couldn't just walk through the door."

I'd done exactly that, because they brought me here after they found me in Kurt's basement. Of course, that wasn't what he meant, but still. Knowing how wrong he was gave me a certain, possibly petty, satisfaction.

"Some people suggested the Sparrow was dead," Gianni said, but his tone was dismissive. Clearly he didn't think so. "If that's the case, maybe one died and it took this long to find someone else good enough."

"You don't believe that," I said. "What do you think happened?" How well had Kurt and my father covered my mistake? Well enough to avoid rumours?

Gianni shrugged. "They could have gone on a really long holiday."

"It's possible their cover was compromised," Reuben

said. "Or they thought it was going to be. They might have thought it wise to step back and let things blow over. And now, apparently, they have."

Damon was watching me intently over his coffee mug. "What do you think happened?"

I tapped the tip of my finger on the table top and frowned while I thought. "If I was an assassin, why would I disappear for years?"

"You don't have to—" Gianni started.

"It's okay." I couldn't avoid talking about it forever. "Kurt ran when he was found out, before you could get to him. It's possible that happened to the Sparrow too. They thought someone was coming after them. Or maybe someone turned on them. Forced them to hide out. Or they made a mistake."

I tried not to look as if I was searching for information in their responses. Some sign of what they knew, or thought they knew.

"This is all conjecture," Reuben said. "Whatever the reason, they're active and we can make use of them. If anyone can find Kurt, it's the Sparrow. I prefer he be found alive, but if that isn't possible, dead will have to do." He nodded to Damon, who picked up his phone and tapped on the screen.

"I've sent the message," Damon said after a minute or two. He lowered his phone back down again. "I'll let you know when I hear back."

Reuben picked up his toast and went back to eating. "Gianni, in two days time I want you and Mina to go to

Dusk Bay to see Daisy Lasalle. Try to find out if Kurt has made contact in any way. If he has, I want to know. And see if he has a twin named Frank."

"You don't think she's working with him behind our back?" Gianni asked.

"No, I don't," Reuben agreed. "But someone who works for her might be. Keep your eyes peeled. Someone out there knows where he is. Sooner or later, they'll make a mistake and we'll be there to deal with them. In the meantime, keep reminding everyone I don't tolerate people operating behind my back. If any of them think they can get away with it, we'll remind them they can't. Painfully or fatally, whichever is appropriate."

I loved it when he got authoritative like that. My clit throbbed in appreciation.

"Got it, boss," Gianni said. "Consider everyone threatened. If I was working against you, I'd be shaking in my shoes right now."

"If you were working against me, you'd have a bullet in your brain," Reuben said.

"Courtesy of me," Damon said.

"Lucky for all of us I'm not," Gianni said. "Especially Damon. He'd really, really hate to have to kill me." He winked at me.

"I'd hate to have to use up a perfectly good bullet," Damon said dryly.

"He'd cry over my grave." Gianni grinned.

"You said 'dance' wrong," Damon said.

"You dance?" I asked.

"No, but I'd make an exception for his grave." The sides of Damon's mouth twitched up in a hint of a smile. As far as I could tell, that was his equivalent of a grin.

"He really does adore me," Gianni said. "We'll probably be buried in adjoining graves. Side-by-side. In death as we were in life."

Damon grimaced. "Remind me to change my will so it says I have to be buried on the other side of Sydney."

"That's still close enough for me to haunt your dead ass," Gianni said.

I exchanged glances with Reuben, who looked amused at their banter.

"It's like having the twins around, but they're older," he said wryly.

I choked back a laugh.

"I think I'll have it revised to say I need to be buried on the other side of the *world* from all of you," Damon said, smirking at us.

"That sounds lonely," I said.

"It sounds quiet," he insisted.

"Quiet is overrated," Gianni remarked.

"No, it's not," Reuben said. "Damon might have a point."

"Says the man who has a family mausoleum that's nice and quiet," Gianni said.

Reuben shrugged, but looked smug.

I didn't much care what happened to me after I was

dead, as long as no one haunted me. Then I'd be pissed off. Honestly, my life was haunted enough now as it was. By Kurt and by that girl.

"Where are my parents buried?" I asked. It hadn't occurred to me to wonder until now.

"On the other side of the city," Reuben said. "Did you want to pay them a visit?"

"We could dance on your father's grave," Gianni offered.

I thought for a moment before shaking my head. "No. I was just curious. My brothers and sister, how did they react? Were they upset? Did they know what happened?"

"All three of your siblings know your parents killed my parents," Reuben said softly. "I told them myself. They had the option of joining your parents or staying the hell out of my way. Rose works for me once in a while, but otherwise they took the second option. I didn't want to have to kill any of them."

"Why?" I asked. He didn't seem reluctant to kill, when and wherever necessary.

He gave me a lingering look in response.

"You thought someday I'd come back and I wouldn't forgive you for killing them?" I guessed.

He really had thought of me a lot more than I would have expected him to. Thinking he was out of my league seemed silly, now I was looking back at the past. What would have happened if I'd gone to him when I had the chance? He might have saved me from going through hell.

No, there was no 'might' about it. He would have.

"I hoped you'd come back. If what your father said about you being married and living in the suburbs was true, I would have kept my peace, but this is your place."

He gestured around himself and the house. "If your siblings chose to make trouble, I would have done what I had to. But not without considering the potential consequences."

"The only one who looks like he has any potential of causing trouble is Dane," Damon said. "He's ambitious and he's always looking for a way in. He'd be right here at the table, if he could, but none of us would turn our backs on him."

"I wouldn't turn my back on him either," I said. For a while, I'd wondered if Dane knew what I was. It was possible he did and thought the Sparrow was inactive because I was living life as a suburban wife and mother.

That thought gave me a moment of panic. If he knew I was active again, he might wonder why. He might come looking for me.

Let him try. He probably wouldn't think to look for me here. If he did, he wouldn't get past the front door without me knowing. I'd have plenty of time to make myself scarce. No one would enlighten him unless I wanted them to. Someday I would, but not yet. Not until Kurt was dealt with.

"Family are the people you choose," Gianni said, his eyes intent on me.

"That's deep," Damon said.

"It's true though." Gianni was unruffled. "You three are family to me. More than anyone I'm related to by blood. The twins too. They're more like my younger brothers. Except my actual younger brothers are assholes."

"Does that mean I'm like a sister?" I teased.

I remembered the way his cock felt in my hand, running my fingers up and down his length and over his Jacob's ladder. The way he came in my hand. The way his cum tasted when I licked my fingers clean. Yeah, there was nothing sisterly about it.

"I hope not," Gianni said. "Because if we're related, I'm in all kinds of trouble. There's nothing brotherly about the things I want to do to you." In a loud whisper he added, "I don't want to do brotherly things to Damon either."

I glanced over to see Damon's reaction. His face was as tightly masked as ever, but his eyes darkened slightly.

In the corner of my eye, I caught Reuben watching us, his whole body rigid. I knew he wanted me, but he spent a lot of time with these guys. Did it go beyond work and brotherhood? If it hadn't, could it?

A shiver of heat passed through me at the idea of these men kissing each other, touching each other. For a few moments, I let my imagination run wild.

Finally, Reuben cleared his throat. "Gianni, make the arrangements to travel to Dusk Bay. Don't let Daisy know you're coming, or anyone else there. I'd rather catch them unaware. If they have anything to hide, we'll find out sooner if they're not expecting you."

"Got it, boss," Gianni said. "If they're up to something, we'll bust it wide open."

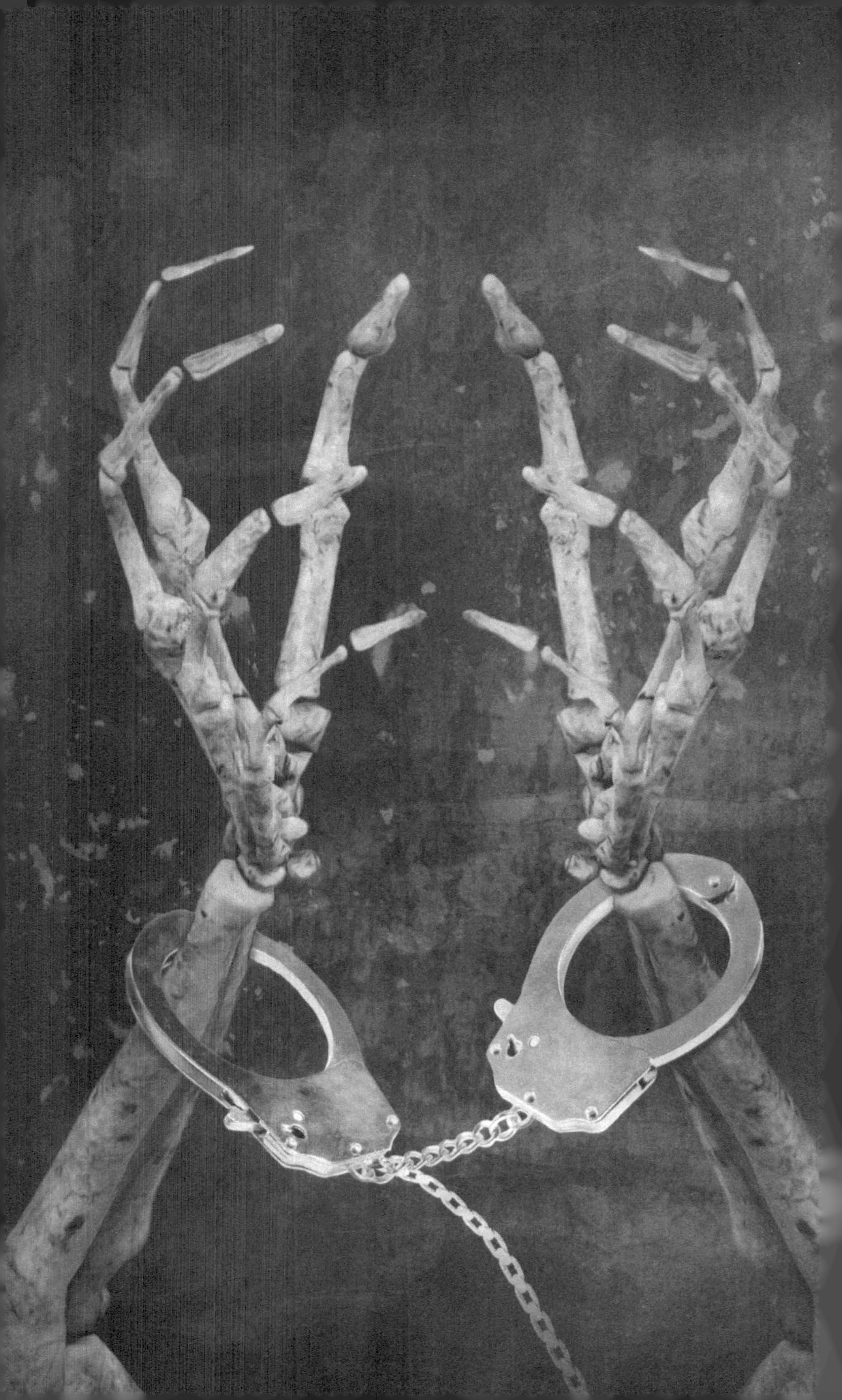

CHAPTER 3

MINA

"I had no idea Reuben owned a private jet." I trailed my fingers along the back of a seat before lowering myself onto the soft leather.

Gianni flopped sideways onto the seat facing me, feet dangling into the aisle.

He grinned. "When he realised Zeke and his band were still flying commercial, he bought this bad boy." He patted the leather beside his thigh. "No one said he couldn't be petty once in a while."

I was smiling as I fastened my seatbelt. "So he bought this to get one up on his brother? Does he ever let him use it?"

Gianni sat around and clicked in his own seatbelt. "There's only one way he'd let Zeke fly in this. If he quits the band and comes back to the family."

"Where would he fit in?" I adjusted the armrest and propped my elbow. "I mean, he wouldn't take the place of you or Damon."

"Fuck no," Gianni agreed. "No one could replace us. Zeke is a good guy, but he's not going to go around crashing SUVs, or killing on Reuben's orders."

"Then why does Reuben want him to come back so badly?" I asked.

"Because he's family." Gianni shrugged. "He's also good-looking and charismatic. Everything I'm not. He could talk people into doing things without needing to threaten them. By the time they realised what was going on, he'd be long gone."

"I can see the value of that," I said. "What about Asher? Does Reuben want him to return to the fold?"

"He'd be welcome, if he brought Zeke back with him. As far as I can tell, they're a package deal. You can't get one without the other."

"That sounds like them," I said. It didn't seem like that changed at all since I was away.

"Also," Gianni continued, "if you wanted Reuben to welcome Asher, he'd do it. Rose or Dane too."

I wrinkled my nose. "Dane would love that. He'd do everything he could to make himself Reuben's right-hand. Or better yet, his heir."

Gianni smirked. "That would be an interesting picture. Dane DiMarco, the new head of the Brantley family. Over the twins' dead bodies. Not to mention Caleb, Joshua and Lucas. He better make sure they're good and dead first, or they'd be coming for him."

"I think it's better not to encourage him then," I said.

That would result in a lot of bloodshed. When things escalated, innocent people tended to come under fire.

"If Dane starts to get too big for his boots, Reuben can always have the Sparrow deal with him."

Gianni had glanced out the window as he spoke and missed seeing me twitch in response. Even an assassin had to draw the line somewhere. I drew it at killing my own family, but to avoid all that bloodshed, I may have to consider it.

"I'm sure that won't be necessary," I said, my voice tighter than I intended.

Gianni's gaze swung back to me. "Sorry, I shouldn't make light of killing members of your family. You must miss them."

"I do," I agreed. Seeing my cousin Ric a couple of weeks ago felt surreal. At some point I'd be ready to see my siblings, but right now I had to focus on the job at hand.

"It's better they keep thinking I'm happily living a suburban life for now." The truth was going to shock the hell out of them.

Unless Asher changed a lot since I saw him last, it would rip his heart out. Rose too.

"You mentioned your family," I said carefully. "If you don't want to talk about them…"

He shrugged and steepled his fingers before pressing them to his lips. "My family is Italian. You probably figured it out from the look of this mug." He pointed a finger at his face. "They're up to their eyeballs in mafia shit. They'd prefer I worked with them than Reuben."

"Why don't you?" I asked.

He exhaled, long and slow. "I've never gotten along with them. They…" He searched for the words. "They don't give a shit who they step on to get what they want. They'll happily step on each other. If you can't even trust your family, then who the fuck can you trust?"

"The family you choose," I said.

He grinned behind his fingers. "Exactly. So I choose Reuben, Damon and you. And not them. Lucky for me, they don't live in Australia, for the most part. Also, Reuben was happy to sponsor me to join the Brotherhood."

I grimaced. "I shouldn't be surprised they're still around."

"The Brotherhood of Kings has been around for a few hundred years; they aren't going anywhere anytime soon," Gianni agreed.

"The Brotherhood, owning governments since the dawn of time," I said sarcastically. Although, that was the truth of it. "Are they letting women join yet?"

"Only as fillies." Gianni's smile was teasing, knowing he'd get a rise out of me. No woman was allowed to join the Brotherhood, but they could become a filly, offering sexual favours in the hope of catching the eye of a powerful man. My parents met that way. Reuben's parents too, probably.

I'd never been interested in hunting for a powerful husband, especially after what I heard about the Brotherhood. They tended to hand women around like they were a bag of chocolate pieces, to be shared, used, and degraded.

To me, that seemed like a high price to pay for money and power. As far as I knew, my brother Asher wasn't a member. I wasn't sure about Dane, but if he could join, he would have.

"Misogyny is alive and well I see," I remarked.

"Running the world has to come at a price." He shrugged. "Would it be better to leave it to politicians?"

I snorted. "No, it would be better to leave it to women."

Gianni grinned. "When you become Queen of the world, can I wash your feet?"

I pretended to consider the matter. "I'll think about it. It depends who does it best: you, Damon or Reuben. Or maybe the twins."

Gianni chuckled. "Don't make me kill the twins to keep them from muscling in on my territory."

"The day I'd be interested in either of them..." I shook my head. "They're too young for me anyway."

"They're closer in age to you than you are to me," Gianni pointed out. "Or Reuben, or Damon."

"Just the way I like it," I said lightly. I glanced out the window as we taxied down the runway. "I've always preferred men who have their shit together."

"I've always had a thing for women who know how

to use a knife," Gianni said. "Who don't let the world hold them back. Who stand on their own two feet. The opposite of the kind of women who fraternise with the Brotherhood. Although, every now and again, there'll be a firecracker. I'm mostly there for the parties and world domination."

"World domination does seem to be a good excuse to hang out and get drunk," I said.

"It's the best excuse," he said. "Let other people have good looks and fame, I prefer power and money. Or to be close to it."

"Who says you don't have good looks?" I asked. He'd said several times now that he was the brains or the brawn, while other men were the attractive ones.

"When I was born, my mother cried," he said. He gave me a lopsided grin.

"I don't believe that for a minute," I said. "I think you're cute." He wasn't as classically handsome as Reuben or Damon, but he had his own charm.

"That's the first time anyone has called me cute," he said. He placed his hands in his lap and cocked his head in contemplation. "I think I like it."

"I'm glad you do," I said. "But I'm sure you've been called that before."

"I tend to think that's a word that applies better to you, but we can share." He reached over to take my hand, his smile replaced by earnestness. "Can I confess something?"

My heart skipped a beat at his touch and the expression on his face. Was there a chance he knew what I was and was about to tell me? If it wasn't that, then when was it?

I forced myself to say, "Of course you can." I wasn't oblivious to the fact we were now in the air. He couldn't shoot me, but I couldn't run. Was I strong enough to defend myself against him if I needed to? I'd have to be, if it came down to that. What then? The pilot might have orders to take me to fuck knows where.

He took a deep breath and looked from side to side before locking his gaze back on mine.

"I hate flying," he admitted. "I know, big badass guy like me shouldn't be scared of anything. But we're a long fucking way up and it's a long fucking way down. I hate heights."

I pushed out a breath of relief and reminded myself to be sympathetic. I didn't need him to wonder why I was on the verge of freaking out. Although, the enclosed space around us *was* unnerving. I could always say it reminded me of the cage.

"There's nothing wrong with being scared of heights or flying," I said. "Everyone is scared of something. Heights, snakes, marshmallows."

He looked surprised, then grinned. "Marshmallows?"

"Yeah." I grimaced. "They're all squishy and sticky." I mimed pressing one of them between my thumb and the rest of my fingers. Imagined the way they felt, soft and sugary. Like flesh, but sweet. I couldn't understand why anyone would want to put one of them in their mouth.

"I like sticky." He chuckled.

Of course he did. Our conversations came down to sex more often than not. The memory of slipping my finger between his lips and letting him suck his own cum from my skin made my skin tingle and my clit throb.

I rolled my eyes. "Not that kind of sticky. I just don't like them, okay?"

He held up his hands in surrender. "Noted. If I make you a hot chocolate, I won't put them in."

"And I won't insist you fly anywhere unless Reuben tells you to," I said. "Although, this is a lot more comfortable than flying commercial."

"It really is." He sank back against the seat and crossed his arms. "I should take a selfie and send it to Zeke. Remind him of what he's missing."

"I bet the twins would do that," I said. I pictured them with identical smug grins, taking several photos and bombing their brother with them. Laughing the whole time.

"They definitely would," he agreed. "Anything to get a rise out of anyone. There's nothing they wouldn't do for shits and giggles."

"They haven't changed either," I said. "Sometimes I think five years changed everything and sometimes I think it changed nothing."

"It changed you," he said softly.

I closed my eyes and sighed. "Yes, it did. What he did to me would change anyone."

What would I be like if I hadn't gone through that? Would I be as carefree as Hunter and Parker? Or would I have been fully consumed by the persona of the cold-blooded assassin? Unfeeling and uncaring.

Either way, sweet, innocent little Mina DiMarco was dead. The woman who sat in her place was a lot more ruthless and driven. I wouldn't kill my family, if I could help it, but I'd destroy anyone who got in my way. Anyone who got between me and killing Kurt.

Let their blood coat my hands; I wouldn't feel a thing. Not until I drove that blade through his heart and watched the life drain away from him.

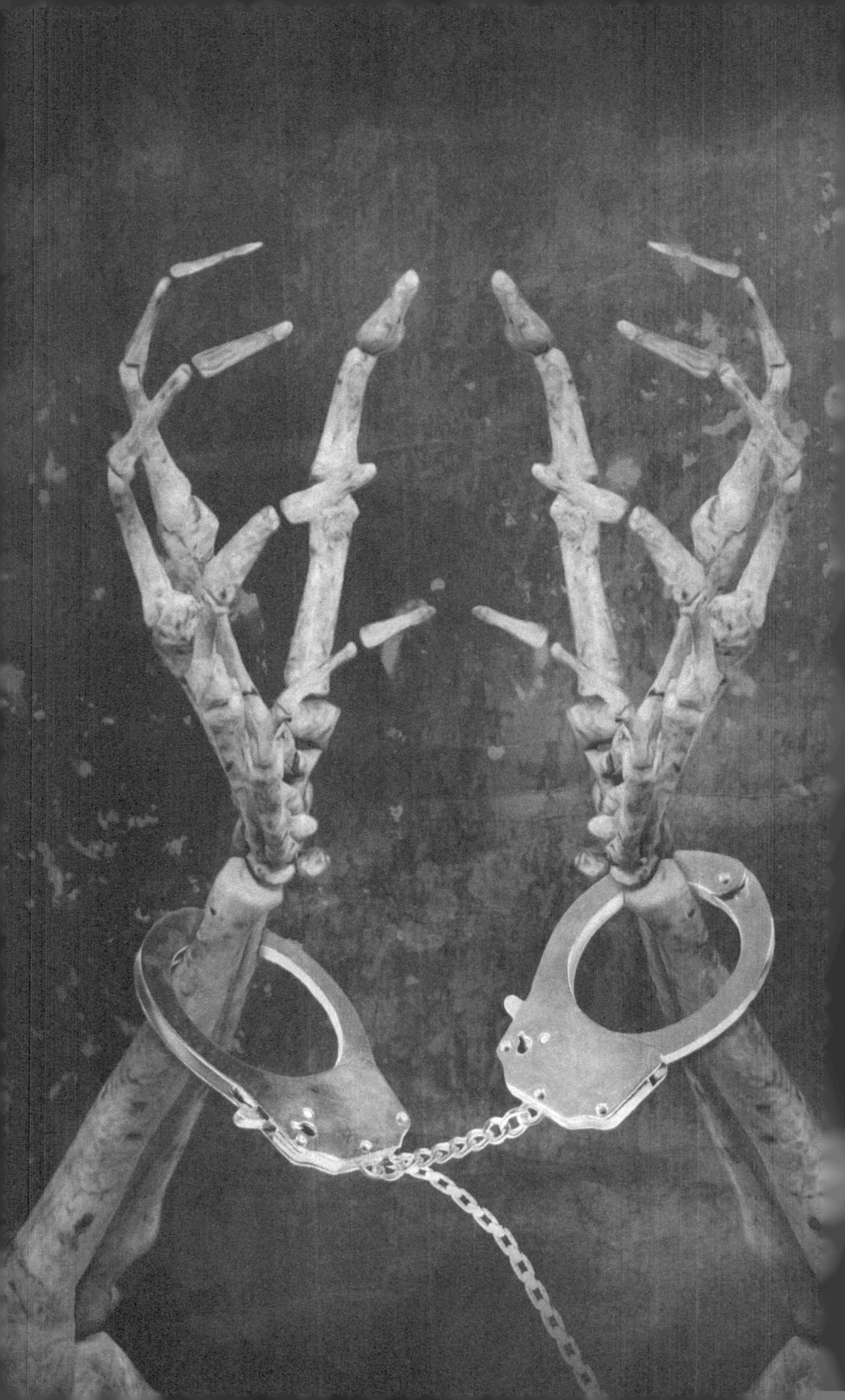

CHAPTER 4

MINA

"Mina." Daze hurried into the room and gave me a hug. If she was disconcerted about Gianni and my sudden appearance, she gave no sign. If anything, she seemed happy to see me.

I hugged her back quickly before stepping away again. Physical contact with another person was still difficult for me. Chances were, it always would be. That was another item on the long list of reasons why I hated Kurt. I wanted to be able to touch, hug and fuck. Not flinch and pull away.

"Sit down." She waved towards a couch in the centre of the room. The walls were lined with bookcases, over-flowing with books.

The mess would give Reuben anxiety, but I found it easier to trust people who had lots of books.

She flopped down beside me. Gianni slipped into a chair opposite.

"What brings you to Dusk Bay? Let me guess, this is about Kurt?" Her smile quickly faded. "We haven't found him. I assume you haven't come to tell me you did?" She looked tentatively hopeful.

"Not exactly." I told her about finding the man who called himself Frank, after the twins followed him from the airport. Her eyes widened when I described the house that exploded just after we stepped out of it.

"Fucking hell," she whispered. "You're right, that sounds like Kurt, but at the same time, it doesn't. He's not usually messy like that. He'd lure you there, then set off a bomb while you were still inside if killing was his end goal. If it was, he swung and missed."

"Twice." I told her about the gunfight on the way home. "Apparently they were sent to tell us to back off from trying to find him."

She snorted loudly. "Good luck with that. None of us is giving up now. I'm guessing Reuben is more pissed off than ever."

"About that and other things," Gianni agreed.

I rubbed my palms together absentmindedly. "Does Kurt have a twin? The man who called himself Frank looked a lot like him."

Daze frowned. "No, he doesn't. We don't have any other siblings. At least, not that I know of. I suppose it's possible we have a half brother, but if we do, his existence was kept from me."

"Who would dare to keep anything from you?" Ric stepped into the room and closed the door behind him.

"Only someone with a death wish." She gave him a fond smile.

He stepped around behind her and started to massage her shoulders. While he worked out her knots, she filled him in on the conversation.

"One Kurt is bad enough," he said. "The world doesn't need two."

"The world doesn't need the one it has," Gianni said.

"We're doing the best we can to rid the world of him," Ric said. "But if he's hiring people to attack Reuben, that's concerning."

"We're starting to think his operation is bigger than first thought," Gianni said. "If he can afford to go around setting off bombs and sending mercenaries after us, then he's doing better than we knew about."

Ric's hands stilled. "That's why—"

The door opened. "This is where you all are.'

I froze like a proverbial deer in headlights when my sister, Rose, stepped through the door. She looked around the room before she noticed me sitting there. Her lips dropped apart.

"Mina?" She blinked a couple of times like I was a mirage that might disappear at any moment.

On unsteady feet, I stood.

"Yes, it's me." My lips moved, but I couldn t think of another thing to say. Then she moved towards me and wrapped her arms around me.

Unlike the hug from Daze, I melted into this one. I put my arms around my older sister and held her firm, like I could have five years worth of embraces in one.

"What in the world are you doing here?" she asked without letting go. "I thought you were…"

"I know what you thought." I rested my head against her shoulder. I'd forgotten how much taller than me she was. I was the shortest in my family, hence the nickname, the Sparrow. I'd always been dainty. I could fit into spaces others couldn't, and sneak around more silently than bigger people. Not to mention, who would suspect a tiny woman of killing people? It was the perfect ruse.

Daze scooted over to make room on the couch for Rose and me. My hands in my sister's, my voice soft, breaking occasionally, I told her everything. Not the part about being the Sparrow, but everything else.

She listened with growing horror, her blue eyes filling with tears for me. Every so often, she stopped me to give me a hug, before sitting back to listen.

"I had no idea," she said finally. She shook her head, her blonde ponytail swishing back and forth. We shared some facial features, but in colouring and body shape, we couldn't be more different.

The expression of fury in her eyes matched the one I saw in the mirror.

"I assume there's a long line to kill this prick?" she asked. "If so, I want in. I never liked him very much, but to do this to my baby sister…" She wiped away tears from under her eyes.

"There's definitely a line," Daze growled. "For the record, I had no idea what my fuckhead brother was doing. None of us did."

Rose glanced at her. "I know you better than to think you'd let it go on a second after you found out about it. No more than I would."

Daze nodded, but looked slightly relieved. There was always a chance Rose might have blamed her.

"I didn't know either," Ric said. "Not until..." He grimaced. "A few weeks ago."

Rose's scowl reminded me so much of our mother. "A few *weeks* ago? You knew what happened to my sister and didn't tell me?"

"I asked them not to," I said. "I wasn't ready to see any of you yet. I'm still not ready to see Dane or Asher."

"But they—" she started. She stopped when she saw the expression on my face. "Okay, when you're ready. What do you need from me?"

"Same as you've been doing," Ric said. "Keep your eyes and ears open. Make sure your contacts know we're looking for that asshole. The minute you do, we want to hear about it."

She nodded. "I can do that. That's not enough though." She shook her head. "No one gets away with doing what he did to my little sister. I'll put everything onto this and I'll be wherever Mina needs me to be."

She wiped away tears again. She'd already cried more than I had in years. She was efficient, and dangerous in her own way, but evidently she wasn't as cold-blooded as me.

Did I have a dark heart or was I dead inside? Possibly both. That would explain my attraction to Reuben and Gianni. Damon too. Like-minded people coming together.

"Thank you," I said softly. What else could I say? I glanced over to Daze. "You had no idea I was coming?"

It was Ric who answered. "If we did, we would have made sure Rose wasn't here." He ignored the way she bristled in response.

"Why *are* you here?" I asked her.

"Taking care of a few things for Ric and Daze," she said vaguely.

I decided not to press the issue. I had some idea of what my sister got up to. I didn't need too many details.

"It's just as well I was here," she continued. "If I wasn't, who knows when I would have seen you and found out what happened. As it is, I was only supposed to be here for a few hours before heading back to Melbourne. I don't suppose I can convince you to come with me? Now I've seen you, I don't know if I can let you go again."

"I have things to take care of in Sydney," I said. "But now you know about me, maybe you can come and visit?"

I felt as though I barely knew her. She was my older sister, by six years as it was, and we'd missed so much time. She must have changed during the last five years.

Did she like any of the things she used to like? I had a feeling she'd want the answers to the same questions and I didn't have them.

Apart from reading, I hadn't paid much attention to the world outside Reuben's house. I hadn't watched TV, listened to music or touched a device that wasn't my phone. None of that interested me. Right then, I was focused on taking things one day at a time.

"Of course I will," Rose said. "Are you sure I can't say anything to Dane or Asher? They'd really want to—"

"No," I said firmly. "You never saw me. As far as you know, I'm off living my best life. When I'm ready, I'll tell them everything." I exhaled softly. "Do you see much of them?"

She shook her head. "I see Dane once in a while and Asher a few times a year. We always get together when he's in town for a gig. Or when I'm in Sydney."

"Is he happy?" I asked in a whisper.

She smiled softly. "He's Asher, he's always happy. He's living the high life doing what he does with his closest friends. Sometimes I envy him. Only sometimes. What I do is fun too. In its own way."

"I'm sure it is," I agreed. In the corner of my eye, I caught the expression on Daze's face. She was looking at me speculatively. I could almost hear her thinking.

"Is there any chance Mina and I could have a few moments?" Daze asked. "It's almost time for dinner. We could meet you in the dining room."

They all hesitated, Rose and Gianni looking at me, Ric looking at Daze.

"It's okay," I said. "We won't be long." If Reuben thought she was a threat to me, he wouldn't have let Gianni bring me here. I was certain I could hold my own if I needed to anyway. Daze wasn't that much bigger than me.

Gianni gave me a long look, but reluctantly herded the others out of the room and closed the door behind us.

I turned to Daze and gave her an eyebrow arch worthy of Reuben. "I'm guessing they won't give us long."

She snorted. "Probably not." Her tongue slid over her lips. "I saw the Sparrow is active again."

"I heard the same thing," I said.

"Interesting coincidence they disappeared right around the time you did," she said.

"It's very strange," I agreed. "What are the chances?"

She smiled. "No one is going to hear about it from me, but I have to tell you I'm a big fan. I've heard so many stories about the Sparrow."

"You can't have a selfie with me," I said deadpan. "At least, not in that capacity."

She laughed. "Of course not. The boys should watch out though. You, me and Rose, and a couple of others, could take over the world."

"The Sisterhood of Queens," I said.

She grinned. "I prefer goddesses, but sisterhood

works. Lucky for them, we need some muscle once in a while. And some cock."

"We have to keep them around for something." I said with a slight smile.

Hers faded when she realised what she said. "I'm sorry, I didn't mean to…"

I shook my head. "I can't live the rest of my life dwelling on what he did to me. Neither can you. Please don't try to tiptoe around me. I get that enough at home."

I understood and appreciated it there, but I didn't want it from her.

"You really are a badass aren't you?" she asked. "Thank fuck we're on the same side or, frankly, I'd be scared of you."

I snorted. "I can't imagine you being scared of anything. Or anyone."

She spread her hands. "I didn't think it was possible either, but here we are. Now, shall we go and join the others?"

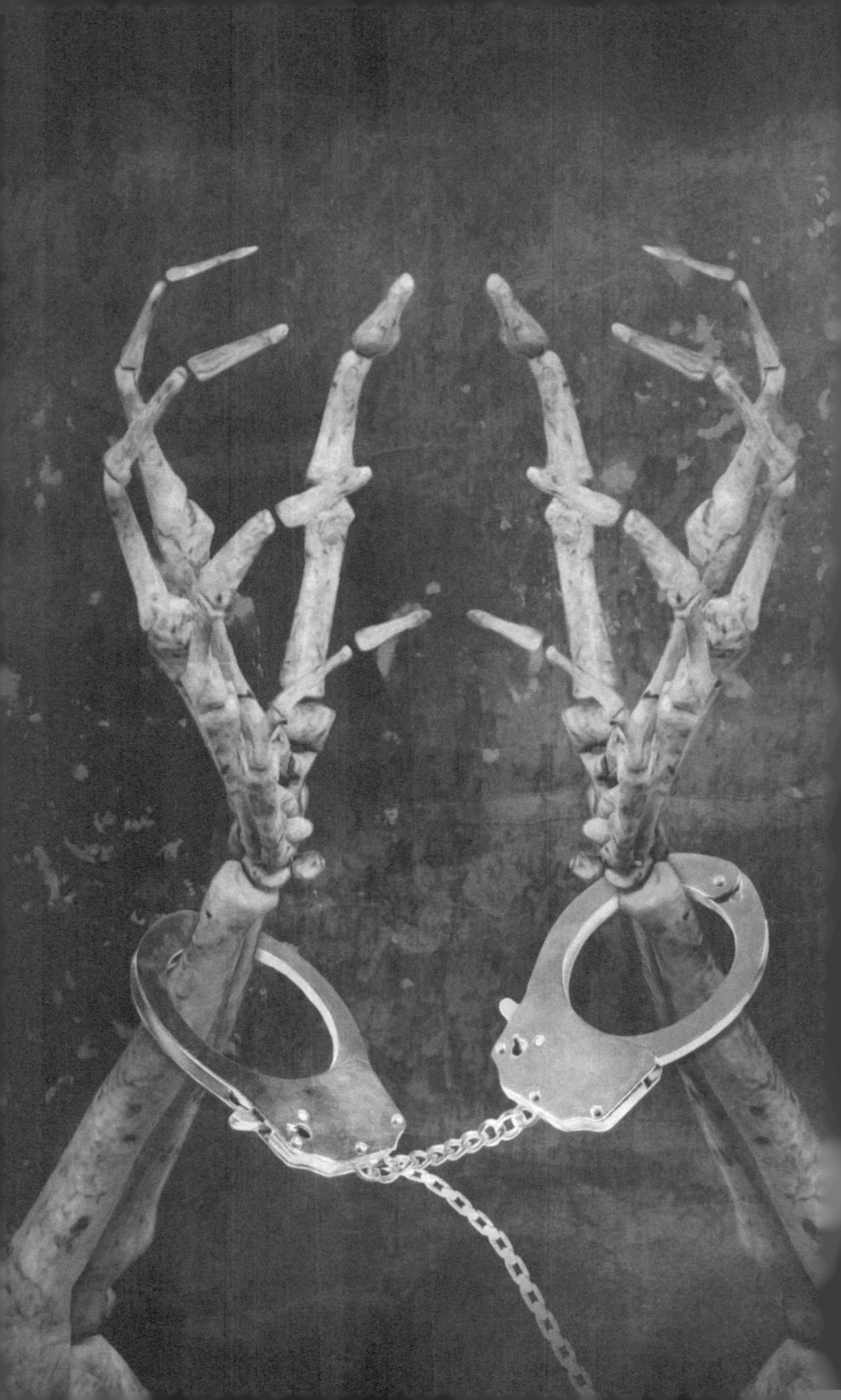

CHAPTER 5

DAMON

"I fucked up." Gianni rubbed his cheeks with the heels of both his hands and grimaced. "I should have looked into where Rose was before we flew out of Sydney."

Reuben looked at him over the top of his desk. "How did she respond?" He seemed more interested in Mina's reaction to seeing her sister than in Gianni screwing up.

Right here was a prime example of why I kept insisting she was a distraction. Not because I didn't care about how she felt, but because Gianni making a mistake should have been a higher priority. He didn't make mistakes like that. Neither did I.

Except on this occasion. I hadn't looked into Rose's whereabouts either. My attention was focused on searching for Kurt. And keeping an eye out for any sign of trouble in Dusk Bay. The city was a cesspool at the best of times. Mostly under Reuben's control, but a cesspool nonetheless. I didn't envy Caleb having to keep a close eye on it. Although, fuck knows if the man fit in better than the rest of us would.

Gianni looked at Reuben through his spread fingers. "Surprised, but happy to see her, I guess. They sat together after dinner and had a long chat. Rose was as pissed off as you'd imagine. She went all mother tiger over what happened to her baby sister."

"That sounds like Rose," I said. Both of us were good at fixing things. I would have brought her in on this earlier if it wasn't for Mina's insistence. Rose had contacts I didn't and vice versa. Between us, we could have Kurt screaming down in the basement by now.

"It doesn't sound like too much harm was done," Reuben concluded. "Have you—"

"Dane is still at Brutham Academy," I interrupted. "Asher is on tour. As of two minutes ago, Rose is back in Melbourne."

Ric contacted me before Gianni and Mina returned from Dusk Bay. I'd anticipated Reuben wanting to know the whereabouts of her other siblings.

Reuben nodded. "They're easier to keep track of than Kurt."

I held back a grimace. The comment wasn't personal, but it was difficult not to take it to heart.

If anyone should be all over finding him, it was me. This was literally my job. I didn't appreciate Kurt making a laughing stock of me, or my network of contacts. I wasn't even one of the first five people in line to kill him slowly, but I'd happily watch.

"I have everything and everyone on this," I said smoothly. "Lasalle is like a ghost. Or a slug. He's left a trail behind, but no one seems to know where he is. If he's paid people to say they haven't seen him, he's paid them well. Not even threats or torture have uncovered anything. If I didn't know better, I'd think he doesn't actually exist."

"Is that possible?" Gianni frowned. "He was in the building where he kept Mina just before we found her. Maybe he ran out onto the road and got hit by a car. He could be a John Doe lying in the morgue somewhere. His face might be so smashed in he's unrecognisable. His teeth all broken up and his ugly face ruined."

He waved his hands in front of his face. He didn't find himself attractive, but he had the kind of face people couldn't help looking at. Intelligence burned in those dark eyes, along with a good amount of deviousness. He fascinated people and in turn, was fascinated by people.

He fascinated me, but he wasn't the only one who held my attention.

"I think you're projecting," I told him. "You want to smash his ugly face in and ruin it."

"Hell yeah I do," he agreed. "So do you."

I shrugged one shoulder. "A bullet between his eyes is quicker and cleaner." I knew Reuben's preference for neat and tidy over messy and sloppy. Truthfully, I shared that preference. Mess got out of control too quickly.

"I don't care how he dies, as long as he dies." Reuben steepled his fingers and pressed them against his lips. His voice was low as ever, a rumble that made my balls tingle.

As long as I'd known him, he'd had that effect on me. Something I barely admitted to myself, much less to him. He was my boss. That was one of many reasons why I had to push those thoughts aside and focus on the conversation.

"I was thinking we could set a trap for him," I said. "Something that will ensure he comes out of the hole he's buried himself in."

Reuben turned those ice blue eyes on me and arched an eyebrow in question. "You have something in mind?"

"We can start by hacking his bank account and draining all the funds," I said.

Until now, we'd been keeping track of them, watching for money to be withdrawn. Hoping the transactions would give away his location. So far, he hadn't touched any of his accounts. Not the ones we knew about anyway.

He may not even notice us empty his accounts, but it would be fucking satisfying.

"Can I have a Maserati?" Gianni asked. "I mean, Kurt's money should go to something useful."

"His money should go to Mina," Reuben said. "She can decide if you should have a Maserati."

Gianni punched the air and grinned. "That wasn't a no."

Reuben smirked at him.

Gianni, as always, was unapologetic.

"Have the twins hack his accounts," Reuben said to me. Parker was studying cybersecurity to prevent anyone from hacking us, but that skill was useful in reverse. "Make sure they don't drain the money into their own accounts."

That was definitely something they'd do, given half a chance.

I glanced over at Gianni.

He looked back at me. "What?"

"I'm waiting for you to wonder out loud if the twins would buy you a Maserati." I leaned against the wall, crossed my arms and cocked an eyebrow at him.

He chuckled. "They probably would, but if that money is meant for Mina, and they tried to take it, I'd have to smash their kneecaps. Then we'd have to transfer the money to her and, voilà, we're back to me asking her for a Maserati."

"I see you've thought it all the way through," I said.

"I always do." He grinned. "To be honest, I thought you would have too."

I rolled my eyes at him, then turned back to Reuben. "If that gets no response from him, we may need to think bigger."

His eyes narrowed slightly. "If you're suggesting what I think you're suggesting…"

"If Kurt knows Mina is alive and well, and with us, that's going to elicit some kind of response," I said.

"Prick," Gianni snapped. "We're not using her as bait."

Reuben bristled too, but waited for me to continue.

"I'm not suggesting we use her as bait. Sooner or later people are going to need to know she's alive and what he did to her. We could let everyone know. Eventually, word would get back to him. People who are loyal to him might turn on him. This might be exactly what we need to draw him out."

"Mina isn't ready to—" Gianni started.

"It doesn't fucking matter what she's ready for," I said. "The fact is, this might be the only way to get to him. I'm not suggesting she walk around the streets waving a red fucking flag. I'm just saying we can let people know she's here and let the rumour mill do the rest."

"You're a red fucking flag," Gianni muttered.

I choked back a laugh. "Pot, meet kettle."

"What's that supposed to mean?" He rounded on me.

"I mean, you're not exactly a middle-class, suburban working guy, are you? We break the law for a living. We kill people. Threaten, bribe and coerce. What's that if not a red flag?"

"Sounds like a green flag to me." He jutted his chin out in defiance. "Women, and men, are attracted to powerful people like us. You need to read one of Mina's mafia romance books. I'm telling you, we're fucking hot. Some more than others." He pretended to fluff the back of his hair.

"Yeah, some are." I resisted the urge to look at Reuben. If he was in a book, he'd be the character readers were drooling over. Him and Mina.

I forced myself to not think about her on her knees, his cock between her lips. I would also not think about me on my knees doing the same thing.

Reuben cleared his throat. "I'll think about it. That's something we'll need to discuss with Mina before we proceed. I'm not going to do that behind her back."

"I wasn't suggesting we should," I said. "She should know the plan before we execute it."

Having her upset after the fact was another distraction we didn't need. She should be told what we were doing and deal with it. She wanted Kurt dealt with even more than we did. She'd understand the need for this.

"If we do," Gianni said firmly. "There has to be a better way."

"You could walk around Sydney waving a red flag," I suggested. "Maybe with the words, 'Where the fuck are you, Kurt?' written on it."

"That would be subtle," Reuben said dryly. "If I thought it would work, I'd send Gianni out right now."

"If I thought it would work, I'd go," Gianni said. "On the other hand, Damon is better looking than me. He'd be much better at something like this."

I ignored the comment. "If I thought Kurt would actually reveal himself for his sister, we could try that. It doesn't seem like there's much love lost between them." Since Daze was one of those top five in line to eviscerate Kurt, I doubted he'd care what happened to her.

"Is there anyone he cares about?" Reuben asked. "A wife? Children? Friends?"

"None," I said. I thought for a moment. "Mina said something about her being given to Kurt as payment for some debt. I've always had a feeling there was more to it than that. I haven't found any evidence of financial debt."

I'd gone through every record I could find from five years ago, and further back. If Mina's father owed Lasalle anything, there was absolutely no record of it. That didn't mean it hadn't happened. Some transactions still took place with cash. That was exactly why the Brotherhood of Kings was pushing for a cashless society. It was much easier to track funds electronically than it was to trace notes and coins.

"That might have been a lie Kurt spun," Gianni said.

"Then how did she end up with him?" I asked. "I don't get the impression he randomly snatched her off the streets. Have either of you dug down deeper?"

"She hasn't been—" Gianni started.

"Let me guess, she hasn't been ready," I interrupted. "She might have to be ready. Anything she can tell us might be the key to leading us to him."

I understood she needed to heal, but we couldn't sit

around and wait forever. If we did that, she may never be ready. Kurt could elude us until the day he died of natural causes. I had no intention of letting that happen. Whatever the cost.

Gianni looked like he was going to continue the argument, but exhaled and nodded. "I'll speak to her. If that's okay with you, boss?"

Reuben inclined his head. "Do that. Damon is right. She might have the answers we need."

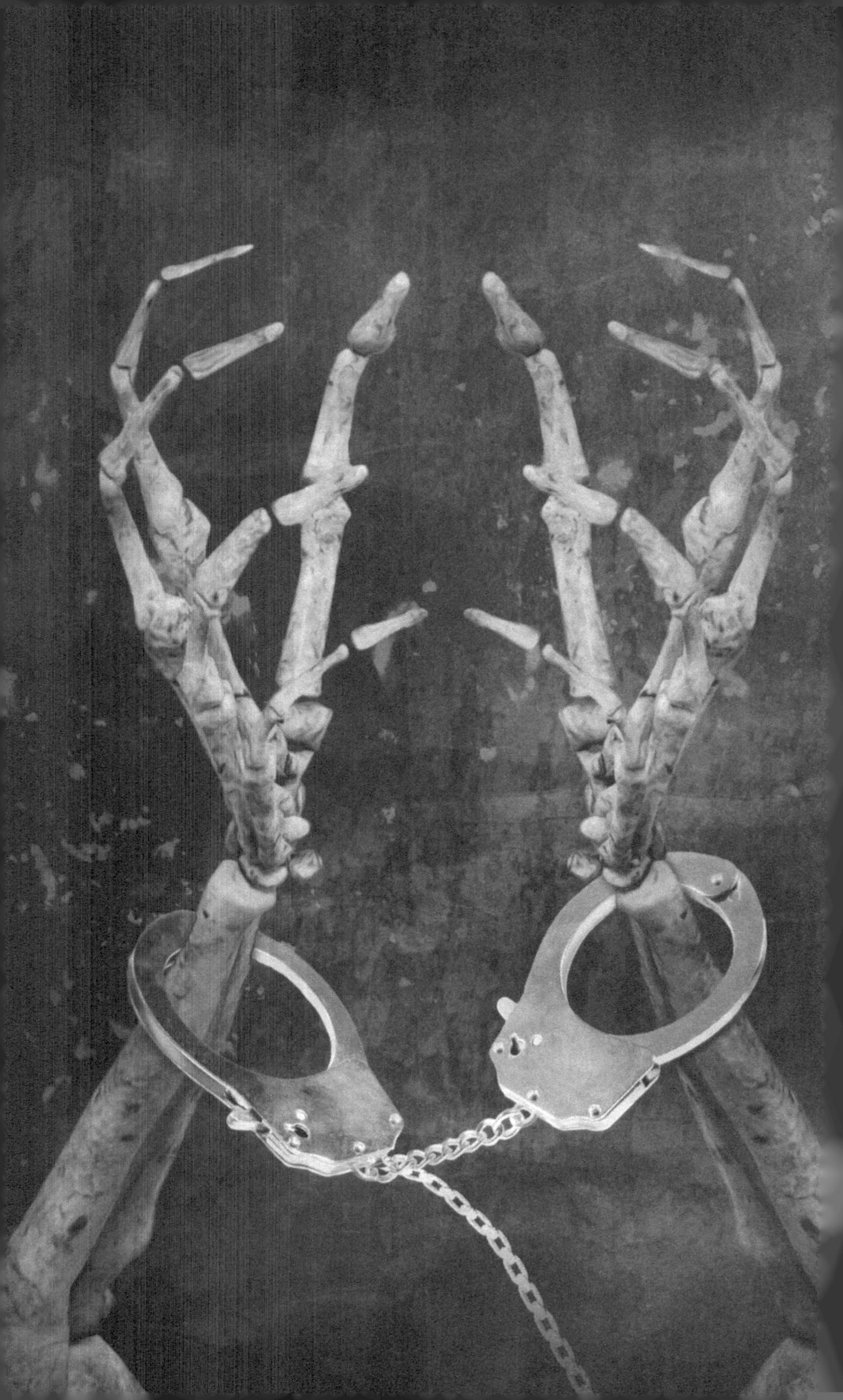

CHAPTER 6

MINA

Terry making crème brûlée was mesmerising One of those little blow torches in his large hand, he leaned forward, careful to let the flames lick the top of the desert, browning them.

"It's hard to believe someone so big can do something so dainty, isn't it?" Gianni asked.

I was aware of him stepping into the kitchen, and over to stand beside me. I didn't need to look to know who it was, even before he spoke. He moved differently from anyone else here. His footsteps were lighter, like a cat.

He made no effort to be quiet, but he was anyway. Like he made it his life's work to be unassuming. Physically anyway.

Terry gave him the side eye, but didn't look away from his work.

Gianni chuckled. "He's a master of making desserts.

Fortunately for my stomach, he doesn't make them too often." He patted his flat stomach. "When he does, they're sublime." He mimed a chef's kiss.

"They smell incredible," I said. Everything he cooked did. To be fair, he could have made toast with butter on it and it would taste like paradise after five years of stale bread and the occasional apple.

"Can we talk for a minute?" Gianni asked.

I looked over to him. "That sounds ominous. Was Reuben pissed off about me seeing Rose?" I was tired after our flight back and the drive through the city, so I'd opted to take a nap instead of attending that meeting.

My continued lethargy was frustrating, but slowly easing as I got stronger. I could spend longer in the gym now, working out. Soon, I'd be back to my full fitness.

Not soon enough, as far as I was concerned.

"Nothing I couldn't handle," Gianni said lightly. He laced my fingers in his and led me out of the kitchen.

"I'm not feeling reassured." I followed him into the library and let him close the door behind us. Was there a chance they figured out who I was? Had Daze told them, even after promising not to?

I decided that was unlikely. The vibe I was getting from him was different to that. He seemed apprehensive, but nothing to suggest he was processing a bombshell that big.

He waved for me to sit down and pulled over a footstool to perch in front of me. "Damon has some…ideas."

He grimaced as if he'd tasted something nasty in the past and was now remembering how unpleasant it was.

"Judging by the look on your face, you don't like them," I said.

His expression relaxed slightly. "I like one of them." He explained the plan to drain Kurt's bank accounts. "Reuben thinks you should have the money."

"I suppose so," I said unenthusiastically.

I couldn't explain why I didn't really need it. Not without telling him why. It wouldn't hurt to have extra funds to put into finding the asshole, I supposed. Anything left over after that could go to charity. I didn't want Kurt's dirty money. I didn't have to fake that. I wanted nothing from him.

"What was Damon's other idea?" I asked.

I listened while Gianni told me quickly and briefly what Damon proposed.

My first instinct was to give in to a spike of panic. If they did what he suggested, Dane and Asher would know where I was and what happened to me. That couldn't happen, not yet.

"I told him this was a bad idea," Gianni said. "I'll tell them both to fuck off." He placed his hands to either side of him on the footstool and started to stand.

Without thinking, I grabbed his wrist, my hand snapping out so quickly I surprised myself.

"What if we put out word someone was found down in the basement?" I said slowly. "We don't have to say who. We don't even have to say I'm alive. Knowing he was keeping a woman chained up down there, in a cage, would be enough to make people think twice about supporting him. They may not turn on him, but they might get sloppy."

Gianni lowered himself back down. "Now I know who the brains of the outfit is. We should have thought of that. I was busy being pissed off at Damon."

"He doesn't like me, does he?" I asked. "He'd happily throw me to the wolves."

"Damon doesn't like much of anyone, including himself," Gianni said. "He has some shit in his past to overcome." He hesitated. "Speaking of the past…"

The subtle change in his tone immediately had me on edge.

"What about it?" I asked carefully.

"Damon can't find any sign of a financial debt between your father and Kurt," Gianni said. "You said you don't know what the debt involved, but I don't remember if you said whether or not you knew Kurt before all of that. Did you?"

I hesitated. This would have come up sooner or later, but was I ready to respond?

"Did you know him before he put you down in that cage?" Gianni asked, gentle but insistent.

I sat back and rubbed my forehead with my thumb and fingers. "Yes I did. My father hired him to teach me self defence." Other skills too, but that explanation would do for now. "I guess he paid him in cash, if there's no trail. Or they found a way to hide the transactions." That wasn't my area of expertise.

Gianni's wide lips dropped apart. "He taught you self defence?"

"And he used everything he taught me against me," I said. "He could anticipate what I'd do."

That only helped him in the moments I tried to fight back. Mostly, he used words, reminding me of what happened that night. Breaking me down, bit by bit, with my own guilt.

"Shit," Gianni breathed. "He really is a prick."

I glanced down at the hardwood floor under my bare feet.

"He said he had a thing for me. I told him I wasn't interested. He decided he didn't want to take no for an answer. I don't know what happened between him and Dad." I shook my head. "But somehow Kurt forced his hand so he'd give me to him."

"That's fucked up," Gianni said softly. "It sounds like he was obsessed. I'm obsessed with you, but my obsession is much healthier than that."

I looked back up at him and managed a small smile. "I never said Kurt wasn't unhinged as fuck. Normal people don't lock people down in basements. They don't starve them until they're too weak to stand. They don't..." I didn't need to elaborate. Gianni knew what happened to me.

"By the time we're done with him, the biggest part of him anyone will be able to find will be his little toe,"

Gianni growled. "I plan to keep him alive until that point. I don't know how, but I will."

"I believe you," I told him. I wished I could tell him everything else. I hated lying to him. Was I as bad as Kurt for doing it? The line was too fine, too blurred, even though I reminded myself I wasn't doing it to be cruel.

"How old were you when you met him?" Gianni asked.

I swallowed to keep the contents of my stomach from coming back up. "I was fourteen. He was about eighteen. Full of anger and arrogance."

I remembered the way he used to throw me, then pin me to the mat and look down at me, like he wanted to devour me. I quickly learned how to throw him off me.

Down in the basement, he'd looked at me the same way, so many times. Usually right before he forced himself on me. Did he ever see me as a person? I doubted it. He thought of me as his possession. A toy he could do whatever he wanted to. As if I had no thoughts or feelings of my own.

"I'm so sorry." Gianni cupped my cheek lightly with his hand. "I wish I could take all the hurt away." He leaned in to brush his lips over mine.

I hesitated for a moment. Pushed my dark thoughts aside to kiss him back. I wanted to think about anything else right now but Kurt. No, I didn't even want to think. I just wanted to feel. I needed a connection to another person that didn't involve fear and violence. I wanted that connection with Gianni.

I wanted more. My body and soul both ached for it.

I took his hand and guided it down between my legs. "Can you…touch me here?" I whispered. "I want to know how it feels to be touched gently."

"Of course I can, sweetheart," he said. He rubbed his knuckles over the front of my jeans, light and tender. My clit throbbed, yearning for more.

I sucked in a breath. Could I do this? I'd be exposing myself literally and emotionally.

It was the latter that had me terrified. With some effort, I forced myself not to switch off and retreat into the back of my mind. Doing that would be an injustice to us both.

I managed to work the button loose on my jeans and draw down the zipper.

After another breath, this one more shallow, I lifted my hips to push my jeans down to my thighs. A thin layer of pale pink lace was the only thing between his hand and my pussy.

His eyes were huge, but reverent, very much aware of what I was asking of him. Very much determined to give me exactly that, what and how I needed it.

He rubbed the tips of his fingers across the gusset, with increasing firmness, until I was rolling my hips, increasing the friction.

"Sweetheart—" he whispered.

"Don't stop," I whispered back. "I want more."

He pulled the gusset aside and slid his fingers against my bare pussy.

I shivered at his touch, but this was nothing like... I didn't want to think his name right now. I'd never been touched like this before. This was gentle and sweet. At the same time, hot as hell.

"Are you okay?" he asked.

"More than okay," I said. "Please—"

"Can I taste you?" he sounded tentative, like he wasn't sure if he was overstepping boundaries. Worried he'd scare me away.

My tongue swiped over my lips. "I— Yes."

He dropped from the footstool, down to his knees in front of me. With gentle fingers, he gripped my thighs, opening me out to him. His eyes on mine, he lowered his mouth to my pussy. Letting my reactions guide him, he started to lightly tease me with the tip of his tongue.

When I didn't freak out, he carefully pressed a finger inside me, then another.

I was trembling, ready to come faster than I ever would have expected. I found myself looking down at him through a glaze of tears, surprised at myself for not freaking out or wanting to run away. For being able to let him touch me without flinching violently.

I blinked away the tears and watched him fuck me with his mouth and hand. Every lick and stroke brought me closer and closer to coming.

I let out a soft moan and pitched over the edge, into the first orgasm I ever had that I didn't give to myself.

I arched my back and ground myself against his mouth, wanting to enjoy every second, every moment for as long as I could. This was what I'd been missing all this time. A pure, loving connection between two people. Sweet touches from a man who wanted nothing more from me than to see me enjoy myself.

He went on lapping at my pussy until I came all the way down from my orgasm and my vision cleared. My pulse raced like crazy, but the rest of me felt like blissed out rubber.

He pulled his head back and grinned. "Sweetheart, you taste like pure heaven. Sound like it too. I've never heard a woman come like that."

He slid his hand out of me and, with a cheeky smile, licked my release from his fingers.

"Thank you," I said softly. "No one has ever done that for me before."

"I should be thanking you," he said. "For letting me do that for you. I could lick that sweet pussy of yours all day long. And all night. You're so fucking perfect. So fucking mine."

When he said it, there was nothing creepy about it. Nothing to suggest he wanted to hide me away from the world and use me. His tone was one of love and genuine appreciation and respect for me. When he said I was his, he meant I was his to cherish, not to possess. At least, not in the way Kurt wanted to possess me. They couldn't be more different.

"If I'm not careful, I could fall for you," I told him.

He grinned. "That's great, because I've already fallen for you. What's that fishing analogy? Cook, line and sinker?"

I laughed softly and lifted my hips to help him put my panties and jeans back into place. "I think it's hook, line and sinker. But yours is good too."

"Mine is more likely to include food," he said. "I've had my dessert, I'm sure you'd like to have yours. They're probably ready by now." He offered me his hand, just as my stomach rumbled.

I took it and stood. I chewed my lip for a moment before saying, "I want to taste you some day."

"Any time, sweetheart," he said. Judging by the tenting in the front of his pants, he was ready right now. I wished I was too, but we had plenty of time.

I hoped.

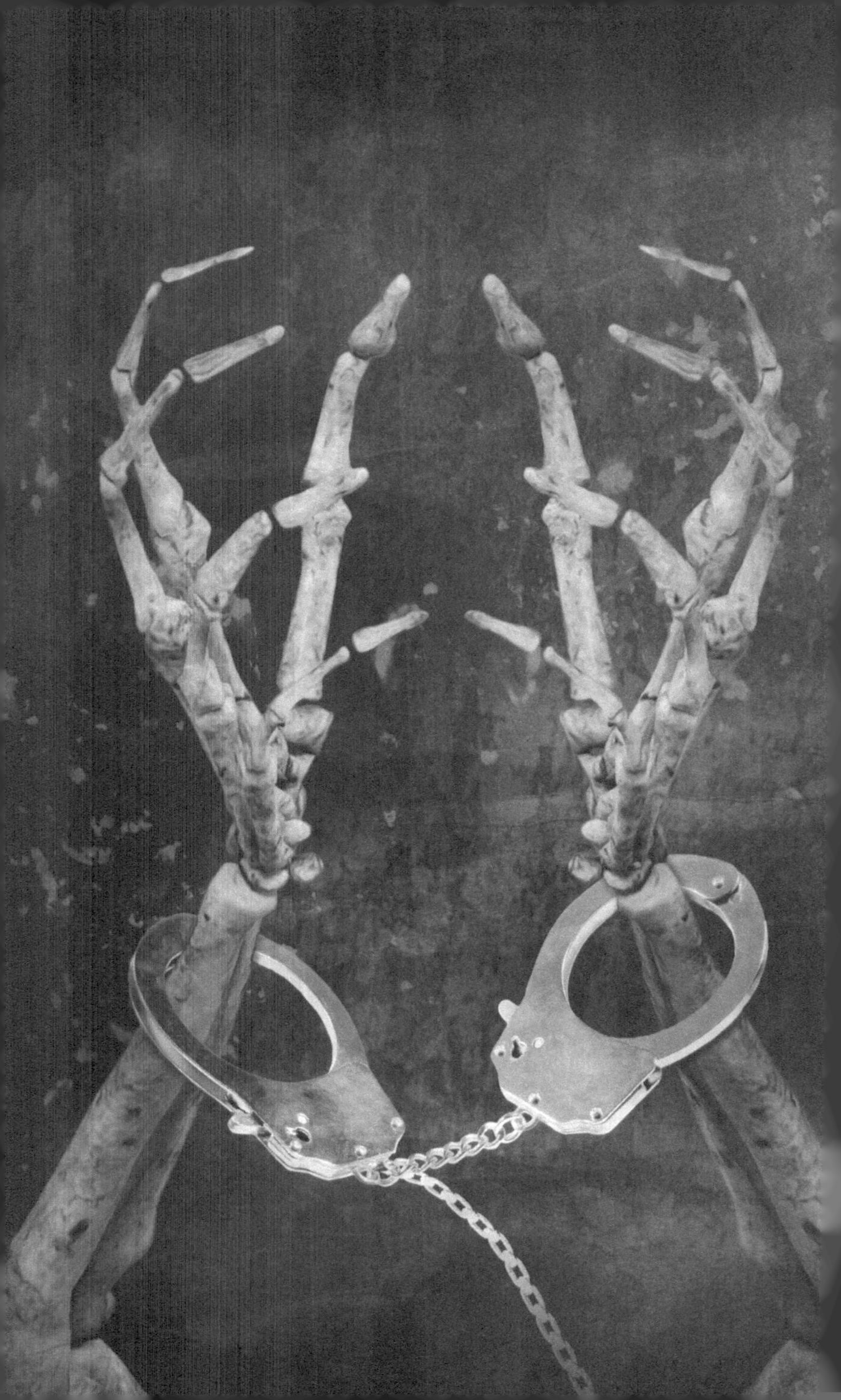

CHAPTER 7

MINA

I double and triple checked the address. Double and triple checked the layout of the building. Moved around it slowly, taking in everything.

The building looked old and tired, but it was a façade. The security system was state-of-the-art. Unable to be disabled or hacked.

Unable, my ass. There was no such thing as a security system that couldn't be bypassed. You just had to know how.

Ignoring the fact it was Kurt who taught me, I pulled a small device out of my pocket and held it up to the touchscreen beside the door.

I pressed my fingers against the front of the device, letting it read my thumbprint. A screen on the front turned on, dark enough that it wouldn't alert anyone to me standing outside in the shadows.

A tap on the screen and it started to run through

numbers and symbols. One by one, it deciphered the pass code. The keypad flashed green and the door unlocked with a faint click.

I shoved the device back in my pocket and opened the door wide enough to slip inside. Silently, I closed the door behind me.

The corridor in front of me was in darkness, but a room at the end was well lit.

I grimaced at the sound of groaning that came from it. It was loud enough that I could have stomped down the corridor and not be heard.

I shook my head and eased forward, stepping carefully across the polished concrete floor. I passed two closed doors and an open one. I glanced in, but saw nothing but darkness and the outline of a bed. No one was in there.

I stepped to the room at the end of the corridor.

A man sat on a couch in the middle of the room. His track pants were pushed down his thighs, his hand curled around his cock.

The groans came from a huge TV on the wall. On the screen, three or four guys were railing a woman who looked as though she was thinking about her shopping list, while they thrust in and out of her pussy, ass and mouth.

"Fuck yeah." He worked his cock harder, oblivious until I stepped behind him, leaned over the back of the couch and pressed a knife to his throat.

He stopped mid-beat, eyes wide. "The fuck?"

"Hi, Stefan. I see nothing has changed. It's just you and your hand." I pressed the blade in slightly. Not enough to make him bleed, but to let him know I meant business.

"Mina fucking DiMarco," he growled. "You scared the shit out of me." His hand was still tight around his cock, like he didn't dare to let go. Just in case I cut it off.

Fair call. I was tempted. Not that I wanted to touch his cock.

"If you have nothing to hide, you have nothing to fear," I said.

He raised his spare hand. "I'm an open book."

"Where's Kurt?" I asked.

He lowered his hand, bringing it down over the other one for additional protection. "I have no idea."

"Mmm." I pressed the knife in a little more, barely breaking the skin. "Wrong answer."

"I can't give you what I don't have," he said. "I swear, I don't know where he is. But—" He exhaled reluctantly.

"But?" I prompted.

"But I have a number to contact him," Stefan said quickly. "Not directly. I send a message and someone passes the message on to him. It's on my phone." He nodded to the table in front of him.

"What happens then?" I asked.

"After a day or two, he sends a message back via, I dunno, whoever the fuck it is. The last I heard was to lay low and play it cool. Seems one of the big heavies is on his ass. Reuben Brantley or Samuel Bell. Kurt was fucking them both over, so I'm not surprised. Dickhead likes to live dangerously."

"You worked with him," I said.

"Indirectly," he argued. "I'm just a fence. People bring me their shit and I sell it for them. Get a nice tidy profit on top of it. Getting involved in things too deeply is above my pay grade. I'm what they call a petty criminal, but you know that."

"I think you're underselling yourself," I said. "Rumour has it you're Kurt's right-hand."

He laughed-grunted. "Not me. He didn't trust me enough for that."

"Who did he trust?" I asked.

"I don't—" Stefan started.

A bead of blood rose where I pushed the knife in a little more.

"Let's try this again. Who did he trust?" There was no doubt in my mind he knew.

That was why I was here tonight. Why I'd snuck out of the house again to deal with him. I had to take the chance he'd speak to me. We weren't friends, but he knew who I was. More or less.

He sat perfectly still, probably weighing his options. If he talked, he was dead. If he didn't talk, he was dead. If he told me everything, he might just have the chance to run and hide before shit hit the fan.

"There's a dude named Leon Graves, he's an old friend of Kurt. He ran a lot of Kurt's operations. If anyone knows where he is, it's him. If I had to guess, I'd say he was the one receiving and relaying the messages."

"There, that wasn't so difficult, was it?" I asked.

"If he finds out I said anything to you, I'm fucked," Stefan whined.

"I have no reason to tell him you said anything to me," I said. "And I know *you* won't."

"Of course not." He took the chance to raise his left hand, as if to promise he wouldn't say a word.

I smirked and sliced open his throat. "You might have misunderstood what I was saying." His blood squirted out onto my fingers, warm and sticky. Better his blood than his cum.

His hand dropped back down with a soft thud. He slumped back against the couch, his hand still wrapped around his cock.

"Sucks to be you," I said with no sympathy. I walked around the couch to pick up his phone. After a couple of attempts to guess the passcode, it opened.

"Sixty-nine, sixty-nine, sixty-nine." I rolled my eyes. "You shouldn't have been so predictable."

His glazed eyes stared back at me. He looked regretful, but I doubted it involved his pass code.

On the screen, one of the men grunted as he came, spilling cum all over the woman's face. I snatched up the remote and turned it off. I dropped the remote back on the table and scrolled through his phone.

His photos contained various candid shots of

women. They all looked like they were taken through a window, or under the door of a public toilet. Their faces weren't visible in most of them, just a breast here, leg or pussy there.

"Looks like I did the world a favour," I said. "One less pervert." I tapped out of the photos and went in to read his messages. As I expected, there weren't many. One or two with a vague address or a thumbs up symbol. The rest were deleted, or he didn't get many.

His contacts were likewise sparse. The pizza place down the street, the number of a ride share, and a couple that might be Leon Graves, or another of Kurt's associates.

I pulled out my phone, copied the numbers and wiped down his phone with a cloth before placing it back on the table.

Leon would change his number if he knew someone took Stefan's phone. If I just had the number, I stood a chance of being able to use it.

"I'd like to say it's been fun, but I hope this was worthwhile," I told Stefan. "Don't worry, someone will find you in a couple of days. If you're lucky."

The man was a snake and always had been. He was also one of the men who carried me down into the basement. I recognised his voice as soon as he spoke. Was Leon Graves another of them? I'd met him a couple of times, and two of the men didn't say a word that night. All I had was vague memories of their faces in shadow, my mind muddled by whatever Kurt drugged me with.

From my phone, I sent a tipoff to one of Damon's contacts, giving them Stefan's name. They'd pass that on to Damon. He could come by and find him like this.

Reuben would be pissed off if he knew I wasn't telling them any of this directly, but I couldn't explain how I got into this building without telling him everything. He'd insist on knowing how I got past impenetrable security.

I wasn't ready to share that yet. Not even with him or Gianni. Not with Damon either, although I still had no idea where I stood with him. He seemed to want me as much as he disliked me.

I respected him, but I wouldn't push. There was no hurry to take things any further. Not yet. When this was over, maybe we'd find time to work things out.

I tucked my phone away and took a few minutes to search around the building. I found a locked room, but no sign of the key. I looked back at Stefan and grimaced.

His pants were down around his ankles. One side looked heavier than the other.

"Really?" I asked, not knowing if I directed the question to him or myself. Either way, I had no choice.

I had to crouch to feel around in his pockets. The heavier one contained a small ring of keys. One said Mercedes on the fob. The others looked like house keys, or keys that unlocked filing cabinets.

Stepping away from him and his now flaccid cock, I tried each of the keys until the door opened.

I half-expected to find a woman caged and chained, but the room was full of boxes.

Guns, gems, phones and cash. One contained what looked like bricks of cocaine. The street value of everything here would add up to several million, at least. This, Reuben would be happy to recover.

I left everything untouched and closed and locked the door behind me. Grimacing again, I replaced the keys in Stefan's pocket and went to rifle through his bedroom. I found nothing but the usual: clothes, shoes, an unopened box of condoms. I picked it up and checked the expiry date.

"Three months ago," I said with a smirk. "That tracks." Stefan was a slimy bastard. The women of the world wouldn't miss him. Neither would the men, for that matter.

I knelt down beside his bed and shone my phone light underneath.

"What do we have here?" I said to myself. I set my phone aside and pulled out the box. Metal and maybe thirty centimetres wide and just as long, it was fitted with a basic padlock. The kind quickly unpicked with the lock pick I kept in my pocket.

I eased open the lid and looked inside.

In the centre lay a phone. The battery was flat, but I decided I could spare a few moments to charge it until the screen turned on. The passcode was simple. There was nothing on the phone but a single app.

I pressed on the screen to open it.

My stomach turned. I felt as though my whole world was tipped upside down. My entire body started to tremble. In my mind, I was right back in the cage, the chain on my ankle.

I slammed the box, shoved it back under the bed and fled out into the night, right before I threw up my last meal.

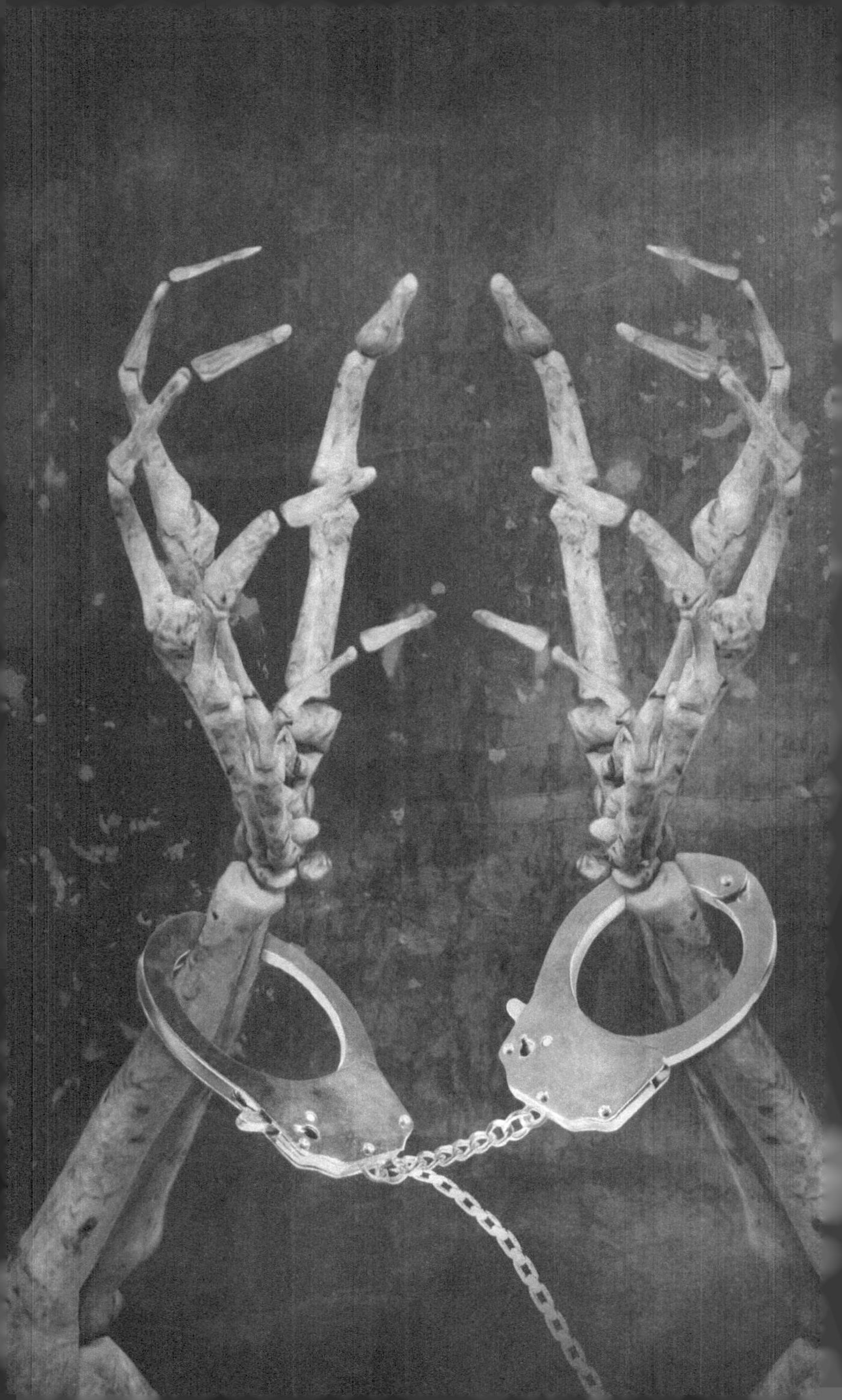

CHAPTER 8

I frowned at my phone as I stepped past Mina's room. It was only a matter of time before Reuben or Gianni moved her into theirs, or stayed with her.

The idea set off a flare of anger inside me. Not just because she was a distraction, although she was.

The real reason… I wasn't ready to admit it to myself. My feelings for Reuben, Gianni and Mina were complicated.

I didn't do complicated. I didn't *like* complicated. I liked my life straightforward, carefully planned.

The message on my phone threatened to disrupt that planning.

A sound from inside her room did the same.

The door was ajar, as it often was. I presumed she didn't want to sleep in a fully enclosed space after what she'd been through.

I peered through the gap. A hint of light shone between the curtains, illuminating a single form on the middle of the bed, wrapped in blankets.

Also nothing new. She was fucked up. Who wouldn't be?

I shoved my phone into my pocket and pushed the door open.

"Mina?" I whispered. If she was asleep, I didn't want to wake her, but I sensed she was awake already. That was confirmed when she startled so violently she almost rolled off the bed onto the floor.

I lurched forward and grabbed her at the last moment.

She whimpered and flinched away, pushing the blankets off and retreating to the head of the bed, where she curled into a tiny ball. Her whole body shook, eyes wide, staring at me as if she'd never seen me before.

"Hey." I sat down far enough from her to give her some space. Close enough to… I didn't know what.

I considered calling for Reuben or Gianni, but couldn't bring myself to move. "Rough night?"

She'd had nightmares since we found her, some nights screaming in her sleep. Others crying out and thrashing before falling still. This felt like something else entirely.

"What happened?" If Reuben or Gianni did anything to her…

I mentally shook my head. If they did, it wasn't on

purpose. They were both gone, as far as she was concerned. They'd cut their own throats before they lay a hand on her in a way she didn't want them to.

Who then? The twins weren't here and they wouldn't touch her either. Reuben wouldn't hesitate to put them both in a shallow grave. Blood ties only went so far.

Her face was as pale as the first time I saw her. In the light, her freckles would stand out. In the gloom, she looked like death.

"Bad dream," she said softly. "I was back in the cage."

"The thing about spending all my time around criminals and liars is that I can pick a liar from days away," I said slowly. "Something else happened. What was it?"

She slid a hand under the blanket near her foot. For a moment, I thought she was going to pull out a weapon.

My body tensed, ready to defend myself.

Instead, she pulled out a phone.

"The pass code is four, three, two, one." She handed me the phone.

I frowned at her, then at the phone. "Okay." I tapped on the screen and entered the pass code. An app was already open on the phone. One that contained photos and videos.

I felt the blood drain out of my face. "Fucking hell, where did you get this?"

She shook her head and curled up again, the blankets up to her chin.

I shook my head and looked down at photo after photo of her. She couldn't have been more than eighteen.

A few candid ones showed her smiling and laughing with her siblings.

After those, were at least twenty of her lying naked, eyes closed. The bars of the cage were around her, the strap on her ankle. She looked peaceful, unaware she was about to wake up in hell.

I found myself clicking on a video, and immediately wished I hadn't. She was still unconscious, but Kurt was laughing, opening her legs and climbing on top of her...

I closed the video and turned off the phone. No wonder she'd unravelled. This would have brought everything back to her like a blade in her heart. Tore open wounds that were finally starting to heal.

"How did you get this?" I asked again. "Did someone send it to you? Let me guess, Kurt." He'd do anything to mess with her mind. He knew all the buttons to push to drive her over the edge. "How long have you had this?"

She didn't answer. I wanted to shake it out of her, but that might be the thing that broke her completely. None of that mattered as much as what we needed to do next.

I tossed the phone onto the bedside table and scooted over closer to her. "I saw you kill a woman. I know you killed that attacker the other night, before they could get to Reuben. You shot those other assholes in the foot. You might be the shadow, but you're a badass. Those photos, that was the old you. You survived all of that. None of that is your life anymore. You're here now, with us."

I placed the tips of my fingers on her shoulder. She twitched, but didn't flinch away.

"Someone took those photos," she whispered. "That video. Someone took them and didn't stop him. They stood there with that phone filming him while he..." She swallowed audibly.

"Do you know who?" I asked. Whoever they were, they'd be missing every finger they used to hold that phone if I got a hold of them.

She shook her head slowly. "I remember one of the men. A friend of Kurt's. His name is Stefan Lowe."

"He won't be a problem anymore," I said. "I just got a message from one of my contacts that he was killed tonight. It seems like someone took a contract out with the Sparrow to end him. I don't suppose you sent the Sparrow after him?"

I was joking, but something about her demeanour shifted slightly. Something that drew both my attention and my suspicion.

"Mina?" I tightened my grip on her shoulder slightly.

"People like Stefan make lots of enemies," she said, her voice empty. "He got what he deserved."

I frowned. "You didn't tell me how you got that phone. No one has been in or out of the house all night. I'd know if they had. They would have set off the alarm. Unless they turned it off. Was it Gianni?" He was known to slip out every now and again, for reasons of his own. Reuben was aware of his movements, so I never questioned it.

"Was it you?" I asked. "You went somewhere in the middle of the night?"

She didn't answer, but I knew I was right. "Where did you go? Did you kill Stefan? That's where the phone came from." I was missing something, but I couldn't figure out what.

"You can't tell Reuben," she whispered.

"The hell I can't." I started to stand.

She grabbed my wrist and held on with a grip that was surprisingly firm. "You don't understand."

I lowered myself back down, pulled my wrist away from her and crossed my arms. "Then make me understand. What the fuck were you doing leaving the house in the middle of the night by yourself? Did you kill Stefan?"

She closed her eyes. "Yes. I remembered him from before and tracked him down. I thought he might know where Kurt was. He gave me the name of someone who used to work for Kurt. Leon Graves. Then I killed him."

She told me about the locked room and finding the phone in the box under the bed.

"I don't understand why you thought you needed to do that alone," I said, while still trying to process every-thing. "We would have gone with you. You're the one who calls this a family, but you felt like you needed to do that by yourself?"

Her tongue darted over her lips. "I wanted to face him myself. I wanted to look him in the eye and know he was another piece of the past I was putting behind me."

"You could have done that with us there," I insisted. I ran through the conversation in my mind and sat back.

Realisation struck me like a hammer.

"I should have seen it," I said, trying to maintain my composure. "Now I think about it, it's fucking obvious. You were gone for five years. So was the Sparrow."

If realisation was a hammer, it hit right on the head of the nail. She didn't move. Didn't breathe.

"You didn't need to hire an assassin to kill Stefan Lowe," I concluded. "You are one. Or you were."

"I still am," she said softly.

I couldn't understand why the hell that was hot, but it fucking was. Mina DiMarco was the Sparrow. Of all people in the fucking world. She was right here, in Reuben's house, where I also lived. Lying on a bed wrapped in blankets, cracked but not broken.

No wonder she survived all those years. She would

have learned a variety of techniques to control her emotions, all of which she would have used, possibly daily.

"You're the fucking Sparrow," I said. My brain spun. "You know Reuben has to know. Gianni too. We can't keep this from them. If you don't tell them, I will."

"Or I could kill you to keep you from saying anything, and make it look like an accident," she said. Her expression was so mild, I wondered what else she got away with.

She might be the best actor I ever met. Sweet on the outside, deadly on the inside.

The perfect woman. Fuck, apparently Reuben and Gianni weren't the only ones who were gone.

"You wouldn't do that," I said.

She cocked her head at me. "Wouldn't I?"

"No, you wouldn't," I said. "First of all, you would devastate Reuben and Gianni. Secondly, you still need me to find Kurt. Third, I know you have a thing for me. Just like you do for them."

She straightened her head and hummed, before replying to each point, one at a time. "They'd get over it. That's an assumption, and that's also an assumption."

I lowered my hands to my thighs and smirked. "No they wouldn't, and both of those are correct. Right now, you're thinking of kissing me."

I'd kiss her if I hadn't found her in a huddle of blankets. Those photos would set her back. Freaking her out would do even worse.

Fuck Kurt fucking Lasalle. And fuck Stefan Lowe for keeping that phone. And fuck him harder for taking that video in the first place. They were both sick. She was right, Stefan got what he deserved. I just wished I'd been there to see it.

"How do you fit that ego inside this house?" she asked.

"It's not ego, it's fact," I said. "I'm actually very humble."

She snorted softly. "You're full of shit."

"You wouldn't be the first to say that," I replied. "Probably not the last either. None of that means I'm wrong."

"You're right," she whispered. She wasn't talking about her attraction to me. "You would have gone with me. If you had, I wouldn't have seen those photos. Not if one of you found that phone first."

"No fucking way we'd let you look," I agreed. I wanted to bleach my eyeballs after seeing the video of Kurt. All of this must be a million times worse for her.

"He doesn't get to win," she said in a shaky voice. "I won't let him."

"*We* won't let him," I corrected. "Family, remember? Even if we are dysfunctional." That was an understatement.

"Right." She raised a hand tentatively and pressed the tips of her fingers against my lips.

I kissed her soft, warm skin. A jolt of electricity

passed all the way through me, but I made no move toward her. This intimacy was enough, for now.

"You're still a distraction," I teased.

She managed a faint smile. "You're still an asshole."

"Absolutely correct," I said. "I hear Terry in the kitchen. Reuben and Gianni will be up soon, if they're not already. If you're not down in the kitchen for breakfast, I'll tell them without you."

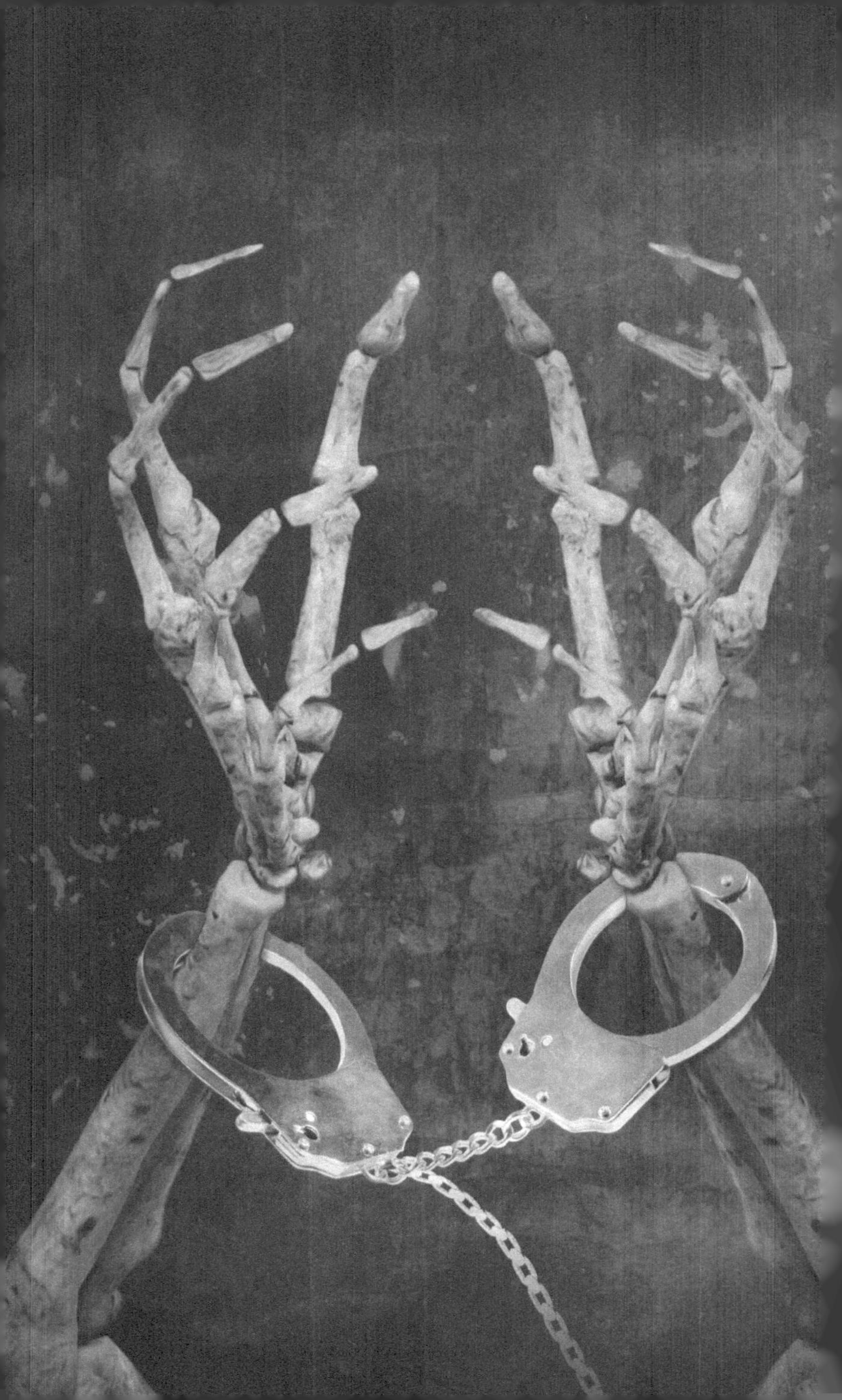

CHAPTER 9

MINA

Reuben flipped through the photos, his expression quietly thunderous. He seemed determined to look at every one of them. Not because he wanted to see them, but because he needed to know what I went through. So I wasn't alone in this. He needed to understand, no matter how difficult it was to see.

Finally, he rose from his seat far enough to hand the phone to Gianni, who nodded.

Gianni carried the phone over to the kitchen benchtop beside the stove. He opened a drawer, pulled out a meat mallet and smashed the phone screen with it.

Terry, who stood stirring a pot, grunted. I presumed he approved. He met my eyes for a moment, inclined his head slightly and went back to his cooking.

"You could have deleted the photos," Damon pointed out.

"Chances are, there's a tracking chip in here," Gianni said. He went on smashing the phone until it was nothing more than a mess of plastic and broken glass.

There wasn't, I'd looked. There was nothing useful on the phone, just the photos and video. Seeing Gianni destroy it was almost as cathartic as doing it myself. He would have let me if I asked, but I didn't want to touch the phone again. Not even the scraps of it.

"Damon was right," Reuben said. "About you being a distraction. I was so distracted, I didn't see what was right in front of my fucking face. You're an assassin."

His whole body was tense with anger, but much of it was directed at seeing those photos. The rest, I suspected, was directed at himself. None at me.

"That's the point of me being the Sparrow," I said softly. Part of me was relieved all of this was out in the open, but in some ways, it complicated the situation even further. "Who would have thought I'd be a cold-blooded killer?"

Gianni raised his hand. "I thought it was possible. Not necessarily cold-blooded, but a killer. All the best people are."

Damon snorted softly. "And some of the worst."

Gianni pointed a finger gun at him. "Good point. But in this room, it's the best."

Reuben ignored them both and kept his eyes on me. "You didn't mention this until you had to. Until Damon figured it out."

"No, I didn't," I agreed. I wanted to look away, but I forced myself not to.

"How did Kurt Lasalle end up with the Sparrow chained and caged?" Reuben asked. "You have skills."

I took a few moments to collect my thoughts and figure out the best way to articulate them. In the end, I decided the best was to jump right in.

"As far as I can tell, my father slipped something into a drink he gave me. When I woke up, I was in that house. Kurt was there with the woman from the ice cream parlour, Stefan and a couple of others. I remember them talking, then Kurt jabbed a needle into my arm. When I woke up, I was in that cage."

Sticky and sore, with no doubt of what Kurt did to me.

"He left me there for three days before he came back to give me something to eat."

He'd taunted me, laughed at me and told me how much he enjoyed fucking me. Reminded me of what I did that night and why I deserved to be there. Guilt kept me from responding, or accepting any food. He'd thought that was hilarious.

"Fucking asshole," Gianni muttered.

"He was obsessed with you. He took the opportunity to have you in a place he could keep you," Reuben said.

"I gave him the opportunity," I said reluctantly. They had most of the story, they might as well have the rest of it. If they turned their backs on me now, I'd manage on my own. I had money and contacts and, like Reuben pointed out, skills.

"I was on a job," I said slowly. "There was a kid. She shouldn't have been there. I saw her standing in the doorway and then, she was dying in my arms." I shook my head. "She had nothing to do with any of this. She was supposed to be with her mother, not her father. He was the one who was supposed to die that night."

"That explains why you looked so upset when you saw Frank's kid," Gianni said.

All I could say to that was, "Yeah"

"I don't understand," Damon said. "You said you saw her, and then she was dying. You killed her?"

I shook my head slowly. "I had to have. I don't remember doing it, but it was only me and her there. Kurt was in another room." I briefly explained his mission was to find information.

"Think back," Reuben said. "Is it possible he did it?"

I frowned. I'd thought about that night a million times. It lived in my nightmares. Her blood, my guilt, were the only things I was certain of.

"If he did, I should have been able to stop him," I said finally. "If I just gave him what he wanted, he wouldn't have forced my hand like that. She'd still be alive now."

"You'd voluntarily sleep with him in return for the life of a child?" Damon asked.

"I'd do *anything* to erase that night," I said quietly.

"What happened to her was my fault. What Kurt did to me, I deserved every moment of it."

"Sweetheart." Gianni slid into the chair beside me. "You did *not* deserve any of that. The only one to blame for this was Kurt. He's a fucked up monster who used a kid to get to you." He carefully slipped his arm around my shoulders. "Her blood is on his hands."

I shook my head. "I should have seen the extent he'd go to. I should have insisted I do my job alone. He could have come in afterward. He shouldn't have been anywhere near there. I misjudged him and she paid the price."

"The only one responsible for his actions is him," Reuben said darkly. "He let his obsession take hold of him and he did something unspeakable."

Damon cleared his throat.

Reuben's gaze slid to him. "There's a difference between distraction, and obsession to the point of imprisoning a woman to keep her." He returned his gaze to me. "Who was this girl?"

"I don't really know. The daughter of my target. He was some kind of politician. He upset someone and they decided to take him out."

My guess was one of his ex-wives, possibly all three of them, if they could afford me. He had a reputation as a massive asshole. Not to mention a serial cheat.

"Kurt was supposed to find information on his whereabouts on a few nights in question. And details about bribes from some construction company."

I guessed his ex-wives wanted to pin his death on them. That was their business. I was just there to carry out the job I was paid to do. There was no benefit in getting too nosy. It wasn't as though I needed the money I get from bribing them. Killing people for money was lucrative enough.

"Did he end up dead?" Gianni asked. "Sounds like he deserved it."

"According to Kurt, someone finished the job a year later," I said. "Unless that car crash was really an accident." Stranger things had happened.

"That seems unlikely to me," Reuben said. "Once someone takes out a hit—"

"It's seen through until the end," I finished for him. "Unless the client withdraws the job. But that's a rare occurrence. Once people are committed to having someone killed, they tend to follow through."

"Have I mentioned recently that you're hot?" Gianni squeezed my shoulders. "An actual fucking assassin. I knew you were a badass. I just fucking *knew* it. You're the baddest of the badasses."

I managed a faint smile. "Yeah, but what happens now?" I looked back to Reuben. "Now you know what I am, and what I did."

"It changes nothing," Reuben said. "You expected us to turn on you?"

"A child died because of me," I insisted. "I expected you to agree that I deserved what Kurt did."

Deafening silence followed my words. Heavier than

a thundercloud ready to break apart and release a flood, accompanied by thunder louder than a Wolf Venom concert.

I'd spent too many years convincing myself I was a terrible person. It was so ingrained by now, I didn't expect any other response. I'd readied myself to defend against them. I'd die or kill them all before I let that happen. The idea of being locked away again was my own personal hell. Whatever I had to do, I wouldn't allow that. Even if I stabbed a knife into my own heart.

I hadn't pictured understanding. Words or looks of concern. Of love.

The anticipated waves of hate and threats of violence didn't come. No suggestion I should go back down into the basement.

"Kurt deserves what we're going to do to him," Reuben growled. "Nothing you've said makes you any less ours. Any less *mine*."

His expression was more intense than I'd ever seen on him. He was the thundercloud, but he wasn't coming for me.

This was the man people were scared of. The one who decided who lived or died with barely a second thought. The one whose absolute certainty that I was his made my clit throb and my heart flutter.

What was it Gianni said? Some people thought love made us vulnerable, but it made us stronger. We were a family, no matter what any of us did.

"If anything, it says you belong here even more than

we thought you did," Gianni said. "You're a fucking assassin. You fit in perfectly."

I finally let myself lean into him and start to relax. "Then you'll understand I have contacts I've reached out to. Contacts who are looking for Leon Graves as we speak. He's next on my shit list. When I find him, I should be that much closer to finding Kurt."

"When *we* find him," Reuben said. "You're not doing this alone. Between us, we have the resources to find both of these pricks and deal with them appropriately."

"I don't know," I said lightly. "Damon might be a distraction."

Our conversation and connection were surprising, as was the intimacy of his kiss on my fingers. They were all distractions, but they were distractions I needed. For their resources and for them. They'd become my safe harbour in an ocean of crazy.

Damon barked a short laugh. "Fucking touché. Doesn't matter though, you need us. Who else knows who you are?"

"Just Daze and Kurt," I said. "My father did. And the people who trained me. If anyone else knows, I'm unaware of them."

"That debt." Damon's forehead creased.

"I still don't know what it was," I said. "Why my father would drug me and give me to him." I was relieved to get all of this off my chest, but that still hung over me. Would I ever get an answer as to why he did that to me? If I didn't, it would linger in my mind for the rest of my life.

"I'm glad I had him killed," Reuben said darkly. "All right, Leon Graves. Anyone else?"

"Not that I can remember, yet," I said. "I'm hoping Graves will shed some light on them." I explained how I got the information on him from Stefan. Including the way I'd surprised him, literally with his pants down.

Gianni laughed. "Taking out a guy while he's jacking off. That's fucking awesome. I love you, Mina 'The Sparrow' DiMarco."

"My middle name is actually Jasmine," I said. "But I love you too, Gianni Covino."

He pulled me closer and wrapped his arms around me. He nestled his face into my hair and laughed softly. "A fucking assassin."

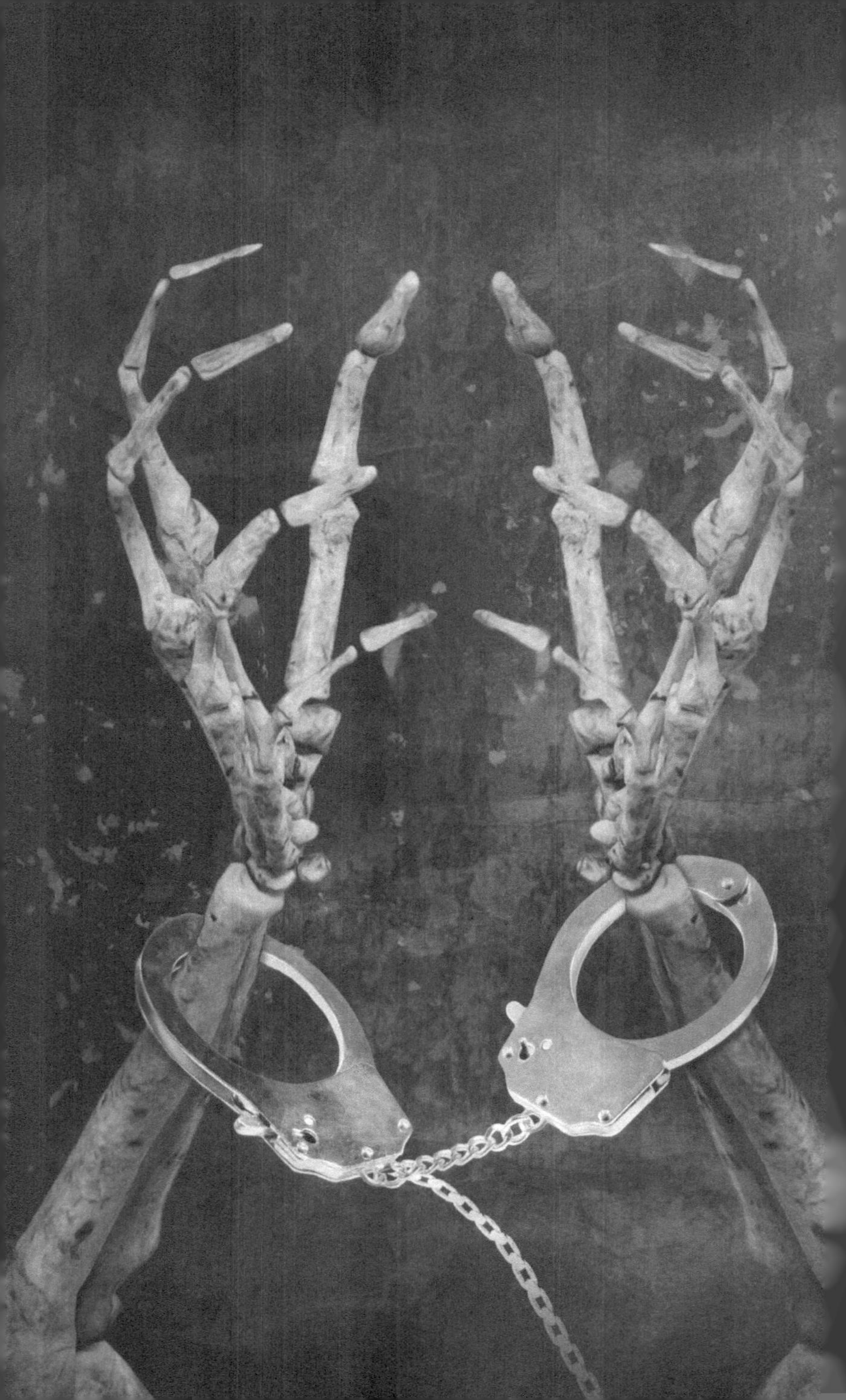

CHAPTER 10

MINA

I sat down on the bench beside Reuben and looked back at the house.

The light was on in the kitchen. Terry moved back and forth every couple of minutes. The night was still, except for the distant hum of traffic, the rustling of birds and sounds of crickets somewhere in the bushes.

"Why aren't you angrier that I lied to you?" I kept my voice low, not wanting to disturb the quiet.

"Because I understand why you did it," he replied after a few moments of pause. "Self-preservation is one of our strongest instincts. The ability to trust is difficult. It often leads to disappointment."

He turned to me. "You trusted Kurt? Before all of this happened. When he was training you to defend yourself."

"I suppose I did," I said reluctantly.

I placed my hands in my lap and leaned back against the trunk of the tree behind us.

"My father trusted him to teach me. Kurt gave me the creeps, but I never had much reason to question my father's decision. Back then, I was still under the misguided belief that parents do what's best for their children. I trusted my father to do that."

"Two people you trusted, betrayed you," Reuben said. "It would be an inconceivable stretch for you to trust me after we'd just found you. Why would you? After everything you went through, why would you trust someone like me? No one who endured that, would be immediately forthcoming. I wouldn't have. That's why I'm not angry. However…"

Of course there would be a caveat.

"If I lie to you again, you'll be furious," I guessed.

"Precisely," he agreed. "I don't expect to know all of your secrets, but never look straight at me and lie, and I'll extend the same courtesy to you."

"I won't," I promised. "I'm not keeping anything else from you, that I can think of. Except…"

In the light coming from the kitchen, I saw his eyebrow arch.

"I've always had a thing for you," I confessed. "You were imposing and so many people were intimidated by you, but I felt drawn to you. I figured a man like you wouldn't be interested in a girl like me. Partly because of the part I played as sweet innocent little Mina, and partly because of what I really was behind that mask. I don't think 'assassin' is in one of the top ten most trusted professions."

"Neither is mob boss," he pointed out. "Although, it should be. Both of us are loyal, driven and ruthless. I consider those to be positive attributes."

He draped an arm over my shoulders and rubbed the pad of his thumb across the side of my upper arm.

"We're more alike than you might think. Including the attraction between us. I was waiting until you were old enough, but with the expectation you'd reject me. Which does come back to the sweet façade. You played that role to perfection. If I knew exactly who you were, I would have made a move sooner. Before Kurt got to you. It's his fault I missed out on all those years with you."

"He has a lot to answer for." So fucking much. "For the record, I never would have rejected you." I leaned against him, enjoying his warmth and masculine scent. "Things could have been very different."

"They could have," he agreed. "You might have been the key to keeping the twins in line."

I snorted softly. "I don't think I have that kind of influence over them. That might have gone the other way though. They could have led me astray." If anyone would try, it'd be them.

"Not if they wanted their heads attached to their bodies," he growled. "I think their survival instincts are too strong to cross that line."

"If not, you could have taken out a hit on them," I

said. "Which I wouldn't have taken, because they're basically family to me too."

"Don't tell them that, it'll go to their heads," he said dryly. "Although, I'm not sure they can get egos bigger than the ones they already have. But let's not talk about them."

He turned his face and brushed his lips over mine. The kiss was tentative at first, the memory of those photos weighing heavily between us.

I'd freaked out when I saw them, but, like everything else, I was determined to put them behind me. If I held back too much, more than I wanted to, then he won.

Fuck that.

I deepened the kiss, tasting his lips and the inside of his mouth with my tongue.

He turned me to him and placed his other hand on my hip.

"Mina…" He said against my mouth.

"Reuben." I pulled back and whispered, "I want to… taste you."

I moved my hand down to the front of his suit trousers. His cock was already hard, straining against the fabric.

"I don't want you doing anything you're not ready for," he said. He seemed like he was about to pull away from me, for my own sake.

"I'm ready for this." I slipped away from him and knelt down on the cool grass in front of the bench.

Hands trembling slightly, I undid the front of his pants and pulled the sides apart. Only his black silk boxers were between his cock and the tips of my fingers.

I touched him carefully, stroking my fingers up and down his erection before I was brave enough to pull down his boxers, letting it spring free.

I ran the tips of my fingers around his head, brushing my thumb over the bead of pre-cum that glistened on his tip.

He quivered under my touch. "Fuck, Mina," he whispered. His expression was strained with the effort to keep from pumping himself into my hand. He wanted this to happen on my terms. There was time later for him to be dominant. Right now, I was the one in charge.

This was the first time in my life I had my face, voluntarily, this close to a man's cock. There was no persuasion, no force. If I stepped away right now, he'd be frustrated, but wouldn't press.

I swallowed and tentatively touched his head with the tip of my tongue.

His skin was warm and smooth, salty and inviting. I ran my tongue all the way around his tip, marvelling at the way he felt in my mouth. He must be going wild, but he let me take my time and explore every centimetre of him before I took more of him between my lips.

He groaned softly and placed his hand on the back

of my head, his fingers stroking and tangling in my hair.

Again, there was no force. He held me in place, but I could have knocked his hand away if I needed to. Instead, he encouraged me to take him in deeper, to close my lips around him and gently suck.

"Your mouth..." he said breathlessly. He kept still while I moved, bobbing my head back and forth, sucking and sliding.

I reached up with my hand to lightly cup his balls. Those too were hot, the thin skin over throbbing flesh and blood.

Throbbing because I did that to him. Me. He was hard as steel because I aroused him. Because I was touching him and making him feel this way.

I looked up at him and sucked harder and faster, then softer and slower. Every drop of control was in my hands. And in my mouth. I knew I had him right on the edge and that was where I kept him for as long as I could. I held him there, deciding when he'd come. If he'd come.

The expression of rapture on his face was all because of me. The control he gave me made me feel powerful. As powerful as I did when I took a life.

I couldn't decide which of those turned me on more.

I decided I'd teased him enough. I sucked him harder and faster, while firmly massaging his balls.

"Mina..." His breath was ragged. His lips moved, but the words wouldn't form.

I kept my eyes locked on his and went on sucking, silently communicating an answer to his unspoken question. Whatever he could give me, I'd take it. All of it.

I was Mina fucking DiMarco and I wasn't going to be anyone's victim anymore.

Kurt could fuck himself, he wasn't going to stop me from being fucked. Or from being loved.

Reuben's grip on my hand tightened as he came. He let out a low cry.

His cum exploded into my mouth, hot and salty. It slid across my tongue, tingling my tastebuds.

I managed to swallow down his release before he sagged, puffing lightly.

"You're incredible," he said once he caught his breath and slid his cock out from between my lips. "I imagined what it would be like to fuck your mouth, but that was so much more." He took my hand and pulled me up beside him, before fixing his boxers and pants back into place.

"It was more than I expected too," I admitted. "Reading about it in romance books is one thing, but I liked it more than I thought I would."

"I have another confession." He pulled me onto his lap. "I've never let go like that with anyone. Never let them take the lead. I'm usually the one who's in control."

I gave him a bland, but teasing look. "I'm shocked," I said, deadpan. "Reuben Brantley, in control?"

He surprised me by chuckling in response. The sound wasn't as carefree and uninhibited as Gianni, but it was just as pleasant. That was another win for me. Making a man who rarely laughed, chuckle.

"I know, it's a difficult concept to grasp," he said, equally deadpan. "I'm usually so passive and in the background."

"No one could ever describe you like that," I said. "You only have to walk into a room to command the attention of everyone in it. Even the twins."

"That might be overstating it slightly," he said. "Those two like to pretend they can ignore me."

"Pretend being the key word here," I said. "They can no more ignore you than I can."

I leaned over and kissed his mouth. My clit throbbed with the knowledge he'd taste himself on my lips.

I'd actually sucked him off. He'd come in my mouth. This was something I could do because I wanted to and he wanted me to do it. Not because anyone was holding me down or telling me lies. Filling my mind with heartbreak.

"I want to do that again," I said.

"Kiss?" he asked, one eyebrow slightly raised.

I poked him in the chest with my fingernail. "You know what I mean."

He leaned in and rested his forehead against mine. "You want to suck my cock again. Consider it all yours.

If you want to put your beautiful mouth around my cock, you can. Any time, anywhere."

"Anywhere?" I echoed.

"Anywhere," he agreed. "I will never not want to fuck your mouth. In the meantime…"

He kissed my mouth. Lightly, gently with more intimacy than we'd ever kissed before. If I ever doubted his feelings for me, I didn't now.

I hoped I conveyed the same to him. I'd been in love with him for as long as I could remember. We'd missed so much time, but we could make up for it.

Someday, it might feel like those five years never happened.

I caught a hint of movement near the back door, leading into the house.

How long had Damon stood there, watching us? I sensed he was there for a while as I sucked Reuben off.

I got a vibe from him. If he could have taken either of our places, he would have.

Apparently, I wasn't the only one with secrets.

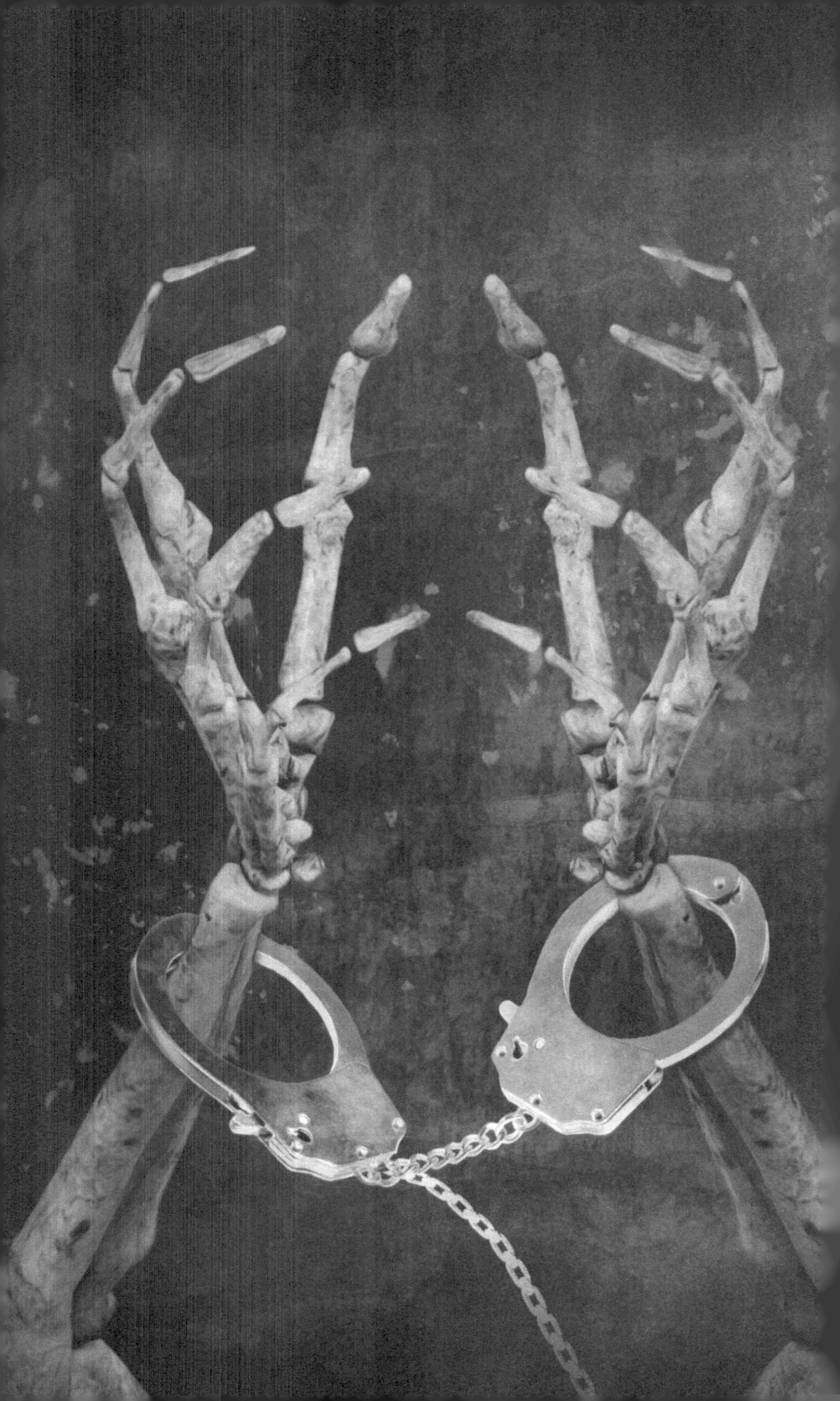

CHAPTER 11

MINA

"You know this is confidential information, right?" I glanced back as Gianni peered over my shoulder.

He grinned, but didn't move away. "I figured I could help. Give you some advice as to which job to take next."

His face was centimetres from mine, close enough for me to breathe in the warm, unique scent of him. He always smelled of lavender, leather and danger.

I turned off my phone screen. "What makes you think I need advice?"

I followed him with my gaze as he walked around the back of the couch and plopped down beside me.

He was completely undeterred. "You probably don't, but there's a shit load of suburbs that didn't exist a year or two ago, much less five. Besides, you might need someone to drive the getaway car."

He raised his tattooed hands to either side of his

face, to gesture at himself. He wore a gold ring on his right hand, which shone in the light that came through the library window.

"I'd suggest you watch too many movies, but I suppose that's Damon's job." I placed my phone down on my lap and leaned against the arm of the couch. "I could ask him to come with me." I couldn't help trying to see if I could get a rise out of Gianni. Naturally, I didn't.

"We could all go." He spoke as if he was suggesting an afternoon out, maybe with a picnic.

"Nothing says 'stealthy assassin at work' quite like a car full of people," I said dryly.

Now I was picturing us turning up in a bright red car, with bright clothes and maybe a neon sign or two. Fun, but it wouldn't go unnoticed.

"What I really need is a current driver's license and a car." Some of these jobs were close, but others were on the other side of Sydney. Many were in different states and a handful were in different countries.

Being an assassin was not only lucrative, but it was a great way to see the world.

If you liked to see cities at night, and didn't mind missing all the things tourists got to do. If I kept turning up in interesting places, people might start to notice. Especially if they coincided with the deaths of influential people.

I might look sweet, but at the end of the day, I was a

DiMarco. Anyone who knew our family would wonder what I was up to.

"Too easy," he said with a wave of his wrist. "We just need a photo and we can sort the license. And Reuben has lots of cars. You could borrow one of his. Or ask him to give you one. If you told him you needed a black Maserati with hot pink seats, he'd have that here in a day or two."

"I prefer black seats," I said. "And something less obvious than a Maserati. Something more inconspicuous, like a small hatchback."

"Does anyone drive small hatchbacks anymore?" He frowned. "You'll be noticed less if you drive an SUV. Everyone seems to have those these days. Preferably bullet-proof and crash proof. And electric. Can you drive?"

"Electric?" I frowned.

That was one of the many changes I was still trying to come to terms with. That and people delivering food on the back of a bike. Personally, I thought that was a perfect front for an assassin. I made a mental note to get a bike and a uniform. It might come in useful.

"I'm a bit rusty, but how hard could it be to pick it back up again?" I shrugged. "I got my license before…"

I didn't need to finish that sentence. We both knew what I was referring to. I didn't want to sugarcoat it, but I didn't want to keep saying Kurt's name either. There really were no good ways to say 'chained and stuck in a cage in a basement.'

"My sister Rose taught me to drive." Asher was too young, Dane was too impatient, my parents too busy or disinterested. Rose took it upon herself to make sure I knew how.

"You two were close," Gianni said. He pulled my feet onto his lap and started to massage one of them.

I fought the instinct to pull them back away from him, and let him touch me.

If a day was coming when I wouldn't automatically flinch, I wished it would come sooner. Now they knew who I was, I felt compelled to live up to my badass persona.

Assassins weren't supposed to be human. We were supposed to be something else, something *more*. The monsters under the bed our parents warn us about.

Sitting in a library, surrounded by books, while one of my boyfriends gave me a foot rub was definitely outside that stereotype. Maybe I should give myself a break and remind myself I was a person first, and my job second.

"We are as close as we could be with so many years between us," I said. "She was just as likely to tell me to get lost as she was to do things with me. Asher and I were closer. We were always spying on the other two, and doing things like waiting behind a tree to throw a water balloon at them."

We'd hurl them, wait for them to connect, then run away laughing. Asher would always make sure I was out of reach of either of our older siblings, even if he had his ass kicked once in a while.

"Dane used to get so angry. He was the one who'd run off and tell our parents what we did." I rolled my eyes. "I think he liked it when we got in trouble, but it was more than that. He wanted us to look bad and for him to look good, like the dutiful son. The one who kept us in line, as if he could actually do that."

Asher and I were more inclined to laugh at him, flip him off, then plan another prank. Not where our father could see.

"Dane wanted to be the golden child. The head of the family. He wanted to be like Reuben."

I doubted Reuben was a snitch the way Dane used to be. He would have given his siblings a glare before slipping off to be by himself and read.

"Who doesn't?" Gianni massaged my toes, one by one. His hands were warm and firm, but gentle at the same time. "Reuben is a powerful man. If I was going to aspire to be anyone else, it would be him. But I don't, because I like being me. So you'd say Dane was the most ambitious one out of you all?"

"Not necessarily," I said thoughtfully. "The rest of us were ambitious in different ways. Rose wanted to be the best at what she does, and so did I. Asher wanted to take over the world with his music. Dane was the one who craved power. When he was at school, he always sought out the popular kids. If he couldn't be the leader, he wanted to be as close to them as he could."

He snitched on the other kids the way he did with us, but only if that was in line with his friends. He wanted to ruffle only the *right* feathers.

"Why do you think he went into teaching?" Gianni asked. He didn't seem as though he was judging Dane, he was just curious about him. Dane was a part of the childhood that helped to shape me. Another piece of my complicated puzzle.

"That's a good question," I said. I wondered that myself. If you'd asked me which of my siblings would be interested in teaching anything to anyone else, he probably would have been at the bottom of the list.

"I'm not sure I know the answer. Maybe he was hoping Brutham Academy would give him contacts, the same way so many men want to join the Brotherhood. Maybe it's something for him to do while he waits for his opportunity. Maybe he just likes teaching."

I laughed slightly. My oldest brother liked ambition more than he liked people. Unless there was something in it for him.

"Everyone has an angle," Gianni said. "I'm surprised he hasn't come knocking on Reuben's door, asking for a job. Unless he has and I don't know about it."

His expression suggested that was unlikely. He had a way of knowing about almost everything that went on around here. He watched, he listened and he learned. He observed and absorbed everything. Like I did. Missing even a small detail could get me killed. Or get someone else killed.

I glanced in the direction of the door, as though he might suddenly turn up outside. When no one knocked, I turned back to Gianni.

"That's what he'd do if he knew I was here," I said. "If he thought I had any influence with Reuben, he'd be right here, looking for scraps."

"Is that why you don't want him to know about you?" Gianni asked. "You don't want him putting you in that position?" He rubbed the ball of my foot. "What about Asher? He's off living his life. I don't get the impression he'd need you to do anything for him."

"No, but Asher, being Asher, he'd be devastated about what happened to me. You know what they say about ignorance being bliss." I didn't want to break his happy, rock star bubble.

"I've heard something about that, but I also know people don't like having other people make up their mind for them," he said. "Whatever you decide to do, I support you one hundred percent. Just think about it, okay?"

His expression wasn't judgemental at all, just offering an alternative perspective. One I had considered, but had to dismiss for now. When the time came, I'd see both of my brothers. In the meantime, I'd let them live their lives.

"Can I ask you something?" I glanced toward the door, but no one seemed to be around.

As far as I knew, Reuben and Damon were in Reuben's office working. Terry was in the kitchen making something that smelled wonderful. The scent of meat and vegetables wafted through the house.

"Of course," Gianni said. "I'm as open as any of these books." He jerked his head towards the shelf closest to the couch. A lot more books were housed there than there used to be. Many I'd read, but lots I hadn't.

"Damon and Reuben," I said carefully. "Have they ever…"

A brief frown flitted across Gianni's brow. "Been intimate? Fucked?"

I swallowed at the mental image his words conjured. "Either of those things. Both. The other night, I got the impression that Damon might want to."

Gianni looked thoughtful. "To my knowledge, no, nothing has happened between them. Unlike me, Damon is a closed book. Reuben too. I won't say I haven't noticed chemistry between them, but whether or not they'd act on it is another thing. Would that bother you?"

"Not at all," I said.

A sly grin crept onto his face. "Would it turn you on?"

My face heated. "It might. I wouldn't ask them to if they weren't interested."

"I would," Gianni said with a grin. "Now you've put that idea in my head, I'd pay money to see it. Just imagine…"

He was interrupted by the sound of my phone

ringing in my lap. The sound was so unexpected, I startled.

The screen lit up. No contact or location, just a number I didn't recognise.

"Who knows your phone number?" Gianni asked.

I shook my head. "No one." My first instinct was to ignore the call, but I picked up my phone and glanced at Gianni before accepting and pressing the screen to put it on speakerphone.

Before I could say anything, a voice spoke.

"Miss me, bitch?"

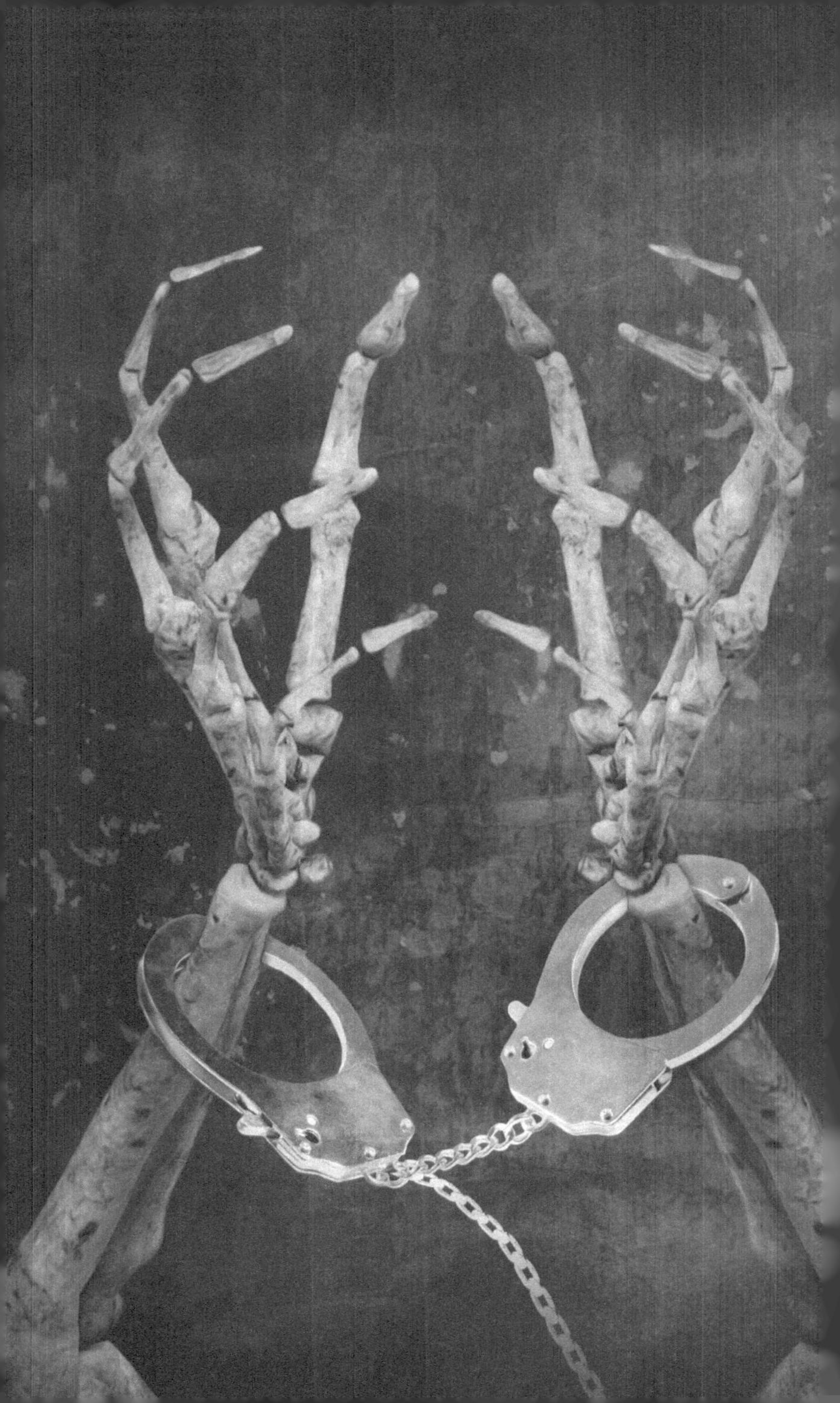

CHAPTER 12

MINA

I almost dropped the phone, but managed to hold on in spite of trembling fingers.

Hearing Kurt's voice again brought everything back in a flood that threatened to swamp me harder than the photos had.

His voice haunted my sleep and waking hours for so long, it was stamped in an endless round of nightmares.

He continued before I could formulate a response.

"You're so fucking predictable, Mina," he said. "Did you think I wouldn't have this number? That I wouldn't know the moment the *Sparrow* was reactivated? The second that happened, I was notified. You think I don't keep track of my property?"

He emphasised my codename, probably hoping someone was in the room with me and didn't already know. He'd be more than happy to expose me. Whatever it took to drag me down. To get under my skin.

Gianni fumbled with his phone and sent off a message. I was vaguely aware of it in the corner of my eye.

I didn't know who he was messaging, or why, until Reuben and Damon all but thundered into the library.

"Did you want something, prick?" I asked coldly.

He laughed. "Is that the best you can do, bitch?"

"I don't know, it's more original than 'bitch,'" I replied.

How I managed to keep my voice even, I didn't know. I drew strength from the three men around me. Every single one of them would have torn Kurt apart if he was here.

They'd hold me if I wanted to lose my cool and cry for a while. They'd also hand me knives if I wanted to carve my initials into Kurt's forehead.

If it wasn't for them, I might well have unravelled on the spot.

"Bitch is appropriate," Kurt said. "Like a female dog, you belong in a cage." He chuckled. "That was why I kept you in one. Don't tell me you didn't enjoy being on all fours in front of me while I—"

Reuben growled. A literal growl. His face was red, eyes flashing with pure fury, as though he might rip Kurt's throat out through the phone.

Silence came through the line, followed by another laugh. "Sounds like the bitch found another dog. I heard a rumour about you being seen with Reuben Brantley. I'm surprised he'd want anyone's sloppy seconds. Then again, he's a Brantley. None of them are known for being discerning."

"I'm going to enjoy rearranging his face," Gianni whispered.

"If I don't do it first," Damon snapped.

"I don't mind sharing," Gianni told him.

"I bet you don't," Kurt said. "Mina has three holes. I'm sure she's told you all about how I've had all of them."

"Did. You. Want. Something?" I ground out. "If you called to remind me what a piece of shit you are, you could have saved us both some time. I have better things to do than think about you."

"Right," he drew the word out. "Like getting back to being an assassin. Does Reuben know about that?"

"Yes, he does," I replied. "He knows what happened to that girl. He's seen the photos of what you did to me. They were on the phone I found at Stefan's place before I killed him."

The silence on the other end suggested Kurt hadn't known his associate was dead. Good, it was about time I got the better of him.

"He was very helpful," I continued. "He gave me all sorts of interesting information about you. It's funny how much people like to talk when they have a knife to their throat."

"You never were a good liar." He sounded uneasy.

I clearly hit a nerve. He wasn't sure what I knew. I could be right outside his door, waiting to step inside and slice him open. Like all cowards, he went on the defensive.

"That's bullshit, and you know it," I said. "Like everything else that comes out of your mouth. Let me tell you, you will regret everything you did to me. We will find you and—"

"Fuck you up," Gianni said helpfully.

"Yes, that," I said.

Kurt chuckled, his ego back in place. "That's where you're wrong, bitch. You won't find me before I find you. Then we'll see who fucks whom up. I know you. You can't and won't hide behind Reuben Brantley forever. The minute you step out, I'll have you. In every sense of the word. I'm going to make that cage look like a holiday. When I'm finished with you, you'll beg for forgiveness and for my cock. Just like you used to."

Before I could respond, he ended the call.

"I hate telemarketers," Gianni said, his expression perfectly serious.

I managed a faint smile before turning off the phone. "Looks like I need a new phone number." Although, he'd likely find a way to get that too.

"These days, most people don't answer their phones," Damon said. "It saves talking to someone they don't want to talk to."

I gave him a funny look. "What's the point of phones then? Don't tell me, people are still watching funny cat videos on social media."

"Exactly," Gianni said. "They also come in useful for

texting and letting the boss and Damon know that prick was on the line."

"I should have realised he'd try to contact me when I switched my status back to active." The rest of the conversation played on my mind, going around and around on repeat. Most of it made my stomach turn.

"Unless he was dead, there was no way to keep that information from him." Reuben lowered himself down into a chair opposite me. "He's smart enough to keep an eye out for any sign of you."

"How did he know I was here with you?" I asked. That was at the forefront of my mind, more than Kurt's threats and reminders. "He said someone told him. The only people who have seen us together work for you or they're dead."

"It wasn't me," Gianni said immediately.

"It wasn't anyone in this room," Reuben said. "It better not be anyone who works for me." The fury hadn't completely evaporated from his expression. He looked like a bomb about to explode.

"What would any of them have to gain by telling him?" Damon asked slowly. "We know Rose wouldn't say anything. Neither would Daze. She'd skin her boyfriends alive if they did. That leaves the twins and Caleb."

"The twins wouldn't," Gianni said. "They may be as morally grey as the rest of us, but they also don't like men who abuse women. Which narrows it down to..."

"Caleb," Reuben said darkly. "If he's working with Kurt, against me, it will be the last thing he does."

I didn't know Caleb well, but I remembered Daze warning me about him. That he was ambitious and would grab any opportunity that arose. How loyal was he to his oldest brother?

"I'll tell Caleb to come here for a little chat," Damon said.

Reuben nodded. "Do it. Better yet, send the jet to pick him up. I don't want to give him an opportunity to run, and if he's done nothing wrong, sweating for a while won't hurt him."

Damon pulled out his phone and stepped out of the room.

Reuben scrubbed a hand over his face. "Are you all right?"

"I don't know," I admitted. I let Gianni take the phone from my hand and look through it.

He tapped on the number Kurt used to call me, but it was already disconnected, if it wasn't fake to begin with. "I suspect it might be impossible to trace him through this, but we can ask the twins to try."

"It can't hurt, but he'll probably be long gone from wherever he is now by the time they figure it out," I said. He was proving to be slipperier than a snake.

"We know one thing for sure," Gianni said. "He's still alive. And while he's still alive, we can find him and remedy that."

"That was a mistake," I said slowly. "If he really was

smart, he'd find a way to convince us he was dead, so we'd stop looking for him."

"I wouldn't stop," Reuben said darkly. "But you're right, he let his arrogance and his obsession for you do the talking. That will be to his detriment."

"We also know he's still in the country," I said.

They both looked over at me sharply.

Reuben frowned. "How do you—"

"I recognise the bird in the background. It's some kind of cockatoo. I only heard it once, and only briefly, but it was clear enough." I shrugged.

Gianni's lips dropped apart. "Not gonna lie, I'm impressed."

"When you have to rely on being stealthy and observant, you tend to notice even the smallest thing," I said. Anything you miss could get you dead, or worse.

"Anything else?" Reuben asked, his eyes intent on me.

I frowned and thought back. "Maybe a car. It was in the background though. Like… He was outside, some distance from the road. Everything else was just him and his bullshit. I wish I could narrow it down further."

"Still in the country is narrower than we had before," Reuben said. "Judging by the way he sounded, he wouldn't have travelled far from Mina. He might well be on the outskirts of Sydney."

"If he is, we will find his sorry ass," Gianni said. "And we'll make it even sorrier."

"You have any idea if there was anywhere he liked to go?" Reuben asked.

I ran everything I knew about Kurt from before through my mind. "He frequented a gym. He was obsessive about fitness. He taught self defence classes there too. And boxing. He also liked to go camping. A couple of times, he wanted me to go with him, but I refused."

"Who trained you to become an assassin?" Gianni asked. "Was it Kurt?"

"No. It was Zara Levin and her sister, Paola. My father wanted me to learn from the best."

"Ohhh, the Sisters of Death," Gianni said in appreciation. "I've always wanted to meet them, but you know what they say. You only meet them once and they're the only ones to survive the experience."

"Only if someone hires them to take you out," I said. "Then your chances of survival are approximately zero percent." If I was scared of anyone in my life, it was the Levin sisters. They were card-carrying badass bitches, if they ever were any.

"They're almost as deadly as the Sparrow," Gianni said. "And now I'm as hard as hell." He made a face and adjusted the front of his pants. "There's something about women who know how to kill that just gets me going every time."

"Is there any chance the Levin sisters are working with Kurt?" Reuben asked softly.

"I doubt it," I said. "They didn't like him and he

didn't like them. I think he was concerned they'd influence me against him." Not that I needed any convincing.

"They were quick to take me up on my request to hunt him down. For a fee, of course." They did nothing for free. Including getting out of bed in the morning. Why should they when they could ask anything they wanted in return for a job?

"That answers the age-old question," Gianni mused. When we both turned to look at him he said, "I'd always wondered who the assassins hire to assassinate someone the assassin wants assassinated. Now I know. The Levin sisters. I bet they hire you too."

"I think people are too scared of them to piss them off. So they wouldn't need to hire someone to kill them," I said. "But that's a job I'd accept."

I owed them everything for all they'd taught me. They'd kept me from losing myself. That was a debt I doubted I could ever repay.

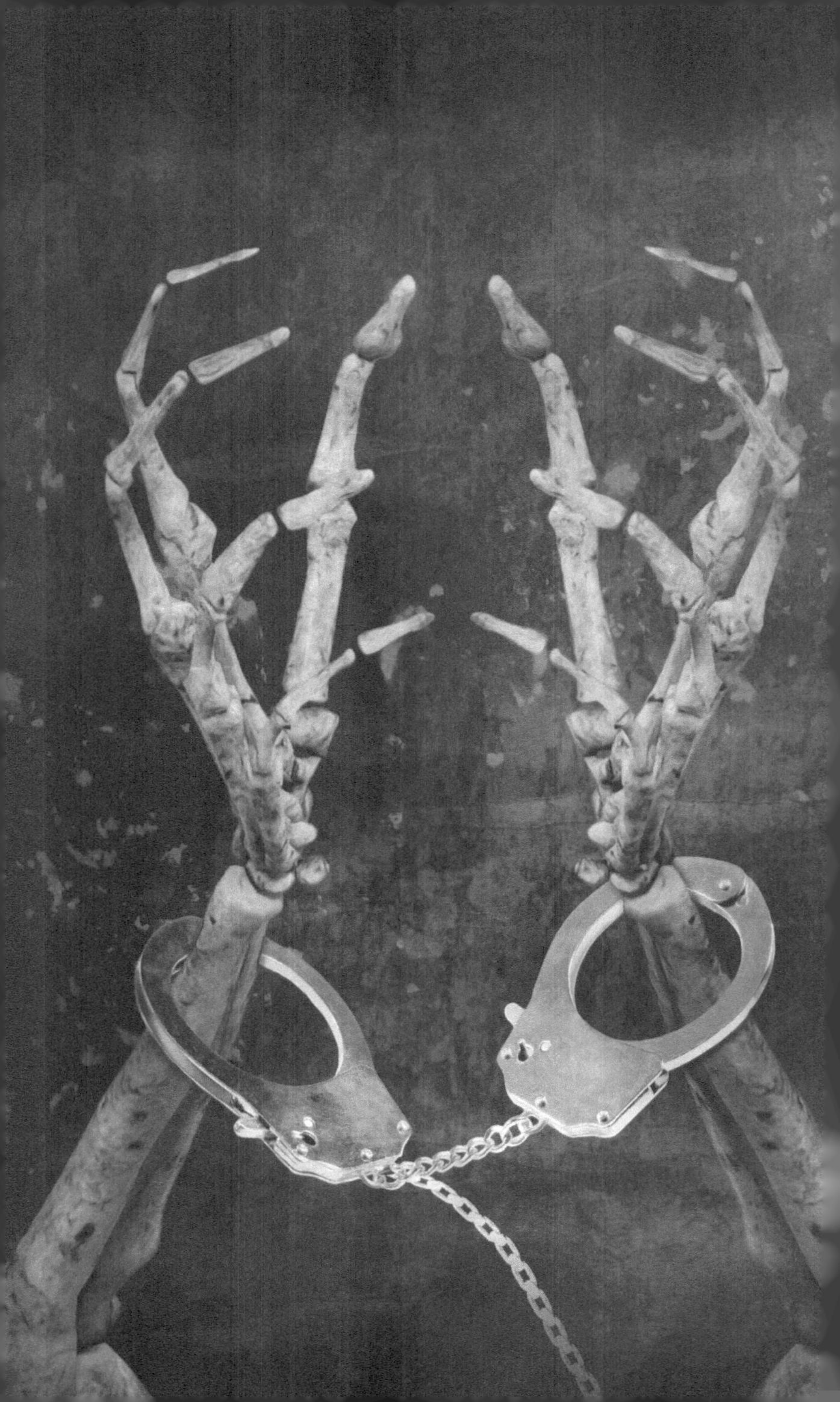

CHAPTER 13

DAMON

"You brought me all the way here to question my loyalty?" Caleb stood with his palms pressed against the top of Reuben's desk, his upper body leaning forward as though he might loom over his older brother.

He was taller, around the same height as me, but he lacked Reuben's presence. Caleb was commanding, but compared to Reuben, he might as well be in the background.

No, I wasn't biased. Much.

"You're always looking for an excuse to borrow my jet," Reuben drawled. "We thought you might enjoy the ride."

"Bullshit," Caleb snapped. He pushed himself back from the desk and turned around, a hand on the back of his head. He stood with his eyes closed for a few moments before turning back to Reuben.

"You think I'm working against you? With a lowlife

piece of shit like Kurt Lasalle? Why the fuck would I do that? I've worked hard all these years to build our family into what it is. You think I'd throw that away? For what?"

"If you thought you could replace me, you might take the opportunity," Reuben said evenly.

Caleb's jaw clenched, but he didn't deny the suggestion. If he thought he'd succeed, he might well step out of line. But if he was going to take that bet, he'd have to be very sure he'd win. Otherwise, he'd be stepping out of an aircraft without a parachute. Literally.

Caleb dropped his hand to his thigh with a slap. "I'm not working against you with Kurt fucking Lasalle."

"Who are you working against him with?" Gianni leaned against the door frame, his head cocked.

Caleb looked like he might lunge at Gianni and punch him in the face, but managed to restrain himself.

"I'm not working against Reuben," he growled. "I have my people looking for Kurt, as requested." He shook his head. "Why are we even having this conversation?"

"Because someone told him Mina was here," I said. I reclined in one of the chairs to the side of the room, my ankle resting on the opposite thigh. A subtle reminder that I was more trusted around here than Caleb. A reminder that didn't go unnoticed, from the glare he gave me.

"Who told him?" Caleb demanded. "You said she was—"

"Yes, I did," Reuben said. "But Kurt had that information anyway." He didn't explain how he knew. Caleb didn't need to be privy to that. Unless Reuben thought he did. He wouldn't hear it from me or Gianni.

Caleb frowned and sank down into a chair, elbows propped on his thighs, where they threatened to wrinkle his perfectly tailored suit. He exhaled, long and slow. "What are you thinking?"

"Either we have a leak, or he was watching on the occasions we left the house," Reuben said.

"We checked the ice cream parlour for cameras," I said. "The only one present was CCTV and we destroyed the footage. The car park was the same. If the house where we found Frank had cameras, we'll never know, since the place exploded."

"If I was going to keep a woman against her will, I'd have cameras on her," Caleb said slowly.

"Sounds like you're speaking from experience," Gianni said. "But there were no cameras in the basement. Not in the rest of the building except outside. We dealt with that one too."

"I know you don't want to hear this, but is there any chance Mina is working with him?" Caleb asked.

I wasn't aware I was about to move, but I leaped out of my seat and grabbed Caleb by the front of his suit to haul him out of his.

"If you ever fucking say anything like that again, you'll be breathing out your ass," I growled.

To his credit, Caleb looked unruffled. He was fully

aware I wouldn't kill him unless Reuben ordered me to. No matter how tempted I was.

"Like I said, you wouldn't want to hear the suggestion, but that doesn't mean it didn't need to be said," Caleb said evenly. "I'm no student of psychology, but Stockholm Syndrome is a thing. We both know people can be made to do all sorts of things with the right level of brainwashing. Isn't that Gianni's specialty? Convincing people that what they think is true, isn't it?" He grabbed my wrists and pulled them off the front of his suit.

I glared at him before stepping back to the other side of the room. If I was too close to him, I might do something I'd regret.

"I have considered the possibility," Reuben admitted. "If that's the case, then she wouldn't be acting on her own choice. What Kurt did to her left her traumatised. Every time she's reminded of him, she looks ready to slice off her own skin and step out of it. When she first saw me, she thought I was going to have her killed. She was *relieved*. She would have preferred to die than stay there."

Caleb nodded and reclaimed his seat. "I trust Daisy Lasalle when she says her and her boyfriends aren't involved. She worked for me for years. She's never spoken highly of her brother. Now, she seems more inclined to make him breathe out his ass." He nodded at me to acknowledge his use of my wording.

"I trust the twins," Reuben said. He steepled his

fingers and pressed against his lips. "What are we missing?"

His brow was furrowed with measured thought and a dose of annoyance. He didn't like it when he didn't know things. When he wasn't fully in control.

"It's possible Kurt was guessing," Caleb said. "You know he was operating behind your back. He would have known you'd come for him at some point. Someone got Mina out of that basement. He might have put one and one together and actually managed to come up with two."

"He could have been fishing for information," I conceded. "But I don't think so. Everything he said seemed calculated. Like he knew exactly what he was going to say. He was sure he knew all the right buttons to press."

"He was very sure one of us would be in the room with her," Gianni said. "I know for a fact there aren't any bugs or cameras inside this house. Not unless we control them."

His words bounced around in my mind for a few moments before they bumped into a firm idea.

I stood up straighter. "Can you excuse me please, boss?" I slipped out of the room before Reuben could even acknowledge I'd spoken.

I slipped down the corridor and down to the last place I saw Mina. The place she seemed the most comfortable, apart from her bedroom.

I stopped in the doorway of the library. Sure

enough, she was sitting on a chair in the corner, reading some kind of sports romance. I didn't realise rugby romance was a thing, but then again my knowledge of the romance genre was limited.

"How do you get into buildings undetected?" I asked.

She looked up at me and frowned. "How do I—" My question sank in. She seemed reluctant, but finally said, "I have a device."

"Where is it?" I asked. "Where is this device?"

She slipped the bookmark into her book and set it aside. "In my bedroom, why?"

"I need to see it." I should have guessed it was something like that. After years of speculation, I had an answer to one of the more interesting mysteries. I'd take some time to think about it later. In the meantime, there were more pressing matters.

Still looking uncertain, she stood. "Okay."

I followed her upstairs, vaguely aware Gianni, Reuben and Caleb stood outside Reuben's office watching us in confusion.

In spite of that, they were behind us when she reached into a drawer, pulled out a jumper and unfolded it.

Inside was a small, black device with a screen on the front.

"This disables alarm systems." She placed it on my outstretched palm.

"Mina is the Sparrow," Reuben said to Caleb, his voice low and reluctant.

Shit.

I probably should have thought of the consequences before I bolted out of the room, but I got an idea and ran with it. If there was a chance waiting might get us killed, then I had no choice.

"How does it work?" I asked.

"It hacks into the Wi-Fi that security systems are run on these days," she explained. "It reads the code and switches the system off."

"So if it hacks, it can be hacked," I reasoned.

"If technology has changed since it was invented," she agreed. "It was supposed to be hack proof. At least, as hack proof as anything could be."

I turned the device over in my hand. In the back were four, small screws. "I don't suppose you have a—"

She reached into the drawer again and pulled out a small screwdriver. She held it out to me with the handle facing me.

I nodded my thanks and accepted it. She really was prepared for almost anything. How many knives did she have hidden in those drawers and around the room? If I was her, I'd have several, in case anyone got past the security system.

The device balanced on my palm, I carefully unscrewed each of the screws and handed them to her. I had to use the screwdriver to pry off the back of the device, but it eventually came off with a pop.

"Bingo." Sitting in the back of the device was a tiny bug. The kind used to listen in and track people. The kind that crunched satisfyingly under my heel.

"He said I was predictable," Mina said, her eyes glazed as she spoke. "I thought he meant coming here, but he didn't. He knew exactly where I kept my phone and that device. He knew if I ever got out of that basement, I'd go back for those things. That could have been inside the device for years. Waiting."

Her face was pale again. That asshole really knew how to get to her. Fuck only knew what else he'd done that we hadn't uncovered yet.

"Mina DiMarco is the Sparrow?" Apparently it took Caleb a few moments to process that information. "How long until Kurt tells the world that?"

Or maybe he processed it immediately and moved quickly to the implications, conjuring scenarios in his mind. His tone wasn't panicked, or even concerned.

His brow was creased as he made calculations in his head. Planning like someone plans moves in a game of chess. Reuben was commanding, but Caleb was the strategic brother. Often several moves ahead of everyone else.

I turned to glare at him.

He shrugged and raised his hands. "Don't say it hasn't occurred to you, because it would have. If this prick has gone to such lengths to track her, then what's keeping him from pulling the pin on this?"

"What would he have to gain from telling everyone?" I asked. "People would want proof. The only way he could give them that would be to throw himself under the bus."

"I wish he would throw himself under a literal bus," Gianni said.

"People like him don't give away information like that," Caleb said. "They sell it to the highest bidder. Can you imagine the amount of zeros information like that would go for? That device Damon is holding in his hand is almost as valuable." He gestured at me.

"The price governments would pay for retribution against her for assassinating their officials would be eye watering. Or better yet, finding out who hired her. Information like that could bring down whole administrations. Hell, countries could collapse. You know the kind of people she was hired to target. I'm not fucking exaggerating." His jaw was set tight.

"We're not letting them torture Mina," Gianni said, his low voice a thinly veiled threat.

"Then we better find Kurt fucking Lasalle before he can offer her up," Caleb said. "Because people aren't going to let any of us stand in the way when there are millions of dollars involved."

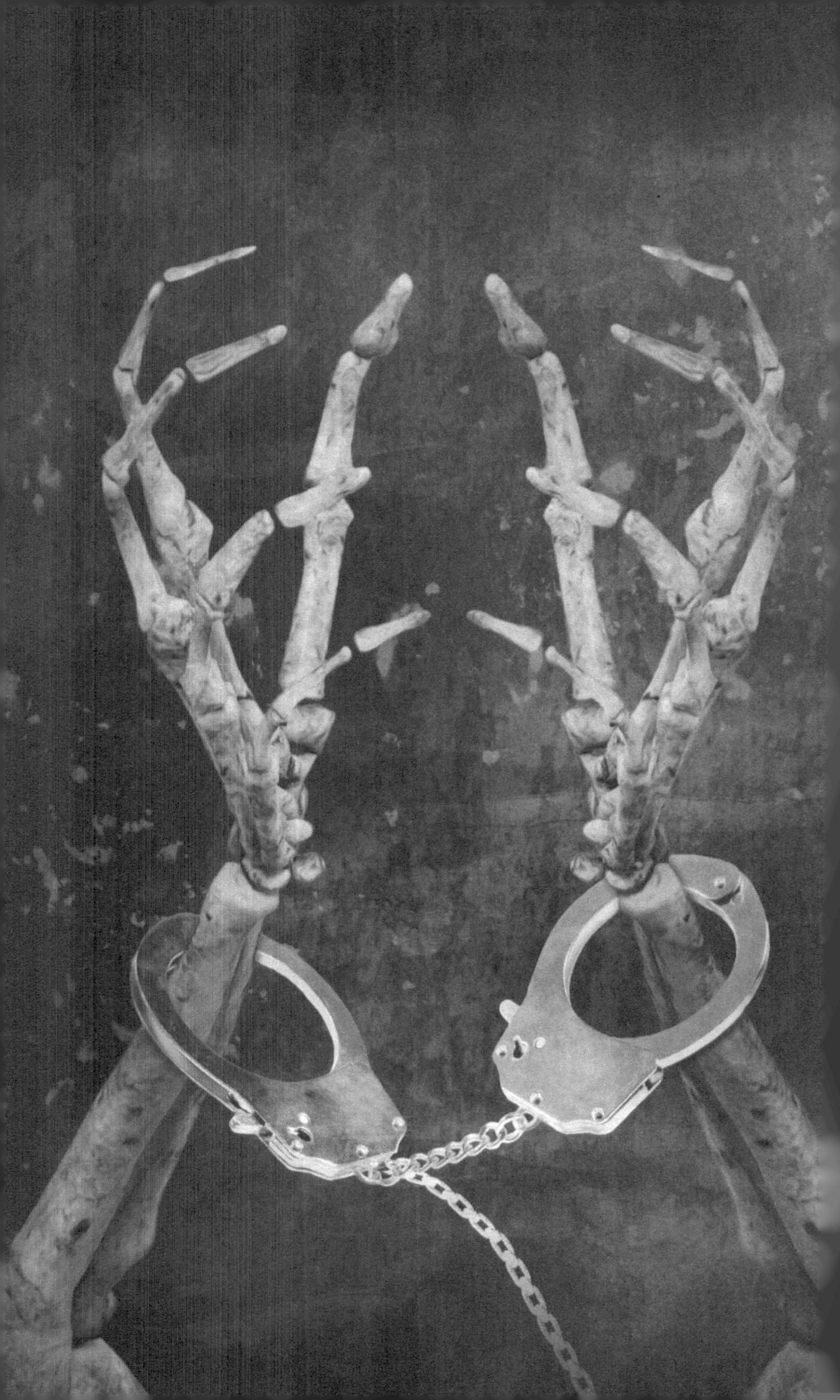

CHAPTER 14

MINA

"Pack as much as you can, " Reuben said. "I want to be out of here within the hour."

"Where are we going?" Gianni followed him to the door.

"Dusk Bay," Reuben said briskly. "My house there is more secure than here. Damon, Caleb, have your connections be on the lookout for any information regarding the Sparrow, especially any offers to sell her identity." Evidently he'd decided to take Caleb's words seriously.

Unfortunately for me, Caleb was right. Kurt would sell that information to whoever would pay for it.

"We could stop him from getting rich," I said softly.

They all stopped to stare at me.

"I could sell that information myself," I said. "Or I could give it away for free."

"No." The word was simple, the delivery soft, but Reuben's expression was firm. "Start packing."

"Listen to what she has to say," Caleb advised. He crossed his arms and nodded to me.

Reuben glared at him, but didn't contradict him. Instead, he leaned against the door frame and looked back at me while I spoke.

"If we release the information, we can control what people hear," I said. "And who hears it. If we leave it to Kurt, he gets to make millions, and he controls who he speaks to and what he gives them. I can't freely disclose information about past clients. Just enough information to satisfy people. They can do whatever they want with that. We can carefully choose what we share for minimal impact on us and our interests. And innocent people. Kurt won't have that kind of restraint."

Reuben looked thoughtful. He didn't dismiss the idea, but he didn't agree with it either.

"I'll consider it," he said finally. "We now leave in fifty-five minutes." He turned and walked out of the room.

"For what it's worth, I think it's a good idea." Caleb nodded and stepped away himself.

Damon waited until he was gone, grimaced and said, "I hate to agree with anything Caleb said, but it is."

"Technically, we're agreeing with what Mina said," Gianni pointed out. "You need help packing, sweetheart?"

"I don't have much," I said. "You should go and pack your things."

"I'll go and organise the jet," Damon said. "And speak to my contacts about putting your plan into action."

"You think Reuben will agree to it?" I asked.

Damon shrugged. "I don't see how he'd have a choice. This is the best way to stop Kurt from having control over this. It might also help to flush him out." He tucked his hands into his pockets and strode out of the room.

I glanced at Gianni.

He looked back at me and frowned. "What?"

"I was expecting you to say something like you wanted to flush Kurt down the toilet."

I grabbed the handle of the suitcase Reuben gave me and pulled it out of the top of the wardrobe. I set it down on the bed and started to toss things inside.

Gianni laughed. "I must be losing my touch if I missed that one."

"Or you thought it was low hanging fruit and weren't going to bother," I offered.

"When it comes to Kurt, there's no such thing as too low." In spite of my assurances that I didn't need help, he started to pull my underwear out of the drawer and place it neatly in the suitcase. "Not even toilet humour."

"I suppose so." I tossed my jeans in beside my underwear.

"So, you can pick locks and have a device that

disables security alarms," Gianni said. "What other tricks do you have up your sleeve?"

"Is that why you offered to help?" I asked, half teasing. "So you could get the gossip?"

"It's mostly because I like your company, but colour me curious," he said. "Caleb was also right, that device would bring in millions, maybe billions, of dollars. Imagine the places we could get into with a few of those."

I cocked my head at him.

"Right, you don't need to imagine. Have you ever been tempted to rob a bank, just because you could?" He matched the angle of my head and smiled.

I scoffed. "I prefer a challenge." My lips moved as I considered adding to that, but I pressed them together and smirked at my own thought.

"What? Where did kid-Mina sneak into?" He pressed his palms to his hips and lifted his chin expectantly.

"Nowhere I wasn't paid to go," I said evasively. I stepped around him to pick up a couple of books from the table beside the bed.

"Where did you *want* to go?" he asked.

"You'll think it's silly." I placed the books down on top of my jeans.

"Have you met me?" He looked at me sideways. "I like silly. I don't think you could say anything sillier than the thoughts that go through my mind on an hourly basis." He raised his hand and gave me a 'give it to me' gesture with his fingers.

I sighed and straightened up. "I had a crush on a popstar once. I thought about breaking into his house and... I don't know. Stealing his underwear or watching him sleep. Something stupid like that." I shrugged.

Gianni smiled. "That's adorable. If he had half a brain cell, you could have just knocked on the door. I wouldn't have turned you away if I was him."

"There's no challenge in knocking on the door," I said. "It doesn't matter anyway, because I didn't know where he lived, or what his real name was. It was just a childish fantasy."

"Those are the best kind," Gianni said. "The problem with growing up is losing things like that. What was his name?"

I made a face. "Bobby Starlight. Like I said, I was young." He sang songs about love, relationships and corny things like dancing under the light of a full moon.

His lyrics and upbeat tunes were a sweet counterpoint to the rest of my life back then. They helped to balance out all the death and gave me a place to escape to. It didn't hurt that he was ridiculously good-looking, with washboard abs and tattoos to spare. He was the fantasy of teenage girls all over the world. The one time I could have seen him on tour, I'd had a job all the way in London. I was gutted, but work always came first. Especially when I was still building a reputation.

"I love him," Gianni enthused. "He hasn't released anything in years, but I bet we could find him." He looked as though he might pull out his phone right now and send a message to his own contacts to find out the real name and address of Bobby Starlight. For all I knew, Asher might have been one of those contacts. Didn't people in the music industry know each other, or something like that?

I shook my head. "We should focus on the present and the shit that matters." I closed my suitcase and zipped it up. That part of my past was so long ago it didn't matter anymore. We had more pressing things to do, like find Kurt, and Leon Graves.

Gianni stepped over to me and placed his hands lightly on my shoulders. He looked me straight in the eyes, knowing I could step away from him at any time, but wanting to get his point across, because it was important to him.

"There's no reason why you can't have childish fantasies if you want to. If I'm too young to give them up, then you are. I know Kurt stole them from you, but I want to help you get them back. Everyone deserves to have some fun once in a while. Especially you. I'm not saying we should break in and steal a person's underwear. Although, I'm not ruling that out either, but we could do other things."

"Don't steal his underwear for me," I said.

I'd be deluding myself if I didn't think he'd do exactly that if I asked him to. I wasn't sure there was anything he'd say no to if I wanted it. He was sweet, but I wasn't going to take advantage. Especially not when I was struggling to find my own independence again.

"I won't steal his underwear for you, but I might do it *with* you," he said with a grin. "Seriously, what did you used to do for fun?"

"Kill people," I said flatly. "I read books and I killed people."

"As hot as that is, you must have done other things," he pressed. "Did you go out and dance all night? Go to the movies? Lie around with your friends, giving each other facials while you gossiped about boys?"

I glanced away from him and let my eyes glaze as I thought back. All of that seemed like a thousand lifetimes ago. It could have happened to someone else, or in my imagination.

"Used to play the guitar," I said finally. "I thought maybe I'd be in a band with Asher some day. Or tour with Bobby Starlight." I snorted at the ridiculous idea. "Can you imagine an assassin touring the world as a guitarist?"

It would be a nice cover, but it sounded like something out of a mafia rock star romance book. Was that such a thing? I'd have to look it up.

"As a matter of fact, I can," Gianni agreed. "You would have been amazing. You still might be. I'm sure Reuben wouldn't mind buying you—"

"I can buy my own guitar," I said, slightly more snappy than I intended.

I exhaled softly. "I'm sorry. I just feel like...that dream passed me by. There's no point in trying to pretend it's going to happen. For one thing, Asher's band already has a guitarist."

"That doesn't mean you can't get a guitar and play it for fun," Gianni said. "I could play with you. We could jam."

"You play the guitar?" I squinted at him. I couldn't quite imagine him doing that.

He grinned. "No, but I can play the triangle. And believe it or not, I'm not too bad on the flute." He mimed playing one, his lips pursed as he blew into an invisible instrument. "You never heard this from me, but Damon is pretty good on the saxophone."

"Don't tell me, Reuben is secretly an accomplished drummer?" I asked.

Gianni chuckled. "I don't think Reuben would be caught dead playing a musical instrument. Besides, I think he's more the bass player type." He mimed playing one of the four stringed instruments, leaning backwards as though he was rocking out to an audience.

A laugh slipped out from between my lips. "That's an interesting visual image. I'm not sure I'll be able to get that out of my head."

"You're welcome," Gianni quipped. "Maybe you can work on him to learn to play. He could use another outlet to let himself relax."

"I might start by getting my own guitar first," I said. He was right, I should give myself the chance to enjoy my life. As much fun as killing and reading were, I enjoyed making music. Even if I was the only one who ever heard it.

"Do you need help packing?" I pulled out my phone and glanced at the time.

I had no reason to believe Reuben wasn't completely serious when he said we'd had an hour. If that was the case, we used up half of that already.

"I'm still packed from when we went to Dusk Bay," Gianni admitted. "Never got around to unpacking. You're going to love the house there. It overlooks the beach. There are stairs that lead right down to it. It's the only way to get there by land. The view is absolutely fucking beautiful."

He grabbed the handle of my suitcase and led me out the door.

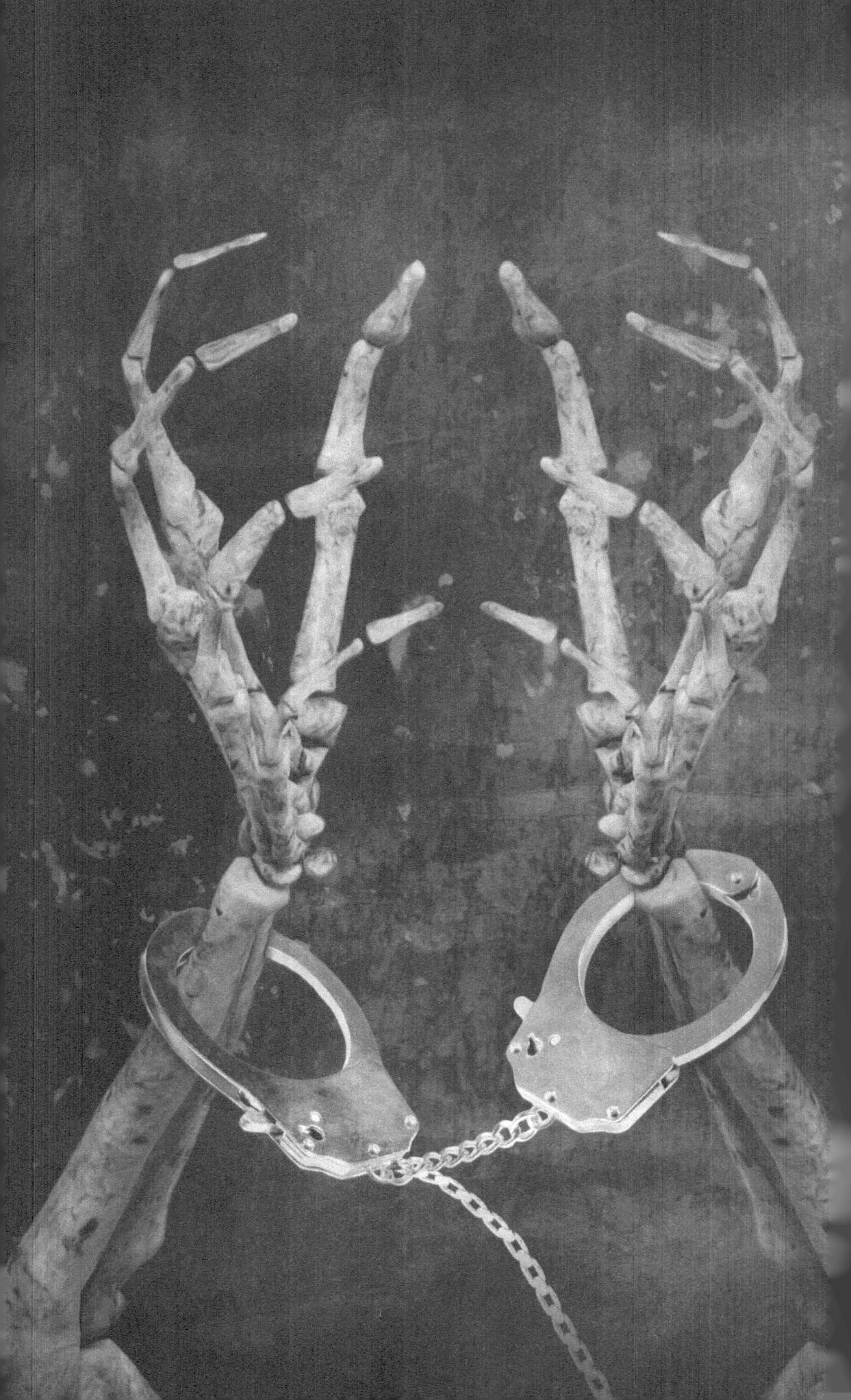

CHAPTER 15

MINA

Gianni was right about the house in Dusk Bay. From the moment we stepped through the front door, the house opened up to the expansive view of the Pacific Ocean.

Easily three or four times the size of the house in Sydney, it was just as tastefully decorated, with light wood, creams and blue-greys. Coastal without looking cliché. Decadent and elegant, but comfortable at the same time.

The rear of the house was a bank of windows that framed the sunlight glittering on the waves.

"This is incredible," I breathed.

I felt as though if I spoke too loud, I'd disturb the peace in this place. "Do you come here a lot?" I stepped over to look out at the water.

Reuben stopped beside me and placed a hand on my shoulder. "A couple of times a year. Not enough."

"It's empty the rest of the time?" I asked.

"Except for the staff, yes." He shrugged. "They keep it clean and well-maintained."

I pictured the expression on his face if he found dust in his house and held back a smile. "It's amazing."

"It's a waste not to be here more often," he said. "Sometimes I consider letting someone else watch over things in Sydney while I live here." He looked contemplative. "There are several rooms for you to choose from, unless you're ready to share."

I expected him to bring that up at some point, but it still knocked the breath out of me for a few moments. Was I ready? Could I do more than share a room, or a bed? I knew what all three of them wanted. I wanted that too, but the idea still left me in a cold sweat.

"You know I won't pressure you—" he started.

"I know," I said quickly. "I think I'd like to share a room. Being by myself at night is lonely and I get into my own head. If someone else was there, it might help." I held my lower lip with my teeth.

"It doesn't have to be me," he said reluctantly. He clearly wanted it to be.

"It's not that," I said. I glanced around to see we were alone. Gianni and Damon must have taken their bags and mine upstairs. I appreciated them giving us some space. "Damon…"

"Cares about you too." A faint frown creased his brow, uncertain as to whether we were on the same page.

Honestly, I wasn't sure we were in the same book.

I cleared my throat. "He cares about you too."

Reuben's brow smoothed. "Ah."

"You know?" I asked.

"I suspected." He inclined his head.

"And?" I prompted. "Can I ask if it's reciprocated?"

"How would you feel if it was?" he asked carefully.

"Happy for you both," I said without hesitation.

"It wouldn't be about us picking each other over you," he said, frowning again. "We both want you as well."

"I was hoping you'd say that," I admitted. "I didn't want to make things any messier than they already are. I mean figuratively messy, not literally." My face heated.

A slight smile tugged at the corners of his mouth.

"But I wouldn't have stood in the way if that was what you wanted," I added quickly. "You haven't said what that is."

"I'm not sure what the answer is to your questions," he said carefully. "There's an attraction there, but we've never acted on it. I wasn't sure if he wanted to, or what it would do to our working relationship. And I thought maybe he and Gianni might have a thing."

"I don't think Gianni would object to anything and everything," I said. "Me, Damon, you. Any combination of the above. But I'm certain Damon wants you as much as I do." I stood on my toes and lightly kissed his mouth. The idea of seeing those three men together was enough to set my panties on fire. How would it feel to be in the middle of all that testosterone and muscle?

Reuben placed a hand on my hip and deepened the kiss. His tongue delved into my mouth, tasting my lips and brushing over my teeth.

"I can't stop thinking about the other night," he said against my lips. "The way your mouth felt on my cock. I've been hard as a rock ever since. All I can think about is tasting you."

His words made me wet before he finished speaking. His voice was a low, compelling rumble that sent my pulse racing.

The only thing I could say in response was, "Please."

He hooked a hand around the back of my neck and kissed me while walking me over to the massive couch that sat facing the view.

Giving me a chance to pull away, he guided me until I was lying on my back, my ass on the edge of the couch. He worked the buttons on my jeans loose and pulled them down to my ankles.

I pushed off my shoes and kicked my legs until my jeans fell onto the floor.

He knelt in front of me and looked at me, his eyes dark with need. "I don't want to go too fast for you."

I swallowed hard before grabbing the hem of my shirt and pulling it up over my head. I tossed it aside and lay back, dressed only in a red lace bra and panties.

My blood was on fire. My body ached to be touched, but my scars made me self-conscious. I wanted to curl up around myself.

I forced myself to lay still and try to relax. He wasn't

going to hurt me, I knew that. He was looking at me like he'd never seen anything so beautiful in his life.

He gently traced a line up my thigh and across my stomach, circling the scars with the tip of his finger like he was worshipping each of them.

"I know you hate these," he whispered. "But they're a sign of how strong you are. After everything you went through, you didn't break. I have scars too, some on the inside, some on the outside. Every one helped to shape us into the people we are today. They say we can be beaten but not broken. They say 'fuck you' to anyone who dared to try."

He pulled down the cup of my bra that covered my ruined nipple. Slowly, he leaned forward to trace circles around it with his tongue. For the longest time, that was all he did, tasting my skin and my scars, like nothing in the world was more important, beautiful or delicious.

Finally, he pulled down the other cup and suckled on my nipple until I was quivering and my self-consciousness was forgotten.

With gentle fingers, he parted my knees and kissed his way up one thigh and down the other. He kissed his way back up and grabbed onto my panties with his teeth.

With a playful expression I'd never seen on his face before, he pulled them down my legs with his mouth before opening his lips and dropping them on the floor. He looked pleased with himself.

I smiled at him before I sat up just high enough to

unhook my bra and slide it off my arms. I swallowed back another wave of self-consciousness. I'd never been naked in front of anyone in daylight before.

"Mina, you're absolutely fucking gorgeous," he said breathlessly. "Every centimetre of you is perfection."

His eyes on my face, he lowered his mouth to my pussy and slowly started to explore with his tongue.

I pressed my palms to the couch on either side of me and let myself enjoy the way it felt to have him tease me, dipping first his tongue inside me, then a finger.

Every so often, he'd look up at me to make sure I was all right before returning his attention to my pussy. He looked fascinated, like he'd never seen anything so incredible in his life.

I heard footsteps on the stairs and glanced over to see Damon and Gianni walking toward us. They both stopped a few steps from the bottom before continuing on.

Eyes dark, they stepped over to the couch and sat down on either side of me to watch.

The expression on their faces pushed the last drops of self-consciousness out the window and into the ocean. They saw my body, with all of my scars, and still looked at me like I was some kind of goddess.

I rolled my hips slowly, adding to the friction I already got from Reuben's tongue. He expertly worked my clit like he knew exactly what I wanted. Like he understood every centimetre of my body and how to give me what I needed.

"Fucking beautiful," Gianni whispered.

Damon hummed his agreement and lightly touched my skin where my nipple used to be, with the pad of his thumb. He ran it up and down as if he wanted to memorise every millimetre, every bump, every bit of red, ruined skin.

Anger flashed in his eyes at how this must have happened, but, like Reuben, this was just a part of me. He leaned over and gave my other nipple the same treatment, making the inferno in my body rise even higher.

Gianni kissed my cheek, then my lips, moving slowly and carefully so he didn't overwhelm me. Having all of this attention from three incredible men could easily have done exactly that. It had the opposite effect. I felt both liberated and loved. Appreciated in a way I'd never been before.

Safer than I'd ever been before. More alive.

Reuben slipped another finger inside me and fucked me slowly with his hand and his tongue. Damon lavished attention on my breasts, while Gianni left me breathless with his kisses.

Gianni broke off and smiled at me, a hint of mischief lurking in his dark eyes. He scooted down until he was almost face-to-face with Damon.

Damon lifted his mouth off my nipple and sat still, close enough that their noses almost touched. Their chins hovered my chest.

I held my breath until Gianni moved forward, brushing his lips over Damon's.

Fireworks went off inside the room. Electricity snapped and crackled.

They deepened the kiss, a clashing of lips and teeth and tongues. Their stubble must have grazed each other's faces, rough but sensual.

Between the sight of the two men kissing and Reuben's mouth and fingers, I couldn't hold back anymore. I arched my back and surrendered to an orgasm that washed over me bigger than the waves outside the window.

I dropped my head back and cried out, while every millimetre of me was engulfed in flame. Instead of burning, it was an inferno of pure pleasure. I held back absolutely nothing, and neither did Reuben. His tongue flicked over my clit. His fingers were firm on my G spot, pushing me to heights I never thought possible.

When I finally floated back down to earth, it was to see three sets of eyes on me, each as hot as the next. Damon and Gianni with their faces just above my nipples and Reuben with his head still between my legs.

"That was fucking hot," Gianni said. "I'm officially rock hard."

Damon grimaced in agreement and shifted his position on the couch.

"It was," I agreed. "Everything."

Damon and Gianni exchanged glances, while

Reuben lifted his shining mouth and sat back on his heels.

Damon broke the silence by clearing his throat and pushing himself to his feet. "I should be working on making sure security is in place."

"Right," Gianni agreed. "I should be checking we have all the weapons we might need, just in case." He rose too and they hurried off in opposite directions.

"I'll show you to your room." Reuben offered me my clothes and his hand. "Before any of the staff appear. It would be inconvenient to have to have them killed because they saw you naked." There was no hint that he was joking. Not even slightly.

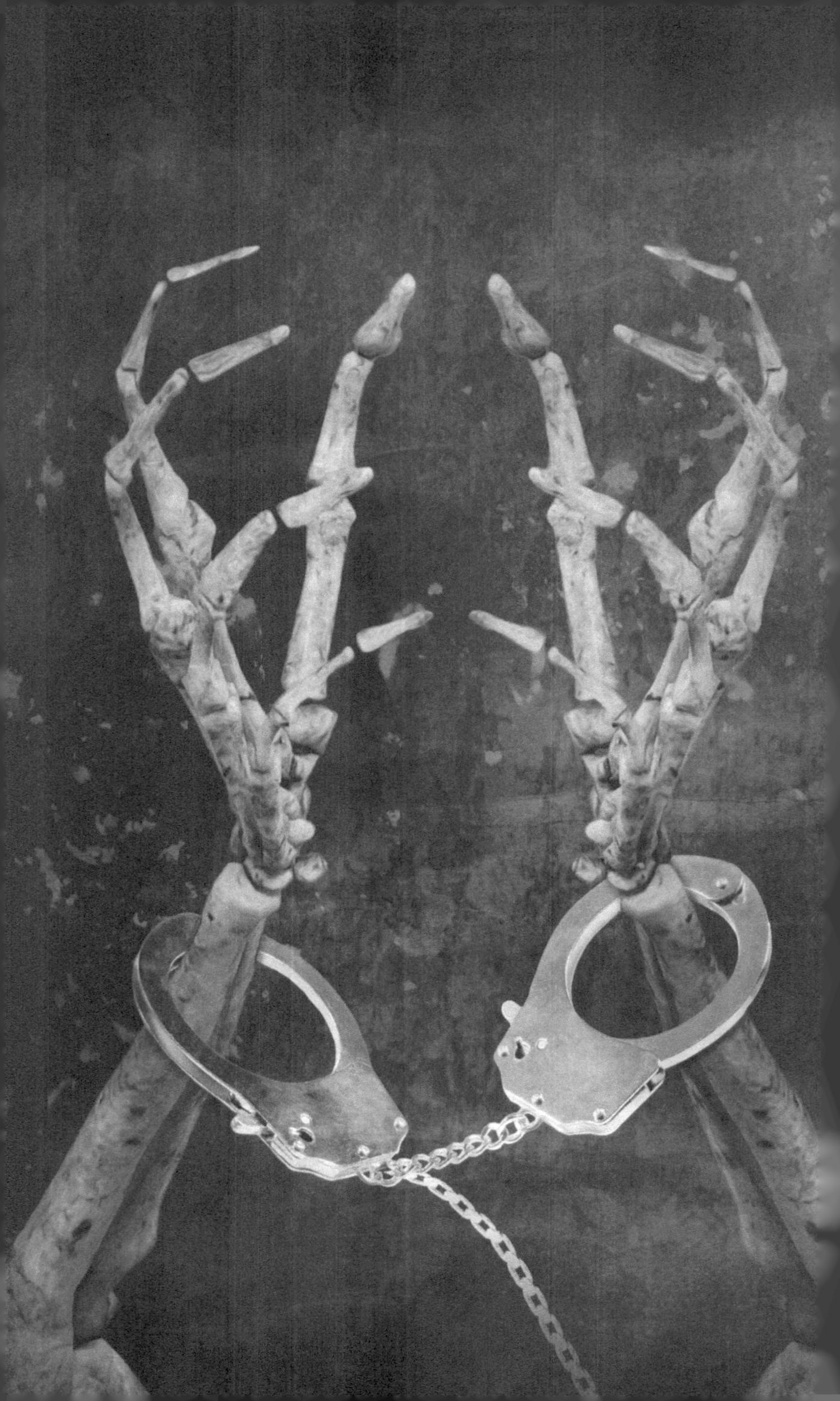

CHAPTER 16

MINA

Caleb put on a pair of reading glasses and looked toward his phone screen. "As far as my contacts have been able to determine, Kurt hasn't made any move to sell Mina's information. Any attempt to trace the phone number he used to call her led nowhere."

"He hid his tracks too well." Parker looked annoyed, as if him not being able to trace Kurt either was personal. "He needs to use more modern technology. Then we'd be all over him. Not literally." He stuck out his tongue in disgust.

"No one thought you meant it literally, Park." Hunter patted him on the shoulder. "If I was him, I'd be going through someone else anyway. Let someone else hang on his behalf. Possibly literally."

"Definitely literally." Reuben sat behind his desk, rubbing his forehead with his fingertips like he had an impending headache.

Hunter and Parker lounged on a couch against the wall. Caleb sat in a chair, his back ramrod straight.

Damon and Gianni both leaned against the wall near the door, glancing at each other occasionally, but looking more comfortable than they had right after they kissed.

I sat perched on top of Reuben's desk and listened, one eye on the view of the ocean behind Reuben, the other on the room. To anyone who didn't know better, I wasn't paying attention.

No one in this room would make that assumption. Even here, surrounded by high walls and abundant security, we were all on alert.

"We have a lead on Leon Graves," Damon said.

Caleb didn't try to hide his scowl. Not because he particularly cared about me, but he clearly prided himself on what, and who, he knew. He didn't want to be bettered by someone like Damon.

Regardless, everyone's attention was immediately on Damon.

"He made contact with one of my contacts two days ago," Damon said, undeterred by the scrutiny.

"We're only hearing about this now? Why?" Caleb asked coldly.

Damon ignored him, his gaze on me and Reuben. "I was just informed about this. She didn't know you were looking for him."

"She, huh? Is she hot?" Hunter asked. He glared at Parker when he elbowed his twin in the ribs. "I was asking for Caleb. He clearly needs to get laid." He gestured towards his older brother.

Caleb turned his glare on both twins. "I suggest you mind your own fucking business. The cliff outside is high. I don't think either of you would survive the fall."

Neither twin looked particularly ruffled, but for once, they didn't respond. Possibly because of the cold death glare all three of them got from Reuben.

His gaze slid from them to Damon. "Where is this contact of yours?"

"Right here in Dusk Bay," Damon said. "I thought we could pay her a visit."

Reuben nodded. "Take Gianni with you."

"I'm going too," I said. "Sometimes a woman will open up to another woman." In the corner of my eye, I saw Parker open his mouth to speak. "Not that kind of open up."

He closed his mouth, but grinned. "A guy could hope."

I rolled my eyes at him but smiled. To be fair, I couldn't blame him. I got off on seeing two men kiss, so why wouldn't he fantasise about two women being together? Or want to watch?

Reuben looked as though he wanted to refuse to let me go, but he finally inclined his head. "Take the twins with you, in case everything goes south."

"We'll be sure to put them between us and any trouble," Gianni said teasingly.

Both twins smirked.

"That would take care of two problems," Caleb muttered.

"He really loves us as much as Reuben does," Hunter said to the room in general. "We're useful to him."

"Occasionally," Caleb said. "I'll keep monitoring the dark web for any sign of Lasalle. There's a lot of chatter about the Sparrow. Mostly curiosity about why they suddenly returned and where they were. I'll keep looking for people asking who they are, or offering that kind of information."

I chewed my lip and looked back at Reuben. He'd still given no indication he'd let me offer up the information myself. I could do it without his help, but I didn't want to go behind his back with this. Besides, it would be easier with him and the other men helping me.

I was tech savvy five years ago, but so much had changed since then. The act of logging onto social media was more complicated than it used to be. Just as toxic though, from the sound of it.

Reuben looked back at me, obviously knowing what I was thinking. He was hoping we'd find Kurt before I had to put myself out there.

I appreciated that on a personal and professional level. Once the world knew what I was, it would be difficult to keep working. Not impossible. The Levin sisters never hid their identity in the way I had. People knew who they were, if not what they looked like.

I didn't even know. They worked and trained with masks over their faces. Zara spoke occasionally, but Paola never said a word in my presence. I could have passed them both on the street and never recognised them.

I supposed I could do that if I was outed. Get myself a mask and a new codename. I'd have to rebuild my reputation from scratch. That would suck, but it wasn't insurmountable.

Reuben seemed to see all of that pass through my mind. Like it or not, we were on the same page on this. For now. If Damon's contact couldn't lead us to Leon Graves, then we might be back to square one.

"I'll bring the SUV around," Damon said. He slipped out of the office, followed by Gianni.

"Be safe," Reuben said to me.

"I will." I dropped down off the desk and walked around to kiss his mouth. I didn't care that Caleb and the twins were still in the room, watching. Let them see. I wasn't ashamed of the relationship between me and their brother.

Fortunately for them, they'd arrived after Reuben tongue fucked me on the couch. I had a feeling there'd be three bodies at the base of the cliff if they saw me naked.

Reuben hooked a hand around the back of my head and deepened the kiss before reluctantly letting me go. "If anything happens to you, Damon, Gianni and the twins better be dead already."

"We'll take good care of your woman," Hunter assured him. He looked like he was about to add something, but after exchanging glances with Parker he closed his mouth.

"Make sure you do," Reuben said.

I stepped back, offered him a smile and followed the twins out of the room.

"How is the—"

Caleb closed the door before I could hear the rest of Reuben's question.

"In case you were wondering, yes, Caleb is always like that," Parker said. "Every now and again, I wonder who is more uptight, him or Reuben. Then we'll get together and I remember, it's Caleb. If you ask me, I think he tries too hard. He's always trying to impress Reuben."

"I got that vibe," I said. "He seems to be good at what he does."

"He is," Parker agreed. "He wouldn't dare not to be. His reputation, and job with the family, count on it. In his universe, those two are the most important things. In that order."

"He really, really needs to get laid," Hunter said. "I mean, we take our jobs seriously…ish…but we know how to have a good time too. Life is way too short to walk around with a stick up your ass. Where's the fun in that?"

"If you're talking a literal stick, not fun," Parker said. "There are other things I'd rather have up my—"

Hunter interrupted him. "Too much information, bro. I don't need to know what you want up your ass."

"As if we don't share a sex life," Parker said.

He looked Hunter up and down, a mock frown on his face, as if he was actually offended in any way. It would obviously take a lot more than that to really get to him. Especially when it came to his twin.

"Yeah, but Mina doesn't want to hear it. Right, Mina?" Hunter asked.

I shrugged. "It doesn't bother me, one way or another. In fact, it's refreshing that you're not shy about shit like that."

Sex wasn't discussed in my family, unless you counted Asher's penis jokes. None of which he ever would have told in front of our parents.

"We've never been shy about much of anything," Parker said. "That's another thing life is too short for. We like to grab every day by the balls and ride that motherfucker for all she's worth."

Hunter nodded. "Accurate. Not literal, but accurate."

I couldn't hold back a smile at their obvious enjoyment of life.

It faded when I wondered if I'd be like that if not for Kurt. I had a vague memory of being more outgoing and bubbly when I wasn't sneaking around assassinating people. I might still be like that. I'd never know for sure.

"If we didn't say it before, we're sorry for what happened to you," Hunter said, in a rare moment of seriousness and sincerity. "That was fucked up. This might sound weird, but you're kinda like a sister to us. If someone does something to anyone in our family, we take it personally. Whatever it takes to deal with Lasalle, we're both in."

"Balls deep," Parker agreed. "Once again, not literally. If I meant that literally, Reuben would probably tear mine off. Since I'm attached to my balls, I will stick to speaking figuratively. But like Hunter said, you're like a sister to us, so that would be fucked up."

"You two are crazy, but you're sweet," I said.

They both grinned.

"That's what we keep telling everyone," Hunter said. "It's about time someone believed us." He offered his twin a fist bump.

Parker bumped, then offered him a high five.

I cocked my head at them. "I'm surprised you don't have a secret handshake."

"Who says we don't?" Hunter asked. "If we showed you, it wouldn't be a secret anymore. Although, if we were going to show anyone, it would probably be you. You're the cool, big sister we never had."

"No one has ever called me that before," I said. Tears prickled in the corners of my eyes.

"Which one?" Parker asked.

"Both," I replied. "Cool, or big sister. I'm the youngest in my family."

"You *were* the youngest," Parker corrected. "Now

you're our family and we're the youngest. As far as we know."

If we kept talking like this, I was going to get choked up with emotion. That wasn't something any of us had time for right now. But I admit, this conversation made me feel warm inside. I'd be happy to have the twins as my younger brothers. From now on, I had their backs and they had mine.

I cleared my throat. "If we don't hurry, Damon and Gianni might leave without us."

They'd do exactly that if Reuben told them to. Honestly, I half expected to step out of the front of the house to see the SUV driving through the gates and away.

Instead, Gianni and Damon sat in the front of the dark vehicle, waiting for us with various levels of patience. Gianni looked relaxed, Damon looked on edge. So, the usual for them both.

I slid into the back and the twins walked around the other side to climb in with me.

Hunter clicked his seatbelt and rubbed his hands together. "It's party time."

"We're just going for a chat," Damon reminded him.

"That's where it starts," Hunter said. "We'll see where it ends."

I hoped a chat was all it would be, but I wasn't naïve enough to think anything would be that simple.

Nothing was yet.

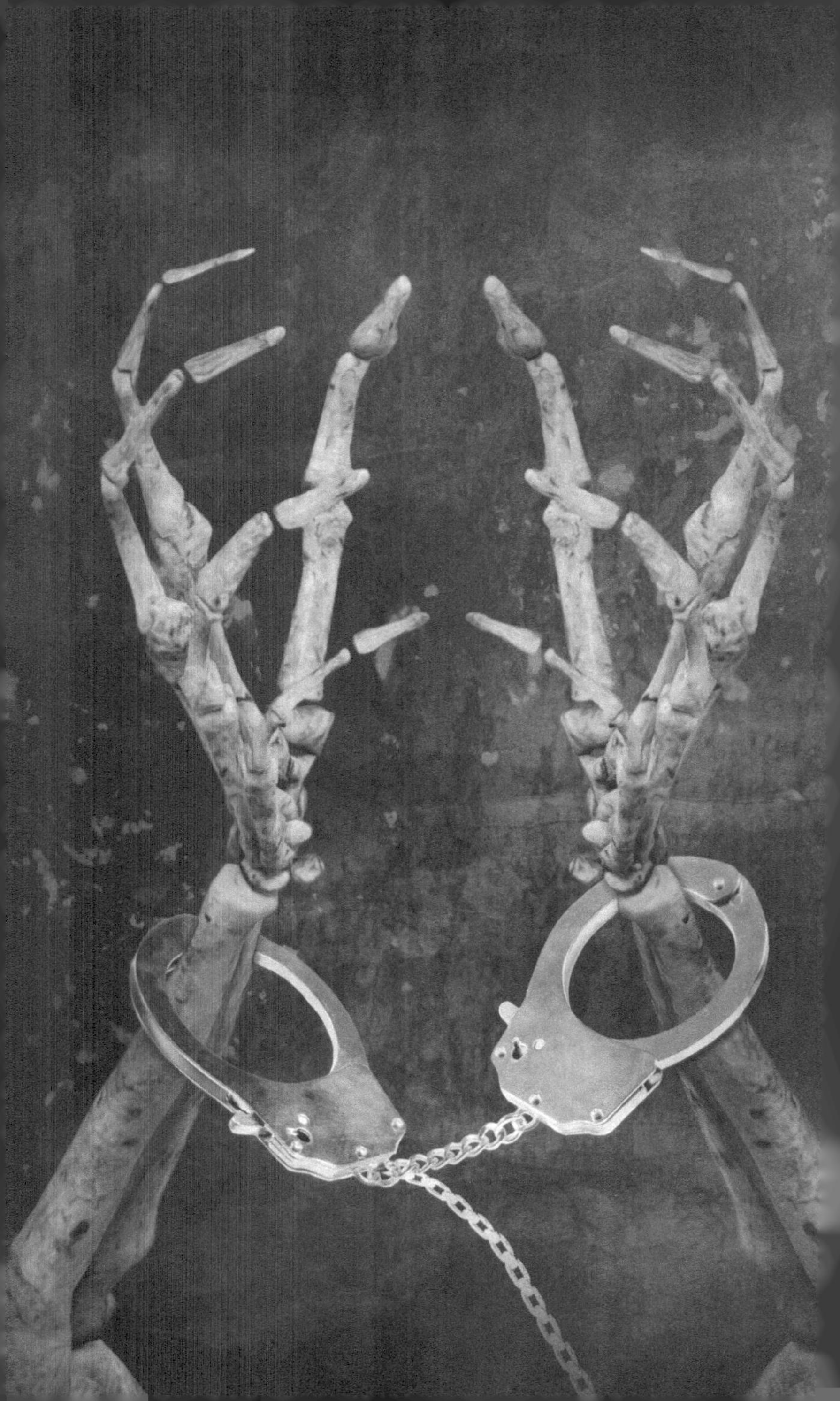

CHAPTER 17

DAMON

"Try not to look too conspicuous." I addressed the remark to Gianni and the twins. I didn't have to tell Mina that. In spite of being stunning, she knew how to blend into her surroundings. She held herself with a casual alertness that wouldn't draw excessive attention.

Gianni and the twins on the other hand, did nothing to disappear into the background.

Hunter and Parker walked behind Mina, and Gianni beside her, looking like a guard of honour. Somewhat appropriate, given she was a queen, but in no way subtle.

"Have you forgotten this is Dusk Bay?" Hunter asked. "Everyone knows us here. They know who we are and what we do. At least three people have crossed to the other side of the road instead of walking past us, and we've only been here for a handful of minutes."

He wasn't wrong about Dusk Bay. Reuben

controlled most of the city. Almost everyone who lived here worked for him, directly or indirectly.

Still, strutting around would draw further attention to us and that would have people talking. We didn't need the scrutiny or speculation. Reuben's presence in town would generate enough of that.

"Maybe you stink?" Gianni teased. He ducked to the side as Hunter took a playful swing at him.

I rolled my eyes and turned my back on them.

"Who is this contact?" Mina caught up to me while the other three were joking around. Her gaze seemed to be everywhere, taking everything in, while focused on me at the same time. How much of that was training and how much was a result of the trauma?

She was hyper-vigilant all the time. I suspected she slept with one eye open.

"Her name is Clarissa, but I don't think that's her actual name," I said. "She runs a vegan grocery store." I waved in the general direction of her business. "We're meeting her out the back."

I led them through an alleyway and around to the rear of the block of shops. In the back was a car park and several large skips. Heavy iron doors indicated entrance to each of the businesses.

The vegan grocer itself was nestled between a gymnastics school, and a shop selling musical instruments and music lessons.

The back door was open and Clarissa herself leaned against the door frame. As tall and sturdy as me, she regarded us all, unflinching. If I had a fistfight with her, I wasn't sure I'd back myself.

"Look what the cat dragged in," she drawled. Her voice was a deep rumble. "Damon Riviello and…friends."

She glanced around me, curious but not intimidated. She offered her hand and shook mine in a grip that made me wince.

"Nice to see you too," I said sarcastically. I shook out my hand and briefly introduced Clarissa to everyone.

Her eyes lingered on Mina before taking in Gianni and the twins.

"I've heard about you two," she said to Hunter and Parker. "Don't touch anything." She waved a thick finger at them.

Both twins raised their hands.

"We wouldn't dream of it," Parker assured her.

She squinted at him, but stepped back inside, gesturing for us to follow.

Mina glanced at me, but followed me over the threshold.

"Nice place," Gianni said.

The storage area was neat, lined with shelves and shelves of boxes. Most would contain stock for the grocery store, but it wouldn't surprise me if some contained guns or other contraband. Where better to smuggle things like that?

Clarissa grunted and picked up a phone from the desk in the corner. She turned on the screen and held it out in front of her. "I got this message two days ago."

Even before she started playing it, Mina's body stiffened.

Instinctively, I moved closer to her, as did Gianni and the twins. A protective wall of muscle between her and the ghosts of her past.

A male voice echoed through the space, tiny from his surroundings and ours.

"Hey, Clarissa, it's Leon. I have a delivery arriving in Dusk Bay in three days and need you to intercept. I'll text you the details." The call ended.

Mina's face was drained of colour. "That's him. I know that voice."

"Did he send you the details?" I asked.

Clarissa's gaze lingered on Mina again, but she tore her attention away and tapped on the phone again. "Just a time and location." She held the phone out to me.

"Any chance he's sending some bacon?" Hunter asked.

The look Clarissa gave him was drier than the Simpson Desert. "Chances are it's bacon, attached to the rest of a person. They're coming here to Dusk Bay. Leon doesn't want anyone to know. He's expecting me to pick them up."

"You work closely with Leon?" Mina asked, her tone this side of dangerous. Any associate of Leon was a potential enemy of hers.

If I thought Clarissa was tight with him, she'd be dead right now.

Clarissa shrugged her broad shoulders. "On and off. He's done me favours and I've done him favours. All within the umbrella of Brantley business. So he claimed. If he was working with Kurt Lasalle against you, I was unaware. I would have told him to fuck off. That's why I'm here telling you about this. I don't want anyone to think I'm not loyal. I like breathing."

"Has he given any indication who he wants you to pick up?" I asked.

"Nope," she said lightly. "What I've shown you is all I have."

I rubbed my chin. "I want you to follow through with the pickup. Don't let on to anyone else that we know. Once we have some idea who it is, we'll move."

Mina swallowed audibly. "You think it's Kurt?"

"Why else go so hard to hide it?" I asked. If anyone was going to arrive like this, it would be him. Trying to sneak in the back door without being noticed. Like the snake he was.

"I'll do whatever you need me to do," Clarissa said. "I've heard some disturbing rumours about Lasalle." Once again her gaze was on Mina. She knew better than to ask and we weren't going to enlighten her, but that wouldn't keep her from being curious.

"We'll be right there with you," Gianni assured her.

"You better, because if he suspects I'm working with you, shit might get ugly," Clarissa said. "I have a feeling you want to get your hands on him before I stab him in the throat."

Of course she hadn't meant that he'd try anything with her, or that he'd succeed. People fucked with her to their own detriment. Personally, I would have paid good money to see her eviscerate him, but that honour went to Mina first.

"Yes, but we don't mind if he loses a few fingers," Gianni said. "Just leave a couple for us."

Clarissa punched him on the shoulder hard enough to make him wince. "I like you."

He grimaced and rubbed his shoulder. "I'd hate to see what you do to people you don't like."

She grinned. "Stay on my good side and you never need to find out."

"I'll keep that in mind," he said. He took a moment to glare at the twins who were both laughing, but keeping a safe distance.

Mina was the only one who didn't look amused at the exchange. If anything, she looked slightly green.

"Stay in touch," I said to Clarissa. I took Mina's hand and guided her back out to the street.

"If it's really Kurt..." She sat down on the curb beside the car park.

"He'll be dead this time tomorrow," I finished for her. I lowered myself down beside her and put my arm around her.

"It doesn't seem real," she said, her tone hollow.

"After all those years, he'll finally be gone. I can put all of this behind me."

My heart ached for her. The fact he continued to breathe was starting to piss me off more and more. It was past time for that to stop, and for her to get on with the rest of her life. While he was out there, she'd be in some kind of limbo. Always looking behind her and wondering if he'd appear. Wondering if she'd wake up in that filthy cage, the strap around her ankle. Her naked body dirty, hair matted. Living through hell day after day. Treated like some kind of wild animal.

She deserved so much better than that. She deserved to be spread out on the couch and worshipped the way we'd worshipped her. The sound of her coming rang through my ears like the most beautiful music I ever heard.

The taste of her skin still lingered on my lips. That and the way Gianni's mouth felt on mine.

I was still trying to get my head around having kissed him. Thinking about it and doing it were vastly different things. I never expected to act on feelings I'd suppressed for so long. My attraction to him and to Reuben were best kept under wraps.

Or so I thought.

Now, I was conflicted, but that was something I needed to think about later. Right now I needed to focus on Mina and tomorrow's pickup.

"Why would he come here?" she asked.

I was wondering the same thing. "I'm guessing he has business here."

"Or he knows Reuben is in town," she said. The wheels in her mind seemed to be turning over, considering all the possibilities.

"Leon sent that message before Reuben decided we'd come here," I pointed out. "He wouldn't know that at the time." Even if he was listening in to all of our conversations, he couldn't have known what our plans were before we even made them.

"I suppose so," she said reluctantly. Her blue-green eyes were slightly glazed, her thoughts clearly dark and troubled.

I wished I could take every one of them out of her mind and give her back the sunshine she used to radiate. The carefree warmth.

"He won't go anywhere near you," I assured her. "If he so much as looks at you, I'll poke his eyes out. We don't need him to have eyes or fingers. Just a pulse. He needs to live long enough to experience the pain he put you through."

"I think to have a pulse, you need a heart," she said. "I don't think he has one of those."

I couldn't disagree with that. People with hearts didn't keep women prisoner. Unless they were the enemy. Reuben wasn't inclined to give leniency to anyone based on sex.

"Whatever he has in his chest to keep him alive," I

said with a shrug. "It won't be doing it for much longer. Twenty-four hours and he'll be dead as a slab of bacon."

"Vegan bacon," Hunter said as he sat down on the other side of Mina. "Never with a beating heart, but still kinda dead."

"Don't ruin bacon for me," Parker complained.

"I think it's already ruined for me," Mina said. "Every time I see it, I'll think of him."

I squeezed her more firmly. "The way Terry cooks it, none of us will be able to resist eating it anyway. Even if it was vegan bacon. Is that actually a thing?"

"Absolutely it is," Hunter said. "Along with vegan cheese, vegan hamburgers and vegan leather. It's a growing industry. Literally." He grinned.

"Anyway, we should get going." I glanced over to see a red haired woman look at us before unlocking the gymnastics studio and disappearing inside. "We don't want to draw too much attention to ourselves, remember?"

"Before we go back home, I want to show Mina something," Gianni said.

I waited for cock jokes that didn't come, before helping her to her feet and following her and Gianni.

CHAPTER 18

MINA

"The 'don't touch anything' rule applies here too," Damon said to the twins.

They grinned and headed over to the drums in the corner of the music shop.

I looked at the drums wistfully. If Asher was here, he'd be right there with them, trying them out.

"I figured this would be a good time to get that guitar you talked about," Gianni said. He gestured towards a selection of instruments that hung on the wall.

In spite of the growing feeling that Kurt was going to pop out of thin air right in front of me, I let myself walk over and take a better look.

In the corner of my eye, I saw Damon appraising the saxophones. I had no trouble imagining him playing one. Which led to me remembering Gianni miming

Reuben playing the bass guitar. A small smile crept onto my face.

"See any you like?" Gianni asked.

I returned my attention to the guitars before reaching for a black Fender Jazzmaster, and holding it carefully in my arms.

"I used to have one just like this." Where was it now? Had my siblings kept it after I left, and my parents died? Rose hadn't mentioned one, but it wasn't something we discussed when we stepped aside from everyone else. For all I knew, they'd thrown it away or sold it. If Dane went through our parents' things, it was definitely gone. He wasn't known for being sentimental.

I plucked at the strings a couple of times before automatically tuning the instrument and plucking again. It felt so natural, like I'd never stopped. My ear was probably off, after all these years, but it sounded better than it had.

I played a couple of bars of *Good Day Sunshine*, one of the first songs I learned to play. Ironic now, but that was the song that came to me first.

"You're good," Gianni said once he finished giving me a clap. "Musical talent must run in the family."

"Unlike some." Damon grimaced in the direction of the twins, who were tapping at the drums with dubious rhythm.

I suspected they were doing it on purpose to get a rise out of him. If they weren't careful, he'd shoot them for being too annoying.

"We're very talented, thank you very much," Hunter called out. "Remind me later to give you a pack of Kink Or Drink cards. They might help you to lighten up." He punctuated his sentence by hitting a drumstick on a cymbal, making it ring out.

Damon rolled his eyes. "I don't need your help to be kinky."

Gianni's eyebrows shot up.

Damon's lowered. "We're not having that conversation here."

Gianni raised his hands in surrender. "I can wait until later." His intention was clear. As long as they had that conversation, he was content to be patient.

I couldn't help being curious. I'd barely started to explore my sexuality, but I wondered how far they'd be willing to take it. Apart from being tongue fucked, sucking Reuben off and letting him and Gianni lick my fingers, I didn't know what I was into. I knew for certain I didn't want to be tied up in any way. Anything else, I had no idea.

Damon pressed his lips together and rolled them a couple of times. A sure sign of his annoyance. "Will you be buying that?" He nodded toward the guitar I was still holding.

I glanced at the price. That was another thing that changed a lot while I was away. The price of everything had gone up so much I couldn't get my head around it. The idea of paying that much for a bottle of milk or a bag of apples seemed crazy, but Reuben didn't blink when time came to pay for them. Of course, he could afford to, but still.

"I don't know," I said slowly. "It seems like an indulgence."

"That's a yes then," he said firmly. "You should have some indulgences. Hell, buy three of them. And a few picks, songbooks, a stand and a good quality amp."

"This quick shopping trip to get a guitar just got real," I said, half-joking. I hadn't even thought beyond the instrument himself. Yes, all of my guitars were a he. I didn't know why, they just were.

The sides of his mouth twitched upward ever so slightly. "If you're going to do it, you might as well do it properly. Why bother doing anything half-assed? Life is too fucking short for that."

All of them had said that to me at some point during the last few weeks. That life was short. They certainly seemed to believe in living each day to the fullest. That was understandable when we could step back out onto the street and get shot, or run over.

Hell, we might get struck by lightning, even though it was sunny outside.

"I'm going to buy it," I said definitely. "And all the other things too. The best of everything."

"That's my girl," he said softly. "Get some of those headphones so only you can hear yourself play. When Reuben is in a mood, you'll need them." He seemed to be speaking from experience.

I nodded and placed the guitar on the counter

before walking through the shop to gather up all the other things.

I finished paying for all of my new purchases when I heard an excited rumble from the street outside. While we'd been in the shop, a crowd gathered. I'd kept half an eye on them, but now they had my full attention.

"What's going on?" Damon snapped to the shop assistant.

She was standing behind the counter, bouncing on her toes. "Wolf Venom is in town to do some promotion. They usually drop in here for a meet and greet with fans."

It was my heart that dropped. Asher was coming here?

"We need to go," I said quickly. I grabbed my guitar and the bag with the smaller items, while Gianni picked up the amp.

"We'll never get out the front," Damon said.

The assistant looked as though she might try to stop us from going through the back, but she thought better of it. With wide eyes, she stepped aside and let us pass.

"What's the hurry?" Hunter drawled. "Their music isn't *that* bad."

I shot him a look and stepped over boxes and packaging material that was spread all through the stock area at the rear of the shop. Past him, I caught a glimpse of the door opening.

I recognised the dark-haired man who stepped through first. Zeke Brantley, lead singer and brother of

Reuben and the twins. He grinned and usherd fans to come inside too. He'd changed a lot since I saw him last. Matured.

My gaze only lingered on him for a few moments before a blonde haired man stepped into the shop behind him.

Asher was also grinning, joking around with his bandmate who followed him in.

Judging by the expression on his face, his bandmate didn't appreciate his humour. That seemed to amuse Asher even more. His grin was so broad he lit up the room.

My heart raced. Part of me wanted to drop everything I was carrying and run over to him. Instead, I was frozen on the spot for a minute or two, watching my brother interact with adoring fans and the other guys in the band, completely oblivious to my presence and scrutiny.

Like Zeke, Asher changed and matured. He kept his hair short, but his chin was covered in a couple of days' worth of stubble. His eyes were still the same brilliant blue, but he had crinkles around them. He wasn't a gangly boy any more. He was tall and muscular, his biceps thick from hours of drumming.

He wore a black T-shirt, tight over what was clearly a fit body. No wonder women were drooling over him. My brother had grown into the perfect rock god he'd always wanted to be.

I could hardly reconcile the man I glimpsed through

the crowds was still the same person I used to share finger paint with, and make plans in whispers to annoy the shit out of Dane. He could have been a completely different person. Why wouldn't he be, I was. A

"Mina?" Gianni said in my ear. "We can stay if you want."

I blinked away the moisture in my eyes and shook my head. "Not today. This is his moment."

He looked so happy, so content. I wouldn't be selfish and steal that from him. I couldn't steal his time from his fans either. They were hanging on every word he said, taking photos and videos while he signed everything they put in front of him.

He leaned in to whisper something in the ear of a cute brunette, who giggled and tugged down the front of her dress so he could sign her breast.

His scowling bandmate scowled even deeper, but didn't hesitate to sign her other breast when it was offered.

"Then we should go," Damon said. He placed his hands on my shoulders and guided me towards the door and out to the street.

Apparently word of the band's presence had got out. People were coming from all directions, going around to the front of the shop, chatting with excitement. Some were even singing what I assumed were their songs. Some stopped to look at me, as if I might be someone famous, being quietly bundled out the back door.

They hurried on when they realised I was no one.

Not one of their favourite rock star idols. Just a regular woman out shopping for a guitar on a Wednesday afternoon, who just happened to get caught in a throng of adoring groupies.

Lucky for them, they realised that before they took any photos of me, otherwise things might have gotten ugly.

"I'll bring the car around here," Damon said. "Stay here and stay out of trouble." He strode away, hands in his pockets. He tried to pretend he wasn't hurrying, but his steps were quick and short.

Gianni adjusted the amp he was carrying. The expression on his face was pensive. I hadn't seen him look uncertain before. It took me a while to realise what the cause of that was. It wasn't that he thought my brother would follow us out at any moment, there was more to it.

"You knew, didn't you?" I asked. Not accusing, just wanting him to be honest with me.

"I had an inkling," he admitted. "I didn't realise they'd come inside, but I thought maybe you could catch a glimpse. You weren't in any danger. I made sure of that. We had a lot of security in that crowd."

How should I feel about him going behind my back like that? I didn't like surprises at the best of times, but he meant well and obviously took precautions to ensure my safety. There was absolutely no malice behind his planning.

That didn't automatically make it all right. If Kurt

found out, he would have taken full advantage. He could have killed me and my brother. He still might.

"It was nice to see he's living his best life, but never do anything like that again," I said, struggling to keep my voice even.

His face fell. "Of course not. It was dumb."

We didn't say another word until we got back to the house and the gates clanged shut behind us.

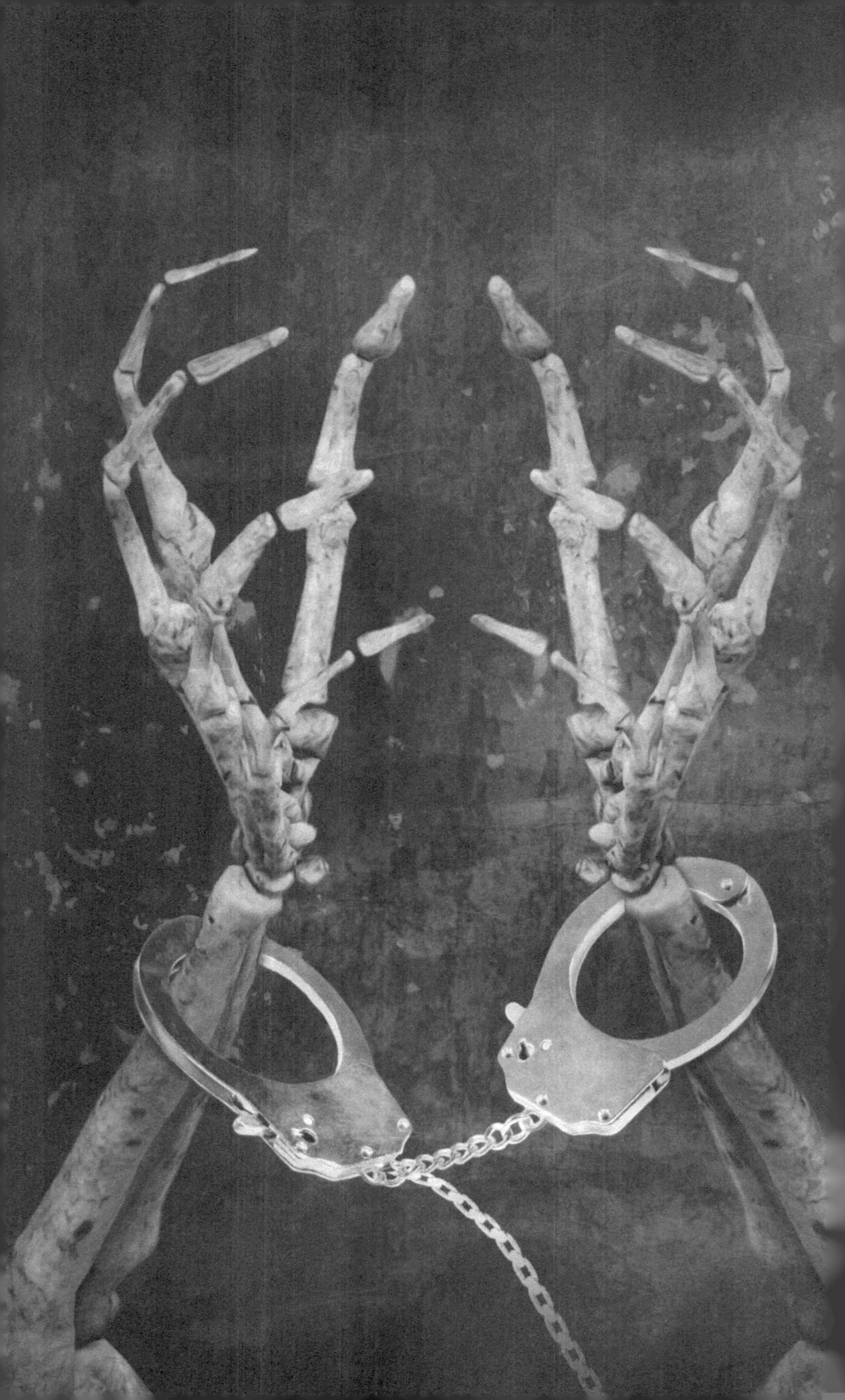

CHAPTER 19

MINA

"You did fucking *what?*" Reuben's voice was low as usual, but laced with a heavy dose of absolute fury. His ice blue eyes snapped with lightning that could have burnt Gianni to a crisp.

Gianni stood his ground. "I had everything under control. I just thought Mina would like to see her brother."

"With cameras and press everywhere," Reuben said. "One image of her would have told Kurt exactly where she was. If she decided to talk to Asher, or he'd seen her, that would have gone viral. Things could very quickly have gotten completely out of control."

Gianni still didn't flinch. "It didn't. Everything went exactly as it was supposed to. She got to see him and the world is none the wiser."

Reuben's gaze slid to me. His expression softened. "Too much could have gone wrong. Risks like that aren't ones I'm willing to take. Not when it comes to Mina." He propped his elbow on the desk and rested his head on the palms of his hands. "Did you get what you needed?"

"Potential information on Kurt arriving in town tomorrow, and a guitar," I said. "You could say I did. And I got to see my brother."

Reuben was right, so much could have gone wrong, but it hadn't. Seeing Asher was soothing in a way I hadn't expected. Knowing he was doing well and seeing it with my own eyes were two different things.

"See, everything worked out perfectly," Gianni said. "Tomorrow we'll get to pin down Lasalle and deal with his ass. For all we know, Asher will still be in town and we can invite him over for a few beers. Or go and see them live. I'm sure they'd have a few tickets left for us."

Reuben grimaced. "Let's deal with one thing at a time. Kurt first."

"I have everyone organised," Damon said. "We'll have people in place hours before the pickup time. If anything looks suspicious, they'll deal with it. When the time comes, we'll be right there. Clarissa will let us know if anything changes."

"Good." Reuben nodded. "I don't want any unexpected surprises tomorrow. No one goes off on their own and does anything rash." He looked directly at Gianni.

"Me, do something rash?" Gianni smiled. "You're thinking of the twins."

"Hey, what did we do?" Hunter protested. He and Parker reclined on the couch, coffees in their hands. "We had no idea what Gianni planned. We didn't even run off and say hi to Zeke."

"No, we didn't," Parker agreed. "We got the hell out of there when Mina said she wasn't ready to talk to Asher. No one ever knew we were there."

"This time," Reuben said. "Which I appreciate. Otherwise we'd be having a different conversation. Tomorrow, I want everyone on the same page. Follow Damon's plan to the letter. If anyone steps a toe out of line, we could be screwed. We could lose this chance at Kurt. I won't allow that to happen because someone feels the need to be a loose cannon."

"My cannon is never loose," Gianni said. He grinned at me.

I rolled my eyes, shook my head and smiled back at him. Nothing ever kept him down for long. Not even been chewed out by Reuben.

"I feel like one of us should have said that," Hunter said. "If Gianni is going to start stealing our one-liners, we might have a problem."

"Not my fault if I'm quicker than you are," Gianni said.

"Being too quick isn't a good thing," Parker pointed out. He grinned and offered Hunter a fist bump.

"Ha fucking ha," Gianni said sarcastically. "I'm never too quick when it matters."

The twins smiled unapologetically.

"That's what they all say," Hunter teased.

"As fascinating as this conversation is," Damon said slowly but meaningfully, "can we get back to the matter at hand? In case you need a reminder, Kurt fucking Lasalle. Remember him?"

I shuddered. I wished I didn't. Remembering him was one of the worst things about waking up in the morning. I wished there was a way I could forget. He still haunted my dreams and nightmares. When I closed my eyes, I could picture him leering at me through the bars of the cage. Looking down at me as he…

"We all remember him," Gianni said as he stepped closer to me. "He's the prick who brought us all together here today. If he was right in front of me, I'd thank him by punching him in the face. Or stabbing him in the dick. Maybe one, then the other." He mimed doing that.

He had a way of making a situation lighter, even when we were talking about someone who, to me, embodied pure evil. People thought of Reuben that way, but he was a pussycat compared to Kurt. Hell, I'd rather be alone with Samuel Bell than Kurt. He was an asshole, but he could be reasoned with. Sort of.

"We all feel that way," Damon said. "But let's not allow our need for revenge to cloud our judgment. The best thing we can do right now, is focus and be cool and calm. Rational. Not rash. If we let our anger guide us, he has a better chance of getting to us. We can't let that happen."

"You missed your calling," Hunter said. "You should have been a motivational speaker."

Damon smirked at him. "I'm not saying anything that isn't accurate. We've all done things in the heat of the moment that could have made a situation worse, or gotten us killed."

"Like driving an SUV into a couple of other cars?" Parker asked.

"That was a completely rational thing to do," Damon said. "I'm sure you'll recall I saved your asses."

"I don't know, it sounds like a heat of the moment thing to me," Hunter said. "Sometimes you have to be flexible, especially when the stakes are high."

"Flexible is good, just don't be stupid," Reuben said. "Any of you. I don't want anyone in this room getting killed."

"I told you he loves us," Parker said. "Not wanting us dead is Reuben's love language."

"Or it might be my way of saying your death would be inconvenient," Reuben said flatly.

"We can read between the lines," Hunter said. "Our deaths would be inconvenient and heartbreaking."

"I'd be heartbroken if I died," Parker said. "As well as inconvenienced."

"Me too," Hunter agreed.

I leaned against Gianni and listened to them banter back and forth. This family I'd found was a little crazy, but they adored each other, in spite of what they might say. If we lost anyone here, we'd all be devastated.

"Maybe we shouldn't go after Kurt," I said softly.

The silence that followed my words was heavy. If I turned into a giant, purple dinosaur, I couldn't have taken them by surprise more than I just had. The only sound in the room for at least a full minute was the pounding of my heart. It beat so hard it almost hurt, but I meant what I said. Like it or not, we had to consider everything.

"What are you saying, sweetheart?" Gianni asked.

"I'm saying he's not worth risking any of you," I said. "It won't change what he did. It won't give me back those five years. It won't erase the memories. I'd rather build new ones with all of you, than take the chance."

"You don't want revenge?" Damon squinted at me.

"I do," I said. "I want that very much. But at what cost?"

"If it costs us our lives, we'll pay that price," Gianni said. "He can't be allowed to walk around, doing fuck knows what to fuck knows who. Not to mention double crossing all of us. We all want our own revenge on him. Whatever it takes, we'll do it. Right guys?" He glanced around Reuben's office.

"I will," Damon said.

"I will too," Reuben agreed. His gaze was so intense my heart skipped a beat or two.

The twins were right, not wanting any of us dead was his love language. If anything or anyone threatened one of us, they'd have him to answer to.

I already cared about him, but those feelings were getting deeper every day. I couldn't imagine living my life without him. Without any of them.

"Us too," Hunter said. "No one fucks with our family and gets away without us fucking back. That's our love language. Like we said, you're our sister now. Your revenge is our revenge. Besides, screwing with people like Kurt is fun."

"It really is," Parker said. "We basically live for shit like this. Some people jump out of planes for fun, we hunt down assholes."

"We'd also jump out of planes though," Hunter said. "And bungee jump. And rappel." He nodded with each new addition to his extreme sport list.

I could imagine him and Parker doing every one of them on a nice relaxing Saturday afternoon.

"You certainly repel me," Gianni laughed.

Hunter flipped him off.

Gianni just grinned. "Bro, you walked yourself right into that one. Don't offer up the opportunity if you don't want me to take it. Because I will, every time."

"Exactly how attached are you to him?" Hunter asked me, clearly joking around. "If you ever feel the need to rid yourself of him, let me know. I'll be happy to oblige."

"That's sweet of you," I said. "I'm capable of getting rid of him myself if I need to. Which I don't foresee happening," I added quickly.

Hunter leaned over to Parker and whispered loudly, "She thinks I'm sweet."

Parker loudly whispered back, "She doesn't know you very well."

Hunter frowned at his twin. "Fuck you too, bro."

Parker chuckled and gave Hunter a hug. "We have to keep you on your toes."

Gianni wrapped an arm around me and spoke softly in my ear. "That was really hot. You saying you could kill me yourself if you needed to. My cock is so hard right now."

I turned my face to him. "I'm not sure how I feel about you getting aroused from death threats."

He wiggled his eyebrows at me. "I can't help being fucked up, but it's more the idea of you killing, in general, than killing me in particular. I'd get just as hard if you threatened the twins or even Damon or Reuben."

"I'll bear that in mind," I said. I wasn't sure under what circumstances I'd threaten to kill any of them. As long as they never tried to restrain or cage me, then I'd have no reason to. If they did, they could expect a blade across their throat, not threats. I wouldn't hesitate if it meant avoiding being locked away again. I couldn't afford to. I wouldn't survive being back in there.

I didn't want to.

"I think we can all agree there's something attractive about a woman who can take care of herself," Damon said.

"And a man who can do that," Gianni said. "Which

reminds me about your remark in the music shop. About being kinky." He cocked his head at Damon and looked expectant but hopeful, like he wasn't sure he'd get an answer, but he wanted one. And if he didn't, at least he got an opportunity to get a rise out of Damon. Although, I suspected he'd prefer his curiosity be satisfied, than teasing Damon. I wouldn't have minded knowing, myself.

Damon cleared his throat. "Can I be excused, boss? I have a few last-minute things I need to check over before tomorrow."

Reuben nodded. "Go. Keep me posted."

Gianni made a disappointed sound in the back of his throat as Damon opened the door and slipped out. "We can have that conversation later then. Good talk."

"I'm sure you all have places to be," Reuben said. He gave us all meaningful looks, but lingered longer on the twins and Gianni. His anger had cooled, but the message was clear. If any of them thought to go out on their own, he'd be pissed off at them. He expected them to stick to Damon's plan and bring Kurt in to be dealt with.

No one said anything about me following his plan.

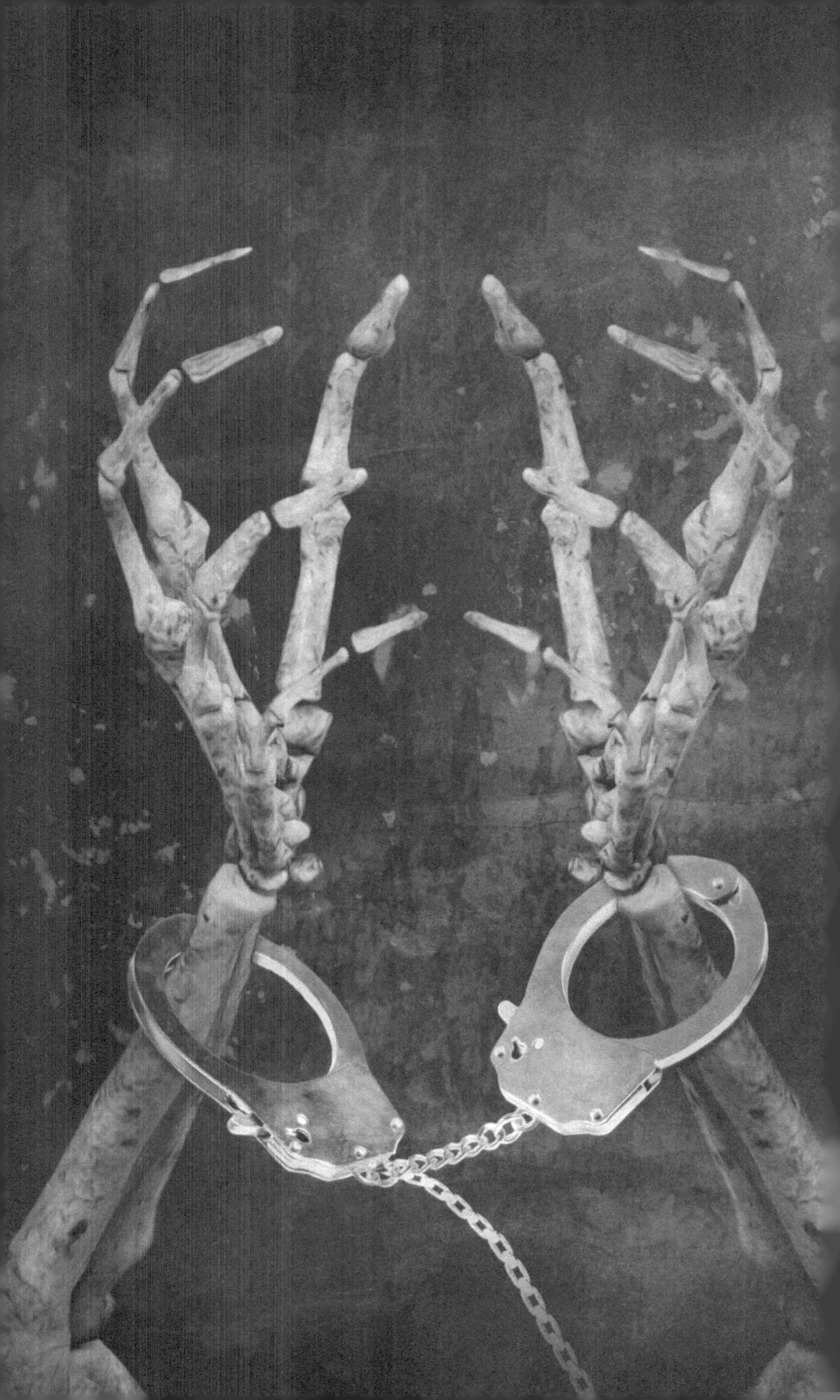

"Reuben is going to kill me for this." Daze drove the car away from the house. She only turned the lights on when we were out of sight.

"I won't let him kill you," I said. "You're only doing what I asked you to do."

"Which I'm only going along with because it was my brother," she said. "I still feel responsible for what he did. I mean, how did I *not* know?"

"My siblings didn't know either," I pointed out. "Don't beat yourself up about it. Save that anger for him." I had plenty of people I could blame for what happened. She wasn't one of them. She reminded me a lot of my sister, but wilder and more outspoken.

"I will, don't worry," she assured me. "I'm going to need some anger to spare, to deal with my guys too. They are going to be pissed off I left them out of this. Ric in particular. He hasn't stopped talking about you and the fact he should have figured things out sooner. I think he's waiting for Reuben to have him executed for failing him, and you."

"If Reuben has my cousin executed, I'll kick him in the balls," I said. "He wouldn't do that. He knows what family means to me. It means the same to him."

She glanced over at me. "I hope you're right. Killing Ric would create all kinds of trouble. It would irritate the hell out of Caleb and put a bunch of our operations back by a long way. Not to mention I'd miss him."

"All good reasons for Reuben not to do it. He'd be shooting himself in the foot. And annoying both of us." I checked the side of my boot for my knife, as well as my hip. If I was right, I needed to be ready. If I was wrong…

But I wasn't wrong. I knew Kurt and the way he thought. He said I was predictable. So was he.

"Reuben wouldn't want to do that," she agreed. "He's always been the pragmatic one. Always the one thinking with his head, not his heart, or his cock. Well, usually. When it comes to us women, they tend to let their body parts do the talking."

"That's why I asked you to help me tonight," I said. "I don't have to worry about you thinking with your dick." I also didn't have to worry about her feeling the need to sacrifice herself for me. She'd look after her own skin, as she should. That made her more impartial than any of my… Could I call them my boyfriends? I supposed I could.

She laughed. "I'd never be accused of that, that's for sure. Lots of other things, but not that."

"I'm sure you would," I agreed. "Mostly by people jealous of you."

"Does that include you?" she asked. "Because I'll be the first to admit I wish I was more like you."

I snorted. "Me? You're gorgeous, strong, smart and powerful. You're exactly the person I wanted to be when I was a kid."

"You're all of those things too," she said. "Especially strong. You're also an assassin, which is the absolute coolest thing I can possibly think of. I couldn't do it. I'd probably trip over my own feet and let everyone know I was there."

I choked back a laugh. "I'm sure you wouldn't. You don't seem like the clumsy type. Besides, it's all a matter of training."

"It's more than that," she said insistently. "You're also dainty, with a face that screams 'I'm innocent, I'd never hurt a fly.' If anyone saw you walking around their house, they'd probably assume you got lost."

I shrugged. "Maybe." That was why I was chosen for the training, but I couldn't have done my job based on looks and build alone. It took years to learn how to move silently, to kill and slip away without looking back.

It was definitely not for the faint of heart.

One of the boys I trained with carried out one kill and then couldn't continue. I vividly remember the first life I took. They never knew I was there. They went to sleep one night and never woke up. Apparently his mistress found him in the morning on blood drenched sheets, his throat cut.

I felt nothing, but a fleeting moment of arousal. The power of having taken a life. The rush of slipping away right after he took his last breaths. Triumph at having a plan executed flawlessly.

After that night, I was forced to accept that part of me was wrong. Twisted, fucked up, whatever. I could have run from it, but instead, I embraced it.

"Definitely," Daze said. "Can I ask you for a favour?"

"Of course you can," I said. She was doing me a big one, I owed her after this.

"I have a daughter, Nova," she said slowly. "I wonder if she'd be a suitable candidate to train as an assassin. She's only five, but I thought maybe…"

"They're never too young to start," I said. "I'm happy to teach her self defence and some of the basic skills, and see how she develops." I couldn't promise more than that. She might not be suitable, but what I could teach her would help her to survive in Dusk Bay in particular, and the world in general. They were skills every girl should have. Skills that might keep her out of the hands of someone like Kurt.

"That would be fantastic," Daze enthused. "Thank you. Nova is going to be so excited. She loves learning new things, especially things that make her more independent. I'm sure she'll be driving the day she's old enough. You know what they say, they grow up so fast."

"I've heard that," I agreed. I'd never given much thought to having children of my own. What would my boyfriends think about it? Assuming I could get pregnant at all.

In that cage, I was too malnourished to menstruate, thank fuck. Having Kurt's baby would have made the hell so much worse. No one deserved to enter the world like that.

The only saving grace was the possibility I would have died giving birth. That was offset by the chance the baby might have survived. That was further nightmare fuel, as if I needed more.

No, thank fuck that never happened.

"It's absolutely true." She slowed the car and stopped where I indicated.

"You should stay in here," I said.

"Fuck that," she replied immediately. "I've come this far. You're not leaving me out now. It's the best way to avoid Reuben kicking my ass later. If you're dead, I better be dead too. Besides, this might be fun." She flashed me a smile and pushed out the driver-side door.

I sighed softly to myself and climbed out of the car. I hoped like hell I didn't regret not insisting she stay behind. I would have left her out of all of this if I thought I could take one of Reuben's cars and not be noticed.

Since that wasn't going to happen, I'd asked her for

a ride into the city, and some help. She's eagerly agreed, saying she hadn't had a girls' night out in too long.

"This is the place," I whispered as we approached the vegan grocery store. We kept to the shadows, moving silently in the darkness.

I glanced down at my phone. "By my calculations, he should be here in a few minutes."

We crouched down near the doorway to the gymnastics studio and waited.

The city was quiet at this time of night, just the sound of passing cars and the occasional shout. The air was cool and laced with the smell of exhaust fumes and Chinese food. Most sensible people were at home, watching the Dusk Bay Demons ice hockey team on TV, or still at the Wolf Venom concert. Not sneaking around at night like a pair of criminals.

"This is where you got to." I heard footsteps right before Gianni spoke. Lucky for him he did, or I would have stabbed him in the neck. As it was, I had my knife in my hand without realising I'd moved. The hilt was cool on my palm, reassuring and familiar. Like holding onto an old friend when you need them the most.

"What the fuck are you doing here?" I whispered. I grabbed his hand and pulled him down into the shadows with me.

"I went to check up on you and you weren't in your room," he said. "Or Reuben's room. Or Damon's room. Or mine. Then I saw you sneak out the door, so I followed you. It's a real prick to drive all this way without headlights on."

"You shouldn't have followed us," I hissed. "Who's with you?"

"Just me," he whispered. "Who's with ycu?" He seemed to be searching and squinting, but he couldn't make out who crouched beside me.

"Daisy Lasalle," Daze said. "You're interrupting our girls' night." She sounded a little disappointed, if glad it was him and not someone else that found us here in the darkness.

Anyone else, and things could be messed up already. Someone would be dead, and it wouldn't have been either of us, if we could help it.

His teeth flashed white in the darkness. "Sorry, but I wasn't going to let you be out here by yourself. Unless you're working, in which case you could have asked me to give you a ride, or borrowed one of Reuben's cars."

"I'm not working," I said. "Not exactly."

I gave him a quick rundown of why we were here. I couldn't see the expression on his face, but I heard the change in his breathing as I spoke. I could almost feel his pulse racing faster and his mind turning over with possibilities. Including wondering if he should contact Reuben or Damon.

"I'm definitely not leaving," he said when I was finished. "First of all, you can't make me, and second of all, you might need my help."

"We can make you if we have to," I said. "But now

you're here, you might as well stay. But I expect you to do what I tell you to do."

I had a plan. I could adjust it to fit him, but I didn't have time to rethink everything. If he followed what I told him to do, everything should go smoothly.

'Should' being the key word. It had to; I had no room to fuck this up. This might be the best shot I got. I was taking it and I wasn't going to miss.

"Sure thing, boss," he said easily. "I live to serve."

"I'm sure you do," I said. "Now, be quiet. We don't need anyone to hear us and find us here."

"Got it," he whispered.

I slipped my knife away and crouched, scanning the surrounding streets and listening carefully.

What was the time? I was certain only a couple of minutes had passed, but I didn't dare to turn my phone on again. The light would give us all away. That was probably how Gianni found us in the first place. One little glance was all it took.

Of course, he knew to look, others might not, but I wasn't taking the chance.

A car roared past, then another. A fourth car was quickly followed by a fifth.

It was the fifth that slowed down and turned into the car park behind the block of shops.

My whole body stiffened with anticipation and a dose of anxiety bigger than I was comfortable with.

I forced them both down. Adrenaline was bad at

times like this. I needed a clear head, precise thinking and exact action.

I took a deep breath, and another, regaining my calm. Forcing my mind to the state where I didn't simply react. I needed to act on instinct and training, with careful precision, not recklessness.

Gianni would have called it assassin mode, or something similar. Whatever it was, I needed it right now.

The car stopped in a parking space and the engine was turned off.

Clarissa stepped out of the driver's side. "I wasn't expecting you until tomorrow morning. I'll have to give myself a few minutes to have a bed ready. I have an apartment above my shop." She gestured vaguely in that direction, her movements illuminated by the light inside the car. The look on her face suggested her passenger was not a welcome surprise.

From inside the car, a male voice responded. Slowly, the passenger side door was pushed open and a man stepped out.

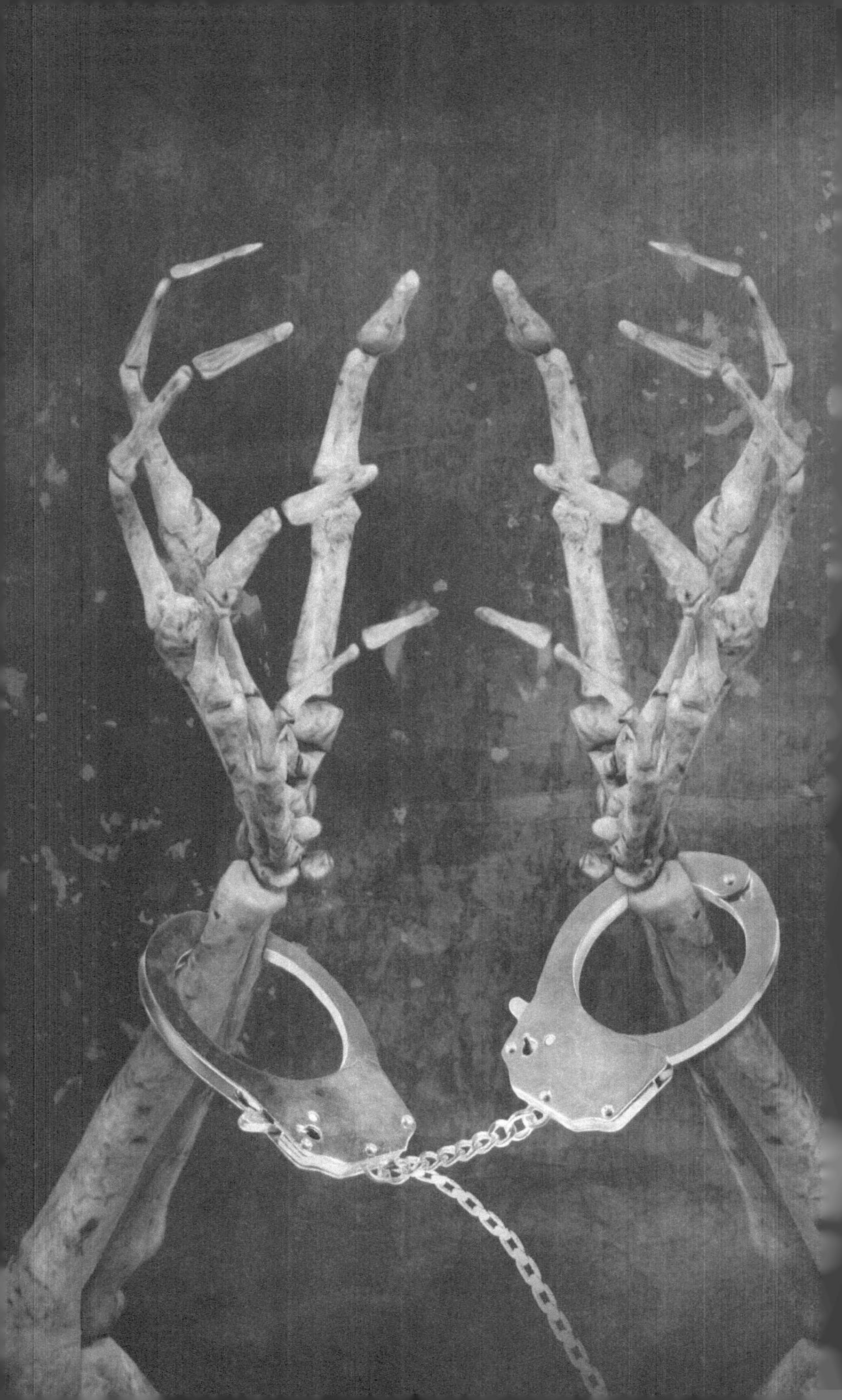

CHAPTER 21

DAMON

I stopped outside the door to Reuben's room. Even this close to midnight, the door was open and a light was on inside. I didn't hear any groaning, so I decided it was safe to push the door open a little further and peer inside.

Typical of Reuben, he was still fully dressed, sitting on a chair near the window reading a recently released, thick epic fantasy.

Not my kind of thing, but they kept him engaged for hours. I'd bet that when he was a child, if he was quiet, it wasn't because he was up to something. He would have been sitting in a corner reading. When he wasn't learning to take over from his father.

I glanced around the room. "Mina isn't in here."

He looked up, his brow creased. "No. I thought she was with you or Gianni."

"She might be with Gianni, but I can't find him

either," I said. "Neither of them are in their rooms, or anywhere in the house as far as I can tell. I tried ringing Gianni, but there was no answer. It's possible his phone was on silent and he didn't hear it."

Reuben slipped his bookmark into his book and set it aside. He sat up straighter, hands on his thighs.

I ignored the way my pulse ratcheted up. This was not the time for that.

"What else?" he asked. He knew me too well.

"One of the cars is missing. According to the tracker, it's in the city."

"It didn't get there by itself," he stated.

"No, and the staff are all accounted for. It's only Gianni and Mina I can't find." I shoved my hands in my pockets to keep from showing the worst of my frustration and concern.

"Fuck," he said softly. "Gianni wouldn't have…"

"No," I agreed quickly. "If they're together, she's a willing participant."

"You think they're together," he said.

"They better be." I couldn't think of another scenario. "I have a theory that Mina thought Kurt might come to Dusk Bay earlier. She might have decided to confront him. Gianni went with her."

"Why wouldn't she come to us?" Reuben asked. He shook his head slightly. "It doesn't matter. You have the location of the car? Wake the twins, we're all going." He pushed himself to his feet.

I nodded. "Yes, boss. I'll get them and the car ready."

"We'll get to her in time," he said half to himself.

"Of course we will, boss. Knowing her, she'll have him pinned down by the time we get there. Tied up and ready for us to bring him back here." I wished I could be so sure.

"Without doubt." He stopped beside me and placed his hand on my shoulder.

If I thought my pulse was going faster before, it was doubled now. My heart was beating so fast I could barely catch my breath. His face was so close to mine, his breath would have brushed my lips if he turned just slightly.

My balls throbbed. Time stopped while we stood there side-by-side, his skin burning a hole in the fabric of my T-shirt.

Moments passed, like a clock ticking slowly.

"We should go," I managed to grind out.

His throat bobbed as he visibly swallowed. "Yes." He dropped his hand and stepped past me.

The moment contact was broken, time started again. My shoulder felt colder than ice, but I shook myself out of my stupor and went to wake the twins.

———

All of the Brantley brothers must be night owls, the twins weren't asleep either. Fortunately for everyone concerned, because I suspected when woken up they came out swinging. Or stabbing, if a knife was close to hand.

I gave them a brief explanation and they were hurrying down to the car behind me. I had to give them credit. They'd fully accepted Mina as one of their own. If she ever needed them, they'd be there for her. At this rate, she'd have her own army.

Reuben was waiting patiently beside the car, with one of the staff who'd sorted guns for each of us. Usually Gianni's job.

I was going to tear him a new one when I saw him next. He should know better than to go out on his own, even in Mina's company.

If anything happened to either of them, I was going to be… I'd have to finish that thought later. Right now, I needed to be cool and clearheaded. I'd leave being rash to everyone else.

"The car is near Clarissa's store," I said. The comment was more or less redundant. Where else would Gianni or Mina have gone?

"I'm surprised," Hunter said. "Knowing Gianni, I thought he would have taken her to tonight's Wolf Venom concert. No one would have recognised her up in the nosebleed seats."

"It was sold out." Reuben looked unimpressed with that suggestion.

"And you know that, how?" Parker leaned forward from where he sat in the back seat.

"It's my job to know things," Reuben said. "Unless

people go behind my back like this." He appeared to be perfectly calm and composed on the outside. We all knew him better than that. On the inside, he was a cauldron of cold fury.

Like I was.

"Just remember, Mina cares about Gianni," Hunter said. "Try not to shoot him too much."

"I'm not going to shoot him," Reuben said. What he left unsaid was clear. If Gianni did anything to her, including encouraging her to leave the house without us, he'd be a lot worse off than if he was dead.

No one asked what would happen if Mina was the one who coerced him.

"Who said Reuben doesn't have a heart?" Parker asked.

"I might have said that in the past," Hunter said. "I'm pretty sure Zeke said the same. And Caleb, Joshua and Lucas. I'm as surprised as anyone to find out he actually does. Much less that it beats for Mina DiMarco."

"Don't make me shoot *you*," Reuben said darkly. "If either of you so much as look at her in a way that's not brotherly…"

"We wouldn't dream of it," Parker said. 'Mina is sweet, but she is not for us."

"Fucking right she's not," I growled. She belonged to Reuben, Gianni and me. No one else. I didn't let myself think about us belonging to each other. That was something we'd have to think about later. Assuming we got a later.

I focused on driving, while the others fell silent.

The drive from the house in Dusk Bay Heights, to the city, wasn't far, but it felt like it tonight. It could have been a hundred kilometres instead of twenty. The traffic was heavier than usual for this time of night, with people heading home from the concert.

Personally, I wouldn't have minded going, but I knew how Reuben felt about his brother's band. That was a conversation not worth having, just to go to a rock concert.

"Still no answer on either of their phones." Reuben sounded frustrated.

That didn't surprise me. If they were up to something, they'd want to keep them silent.

Mina always did now, after that call from Kurt. She had little reason to accept incoming calls anyway. Anyone who had her number, could either text or speak to her in person. The rest of her communication was done via some app on her phone I'd only gotten a glimpse of. Something, I presumed, was only for assassins, not everyday people like me.

"We'll get to her in time," Hunter said. "If there's anything I know about Mina and Gianni, it's that they have each other's backs. They won't let anything happen to each other."

"They better not," Reuben growled.

I'd never heard that much emotion in his voice before. If anything happened to either of them, he'd be as gutted as I would. He'd burn down the whole world in retribution.

I'd hand him the matches.

"Park around the corner from where the car is," Reuben said as we drove into the city. "We don't want anyone to know we're here."

"Got it, boss," I replied automatically.

I ran through the best places to park, finally settling on a side street around the corner from the vegan grocery store. It was empty at this time of night, apart from a darkened delivery truck and a couple of wheelie bins.

I killed the engine and was the first out of the car. My shoes barely touched the ground before my gun was in my hand.

"Just making sure you're all aware this might be a trap," Hunter said carefully.

"Of course it might," Reuben said. "Be alert for anything."

"Okay, just checking." Hunter nodded and made sure his gun was loaded and the safety off. "Wouldn't want to walk into anything fatal."

"We won't," I said. I'd considered the possibility Gianni and Mina had. There was a chance they might both be…

I wouldn't let myself finish that thought.

I led the way down Riley Street, all the way to the corner, where I stopped. I raised a hand to indicate that the others should wait, then peered around the corner.

The street that stretched out in front of me was quiet. The other of Reuben's cars was parked by the side of the road, engine off, in darkness. Intact, as far as I could tell. And empty.

"I'm not seeing anyone," I whispered. "Living or dead."

A light was on above the grocery store. Clarissa's apartment. I squinted, but if anyone was inside, I couldn't tell.

"Have you tried communicating with Clarissa?" Reuben asked.

"I sent her a text to confirm there were no changes from the plans we made earlier today," I said. "She replied that everything was under control."

That was when I started to suspect something was wrong. I started searching the house for Mina and Gianni, and any missing cars. Only when I was certain did I take the information to Reuben. He didn't appreciate people going off half-cocked and making assumptions without looking for the evidence. No, I had to be sure before I bothered him with it.

After all, Mina and Gianni could have been out in the garden practising knife throwing, or fucking.

"That's a weird way of saying yes," Parker said.

"Sounds like a thinly veiled no to me," Hunter said.

"Funny, I was thinking the same thing," Parker agreed. "That sounds like something I'd write if I was under duress, with someone looking over my shoulder. Someone like Kurt."

"Exactly," I agreed. I rubbed my chin with my thumb and pointer finger.

The stairs leading up to Clarissa's apartment were narrow. Only one and a half people could walk up them at the same time. Anyone at the top could pick us off one by one. If he was there, we might have a hard time reaching him.

If Mina was up there with them, we'd fucking try. I didn't care if I died, as long as she didn't, and wasn't taken by him. Those options weren't even on the table.

The question was, where did Clarissa fit into all of this? Had she double crossed us? I didn't want to believe that, but right now, all possibilities were up in the air.

I ducked aside as a car slowed and came around the corner. If they saw us in the shadows, there was no sign from inside the vehicle. They didn't stop to look or turn the headlights on us. They drove on until they reached the car park behind the grocery store.

With practised precision, the car slid into a parking space. The engine was turned off and the driver's side door pushed open. Clarissa stepped out.

I gestured the others forward and moved around the corner silently as the passenger door opened and a man stepped out.

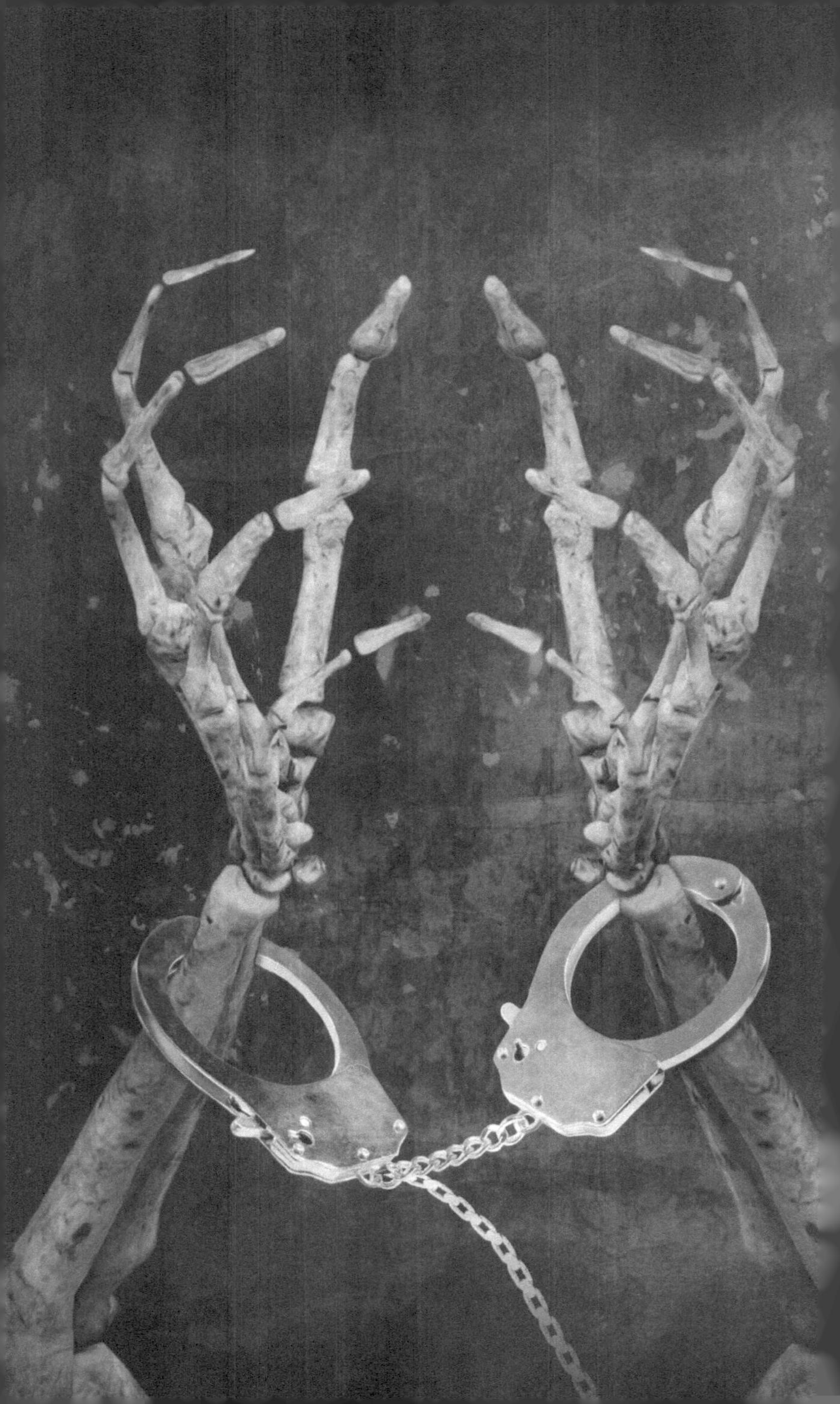

CHAPTER 22

MINA

"That's not Kurt," Gianni whispered.

"No, it isn't," I agreed. "It's Leon Graves."

Fuck.

Fuck.

I knew there was a possibility it would be someone other than Kurt. That Leon had contacted Clarissa on behalf of himself. I'd wanted to assume it was Kurt so I could end this. If he was standing right in front of me now, I'd lodge my knife in his brain. Or somewhere lower, to give him a slower, more painful death.

It was some consolation that I was right about one thing. Leon arrived earlier than originally planned. The question was, why?

Clarissa's eyes swivelled from side to side, as though certain we were waiting in the shadows. She looked nervous, anxious.

So she should. If he'd contacted her to change plans

and she hadn't told Damon, she might be taking her last breaths herself.

"I guess you can come on up," she said reluctantly. She didn't seem to want him near her any more than I did.

"Relax," Leon said. "I'll only be here for a couple of hours to put some things in place. Then you can drive me back to the airport."

"Great," she said flatly. "So you won't need a bed then?"

"Just a chair, coffee and Wi-Fi," he said. "As always, you'll be rewarded for your discretion."

"Yeah." Her expression suggested that was what she was worried about. She rattled the keys in her hand and walked over to unlock a door I presumed led up to her apartment. "After you."

Yeah, I wouldn't turn my back on him either. Apparently he had no such reservations where she was concerned. He nodded and headed inside.

Clarissa lingered near the door, her hand on the handle. Eventually, she stepped inside and closed the door behind her.

"Unless that locks automatically…" Gianni started.

"Then it's unlocked," Daze finished for him. "That could make life easier."

I hummed my agreement. "Let's give her a couple of minutes to get him settled, then we'll pay them a visit."

The hairs on the back of my neck rose. My skin prickled. Someone else was here. I hadn't heard them, but my instincts were screaming at me that we weren't alone.

I'd considered the possibility this was a trap, but until now I hadn't seen any sign to back that up. Of course, they'd wait until Leon was safely inside before converging on our position.

"I feel that too," Daze whispered. She must have felt me stiffen. "Behind us. On the corner. I saw a movement."

"There might be people in front of us too, trying to pin us in," I said. "We need to get out of here before that happens."

I cast a long look at Clarissa's apartment. Shadows moved past the blinds. Her and Leon. If he knew where to find Kurt, I couldn't let him slip away. But if this was a trap, I had no choice.

Fuck. I didn't like being pushed into corners.

"I'll lead them away from you," Daze said. "I'll try to give you enough time to confront Leon."

"Me too," Gianni agreed. "We can hold them off."

I wanted to tell them no, but I saw no other way. I could handle Clarissa and Leon by myself if I had to. If she wasn't on our side, it would be more difficult, but not impossible.

I sighed softly, but nodded. "Stay safe." I reached out to find Gianni's face and kissed him quickly.

"You too, sweetheart." He crept away, moving at right angles to whoever was at the corner.

Daze was right on his tail.

I waited until they were a few metres away, before I slipped through the shadows toward Clarissa's door.

As I'd hoped, it was unlocked. I winced at the slight creak of the hinges as I eased it open. It was only audible this close, but it sounded as loud as a gunshot to me.

Calm your tits, I told myself. *No one heard it but you.*

Lips pressed tight together, I slipped inside and closed the door behind me without making another sound.

The stairs were in near total darkness, broken only by a light that peeked under the door, at the very top. I paused to listen.

When I decided no one was waiting to ambush me, I headed up the steps, one at a time.

"The best thing about Dusk Bay is the fast Wi-Fi," Clarissa was saying. "One of the fastest in the world. Of course, the city is also a beautiful place to live, but the Wi-Fi is a bonus. I've lived in some places where it was barely better than dial-up. It's ridiculous, I know. In this day and age, we should all have decent Internet. But here we are."

Leon's response was mumbled, something along the lines of, "Good to know."

"I know, right?" she responded. "That's one of the reasons I moved here. That and the fact people are mostly nice here. For a bunch of criminals. I mean, not everyone is a criminal here, but you know that. Oh, sounds like the kettle has boiled. Excuse me for a minute, I'll make you a coffee. I might even have one myself, even though it's late. Wouldn't want to fall asleep when you want me to drive you. How do you have it? White with two sugars? Okay I'll just be a moment or two. I might even have some biscuits around here. You must be hungry."

"Yeah, whatever," Leon replied vaguely. Apparently he wasn't impressed with her hostess skills. Or maybe he was an ungrateful prick.

I pictured him hunched over a table, laptop in front of him while she hurried around the kitchen, making him a coffee and hunting around for a snack. She seemed to be making as much noise as she could.

She knew I was there, or at least suspected. She was talking to cover any noise I might make.

I smirked at the idea. I made mistakes, but never noise, not when I didn't want to. Who was she expecting, if she wasn't expecting an assassin?

She might assume Reuben would send the twins to collect Leon. A fairly accurate assumption to make, most of the time. If Reuben knew Leon was here, Hunter and Parker would be knocking the door down by now. Me, I preferred to catch Leon unaware.

That meant continuing to move soundlessly, like the shadow Damon once told me I was. At the time, his remark hurt, but I embraced it now.

I was part of the shadows. Darkness inside and out. I didn't need the sunshine to feel whole. I needed this.

To be the cunning predator moving through the night, ready to claim my prey.

Like the door at the bottom of the stairs, the one at the top was unlocked. I pushed it open slowly and stepped through.

Damon

"Graves went inside with Clarissa," I reported.

What game was she playing? She'd sent me a message that would raise my suspicion. She must be hoping we'd turn up to take him off her hands.

We'd done the first. We could do the second, but it was too easy so far. If Kurt was thinking a couple of moves ahead of us, this was just about to go south.

If Clarissa was working with him, she'd also go south, to an early grave.

Although, was it really early, in our line of work? Now I thought about it, it was probably about average.

Either way, she'd end up dead, which would be unfortunate. Up until now, she'd been invaluable and trustworthy. Maybe she still was. There was time for her to prove herself yet. If she could.

She'd know as well as I did, once the seeds of suspicion were planted, they tended to take root and grow. Coming back from this would be difficult.

In the corner of my eye, I caught a hint of movement. Then another. There were two people on the opposite corner. No, three. Four. I couldn't make out any more, but fuck only knew who else was hiding in the dark around here.

Across from them I caught another hint of movement. Someone walking up the street toward them. Someone making no effort to avoid being noticed.

Gianni. And someone else. Someone taller than Mina. Daze? What the fuck?

Neither of them were usually that sloppy. Given they were now, they were doing it for a reason. They wanted to be seen. They were trying to draw them away.

As far as I could tell, they didn't know we were there yet, so they weren't trying to distract attention from us.

Where was Mina then? She didn't seem to be with them. They were trying to lead any potential attackers away from her.

Was that brave, stupid, or both? It was classic Gianni. He'd take risks others wouldn't, especially when family was involved.

I made a mental note to throttle him later for trying to do this. Daze too.

Across the road, someone spoke. A light flashed on, aimed directly at Gianni. He threw himself to the side as a shot rang out. It must have missed him by a hair.

The bullet hit the wall instead. This was Dusk Bay,

no one would notice another one lodged in the side of the building. Eventually, someone would come along and paint over it.

I didn't think.

I aimed for the light and squeezed the trigger. The gun recoiled in my hand. The gunshot echoed, followed by a cry of pain.

The phone dropped to the ground, offering a faint glow from the screen. It wasn't much illumination, and it'd turn off quickly, but it was enough.

Taking a leaf from Mina's book, I aimed for the visible feet.

"Fucking hell!" a male voice called out. He slumped to the ground, hands on his ankles until Hunter put a bullet in his head.

Parker took out another with a shot through his chest, but the last of the would-be attackers turned and ran.

"Go after him," Reuben told the twins.

"On it, boss." They both sprinted across the road and disappeared into the shadows.

Gianni emerged from them, followed by Daisy Lasalle. What the fuck was she doing here anyway?

Gianni picked up the phone and shone it across the two bodies. The third person lay a couple of metres away, groaning in pain.

It was a woman who held the phone; she was now missing a hand. A moment later, courtesy of Gianni's knife, she was missing a whole lot more. Bleeding out onto the footpath before dying quietly.

"Perfect timing," Gianni said cheerfully. He wiped his knife clean on his black T-shirt and tucked it back away, out of sight. "I'm guessing you have a few questions for me. Let me start by saying—"

"Where's Mina?" Reuben interrupted.

"She went inside." Gianni gestured. "It wasn't Kurt that turned up tonight."

"We know." I clapped him on the shoulder. "It's good to see you, but if you sneak off like that again, I'll put a fucking bullet in your knee."

"I love you too," he said lightly. He drew me in for a quick hug.

I stiffened for a moment, before hugging him back. Later, I'd have time to think about how right it felt to hold him, but right now, we had work to do.

"Have you seen anyone else around?" It was possible Kurt only sent four people to ambush us, but none of us would rule out anything at this point.

"Just you reprobates," Daze said. "And these dead ones." She gestured towards them. "And Clarissa and Leon Graves. It's been pretty quiet apart from that."

"Right," Gianni agreed. "If Wolf Venom was still playing, we'd be able to hear them from here."

"Too quiet," Reuben said.

"Boss?" I asked carefully. He was visibly as torn as I was. We both wanted to go up those stairs to Clarissa's apartment. To Mina. If there were others around, they could pin us all in. Including her.

"Search the area," he said finally. "We need to make sure it's not—"

"Full of people who look like they want us dead," Hunter interrupted. He and Parker trotted back toward us, guns still in their hands. "There's another four on the next corner over and four on the opposite one. Now might be a good time to call for some help."

Reuben grunted in annoyance. "Do it. We'll deal with them and then we'll go for her."

"Got it, boss," I said with some reluctance. I pulled out my phone and started to make the call.

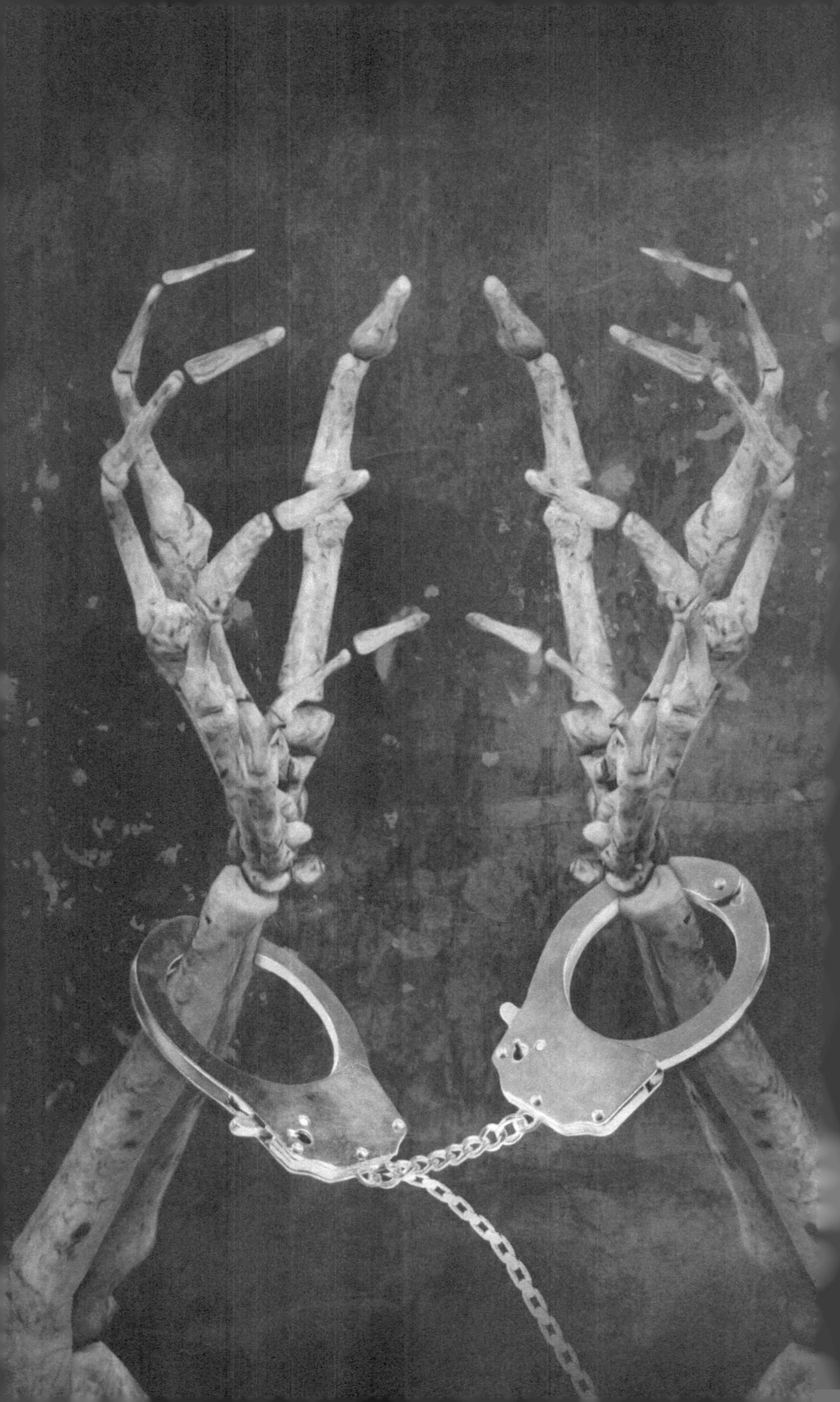

Leon was engrossed in something on his screen when I stepped through the dark entry hall, towards the living room. He didn't look up, but I knew he was aware of my presence. His body language was too relaxed, one leg draped over the side of the chair. His face was turned towards the laptop, but he wasn't seeing anything on there.

"Kurt said you were predictable," he said slowly. He swivelled around in his seat and looked over at me.

I lounged against the door frame, knife held loosely in my hand. "Not as predictable as him. Or you. You might as well have taken out an ad to say you'd be here tonight instead of tomorrow."

"That was the point, silly girl," he said, looking down his substantial nose at me. "He knew you'd figure it out and turn up. He has lots of people outside waiting for your friends. When they're done with them, they'll be up here for you." He leaned forward. "Lots of them. Too many for one little girl to deal with."

He sat back and took a sip from his coffee.

Smug prick.

"For a little girl, it took four of you to carry me down into that basement," I pointed out. "And a cage and a chain to keep me there. But you know all of that. Because you were there. Were you the one with the camera, filming Kurt violating me while I was unconscious? So brave of him that he couldn't even deal with me when I was awake."

I snorted softly and ran the tip of my knife up and down the side of my finger.

"It was Stefan who took the photos and video," Leon said easily. "He thought it was hilarious. So did Kurt, Hammer and Jase."

Apparently he had no trouble throwing his associates under the bus. People like him never did. At the end of the day, he was nothing but a coward. One who thought he had the upper hand. He was absolutely certain of it. Otherwise he wouldn't dare to taunt me. Even if he didn't know what I was, I still carried a knife I knew how to use.

"And you, no doubt," I said. It was taking all the restraint I had not to throw my knife, and put it through his eyeball. From there, it was a quick trip into his pathetic brain.

Watching him die would be as satisfying as hell, but

that would be too quick. He had to at least live long enough for me to twist the blade.

Leon shrugged. "It was just a job. I was paid well to help Kurt to get you down there. What he did to you after that was not my business."

"So you're okay with women being raped?" I asked coldly. "You were happy to see him cage me? You walked away and never gave me a second thought, as long as you got paid? That's fucked up."

It was way beyond fucked up. It was psychotic, disgusting, and made my stomach turn. What kind of man does the things he'd done? I didn't know how he slept at night. He deserved the nightmares I was tortured by.

He shrugged again. "Like I said, it was just a job. When it came to you, he was unhinged as fuck. I wasn't going to get in his way. The one person who tried ended up dead."

I couldn't help the surprise that flitted across my face.

Leon smirked. "You didn't know that, did you? Some guy named Prior, or something like that. He told Kurt he was fucked up and should let you go. He tried to stop him from touching you, but Kurt put a bullet between his eyes. The rest of us, we weren't going to argue."

I didn't remember anyone named Prior, but I respected his attempts to help me. If there was an afterlife, I sent him my thanks, along with a dose of regret that he died trying. And that he failed.

"He had bigger balls than all of you put together," I said. "Where's Kurt?"

"It doesn't matter." Leon shook his head. "There's two ways this goes down tonight. One, people are about to walk through the door, take you and give you back to Kurt, or two, you die. You don't need to know where he is. Just stand there and wait and they'll take you to him."

"And you're going to sit there and let it happen," I said darkly.

If he was right, and people were coming for me, I'd choose death. But I'd fight like hell first. "Don't tell me, you're paid well to do nothing."

"Exactly," he said. "You're finally catching on. Personally, I never understood what he saw in you."

I snorted. "Am I supposed to be offended by that? The last thing I want to be is your type. Besides, someone with balls as small as you wouldn't be able to handle a woman like me."

"Ohhh, your insults sting, little girl," he sneered. He picked up his coffee and downed the rest of it.

"Not as much as my knife will," I said. "Maybe you're right, and there are people coming for me. But I can't think of a single reason why I should leave you alive to see it."

I tapped the tip of my finger against the tip of my

blade. Not hard enough to break the skin, but enough to make his eyes widen.

He glanced backwards slightly, in the direction of the kitchen. Presumably this was where he expected Clarissa to come out and do something. Maybe help him pin me down until help arrived.

Clarissa didn't appear.

He blinked a couple of times, like his eyes were becoming heavy.

"Is it too late for you, old man?" I taunted. He couldn't have been more than in his late twenties. "Do you need a nap? I'm sure Clarissa can find you somewhere to lie down for a little while."

He blinked again and shook his head. "I'm fine."

He was clearly not fine. He was struggling to keep his eyes open. His body swayed to the side. He grabbed the table to keep from tumbling over.

"Are you sure?" I asked sweetly. "You look like you're about to pass out. I'd be very careful about doing that, if I were you. You never know what might happen to you while you're unconscious."

"You wouldn't fucking dare," he snarled, but there wasn't much force behind his words.

"No, I wouldn't, because I wouldn't want to touch you," I said. Unless it was to open a vein or two.

I moved towards him, my knife still in my hand. There was always the possibility he was faking.

If he was, he was doing a good job of it, especially

when he toppled to the side and hit the floor with a painful thud. His head rolled back and he lay still.

Clarissa stepped into the doorway that led to the kitchen. "Oops. I might have accidentally-on-purpose slipped something into that coffee. My bad." She grinned.

I managed a small smile back and slipped my knife away. "I had a feeling you were a badass."

"Through and through," she agreed. "If there's people coming for you, we better get him out of here quickly."

She stepped around him and locked the front door. "That'll slow them down," she said before grabbing his feet and dragging him towards what looked like a bedroom.

"What are you—" I started.

"There's more than one way out of here," she said. "Give a girl a hand?"

I leaned over to grab Leon's wrists and heft him up off the ground. Together, we carried him into the bedroom and over to a wardrobe.

"Wild guess what my favourite books were when I was a kid." She opened the wardrobe door and pushed the clothes aside to reveal a trapdoor in the floor. She pulled a key out of her pocket to unlock it and tugged the door up and out of the way.

Under the trapdoor was another set of stairs leading down.

"Motherfucker is gonna have some bruises when he

wakes up." Her smile suggested she was pleased by the idea. She grabbed his feet again and started to drag him down the stairs, his head bumping on each as they went.

"I'm struggling to feel bad about that," I said. If all he got was bruises, he was getting off lightly. "Where does this end up?"

Wild guess it wasn't Narnia. Although, I could use some Turkish Delight right about then.

"Down to a tunnel that goes under the street," she said. "Up some more stairs to the back of the next block. I may keep a spare car there."

"I want to be you when I grow up," I told her.

She laughed and waited until I was at the bottom of the stairs, and could grab up Leon's wrists again. We carried him through a dimly lit tunnel that smelled of moisture and disuse, and strained to lug him back up another set of stairs.

We set him down beside a door and I pulled out my phone.

"We could use some help." I sent off a quick text to Daze and Gianni to meet us outside, if they could.

A few moments later, Daze texted back that she was on her way.

I frowned at the lack of response from Gianni, but he might be busy dealing with Kurt's minions. There was no way in the world he could be dead. He was too smart for that.

I rubbed my forehead with my fingers. I was

starting to get a headache. I was also starting to wish I told Reuben of my plan.

I hadn't wanted to put any of my men in danger, but that was exactly what I'd done. I knew Kurt had something like this planned and I'd walked into it anyway. If it wasn't for Clarissa, I might be well and truly fucked.

I startled as a knock sounded on the door right beside Leon's unconscious body.

"I'll get it," Clarissa said. "In case it's not anyone friendly, I can pretend I'm working with them. I'm just trying to help Leon escape from the clutches of the enemy." She pressed the back of her hand dramatically to her forehead and grinned.

I nodded and stepped back out of sight.

She must use these tunnels more than I thought, because the bolts slid free easily and the door opened on almost silent hinges.

"Hey." Daze's voice echoed through the space. "I see you brought a friend."

Relieved, I stepped back, but grimaced at her wording. "He's no fucking friend of mine. We need to get him out of here, to Reuben's. It won't be long before…"

I caught the look on Daze's face. "Reuben is here."

"He's somewhere around here," she agreed. "He and the other men are dealing with a few bad guys. Nothing they can't—" A gunshot rang out. "—Handle." The first gunshot was followed by a second and a third.

"Just another night in Dusk Bay," Clarissa said. "Let's get this asshole into my car. He should be asleep for another few hours, but it's always a bit of a hit or miss, because it depends on their body weight and whatnot." She moved her hand back and forth, before grabbing Leon's ankles once again and dragging him out the door.

Daze and I exchanged glances before taking a wrist each and helping to throw him into the boot before Clarissa slammed it shut.

"I hope he doesn't vomit in my car," she remarked. "I hate when they do that."

I made a face and leaned against the car to send a text to Reuben. And then one to Damon. Leon better have some good answers as to where Kurt was, because I had a feeling I was going to get bawled out very soon.

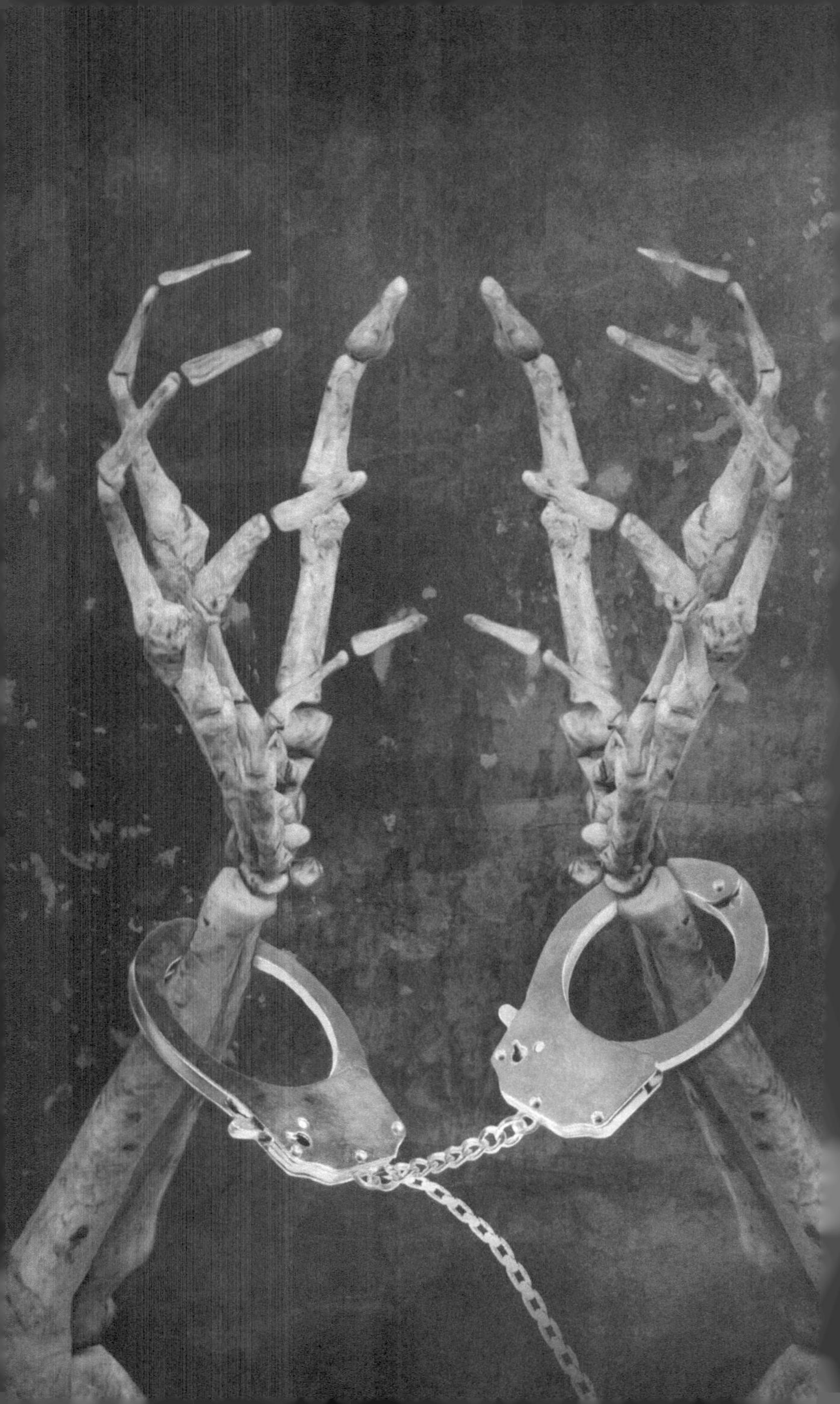

CHAPTER 24

DAMON

We'd barely finished dispatching the last of the attackers, when my phone vibrated in my back pocket. Impatiently, I tugged it out and glanced at the screen.

"It's Mina," I said. "It seems she's taken care of Leon Graves and would like to meet up with us if we're not otherwise occupied." Those weren't her exact words, but close enough.

"So I see," Reuben said dryly. He looked down at his own phone. "I trust Daze is with her."

At some point during the last hour, she'd said she was needed and darted off into the night.

She was going to be hearing about that from me and from Reuben. She was supposed to be following our orders, not hers, or even Mina's.

"That's what my message says," Gianni said. "Daze is with Mina and Clarissa. Just over..." He turned a slow circle, eyes on a map app. "Two blocks in this direction."

"Hunter, Parker stay here and wait for cleanup," Reuben said. "I want all of these bodies gone before morning. The rest of you, let's go."

"Later, bro." Hunter saluted Reuben before we turned away from them and headed away down the street.

"This has been an interesting night," Gianni remarked.

"That's one word for it," I agreed. "Except the evening part." I nodded to the east, where the sun was starting to peek above the horizon. Morning wasn't far away. Chances were, the cleanup crew would be working in daylight.

"It's been a while since we've pulled an all-nighter," Gianni said. "Does that mean we're getting old?"

"Probably." I rubbed the heel of my hand on my forehead and blinked away the weariness that began to descend. Between being up all night, running around the streets being shot at, and killing, I was exhausted.

Far from old, but feeling it right now.

"It means we have other people to do this, most of the time," Reuben said. "People we would have left this to if not for Mina." He narrowed his eyes on Gianni.

"For what it's worth, I followed her," Gianni said easily. "If I knew what she was doing, I would have stopped her and we could have done just that. Sent someone else to pick up Leon." He spread his hands to either side. "But don't tell me you didn't have fun. At least a little bit."

The glance Reuben gave him would have withered anyone else, but Gianni just grinned. "It's not like you sleep anyway."

Reuben grunted.

I shouldn't have found that sound hot, but even in my state of tiredness, I did. Maybe *because* I was so tired. I was done fighting how I felt.

"Took you long enough," Daze drawled as we rounded the corner of the building to see her standing beside a car, Clarissa nearby. "We've been waiting for ages."

"For the record, when I told Ric you were here, he said something about putting you over his knee and spanking you," I said.

She grinned. "Don't threaten me with a good time."

I smirked.

"He knows better than to think he can keep me in line anyway," she added.

The door to the back of the car was open. Mina slipped out, looking as weary as the rest of us, but more beautiful than ever.

"Thank fuck," Reuben said softly.

She trotted over to him and threw her arms around him, before dragging me in for a hug. Gianni invited himself, until we were all embracing each other. Hard bodies pressed against hard bodies. The smell of guns and blood clung to all of us. Heady, but all too real.

"Speaking of spanking," I growled.

"Any time," Gianni said. "If that's your idea of kinky, I like it."

I should have expected him to respond like that. He'd always be himself. Irreverent and possibly crazy, but always charming and, if I was going to admit it to myself, compelling.

"Be careful what you wish for," I muttered.

"If that's on the cards, I'm there for it," he said. "I have a thing about pain. I'm happy to let Mina and Reuben watch."

"I don't want to interrupt the reunion, but we only have a few hours before our guest wakes up again," Clarissa said. "I assume you're going to want him tightly under wraps before then. Not that you can't deal with anything, but…"

"Yes," Reuben said, his voice strained. "Let's get him out of here and back home."

"Is it wrong if I say I don't mind seeing him chained?" Mina asked. "I wouldn't object to him being in a cage either. He didn't mind it happening to me." She scowled in the direction of the boot of the car. I presumed Leon was safely stashed inside.

Telling my cock to behave, I made a mental note never to piss her off. I had a feeling if she served up revenge, it would hurt like hell. She really was the perfect woman.

"Whatever you want, sweetheart," Gianni said. "We can make it happen. Even if you want him hung upside down by his balls. It'll be icky, but I volunteer to touch them."

"I don't think they'll be big enough for you to fasten anything to them," she said dryly. "I'll settle for him being restrained and scared."

"I like a woman who holds a grudge," Gianni said.

"She holds one with good reason," I said.

I made another note to myself. This time to do some searching online when we got home. I had an idea for something that would make her feel much better.

"Gianni, travel with the women," Reuben said. "Damon and I will be right behind you."

"I'll try not to run into the back of your car," I said. With the right amount of force, Leon Graves would be a dead man.

"Only if you want to pay to replace it," Clarissa said. "I don't take kindly to having people…" She paused to choose her words carefully. "Ramming their car into the back of mine."

Gianni grinned.

I rolled my eyes at him before turning back to Clarissa. "I'll try to restrain myself. For the sake of your vehicle."

"I appreciate that." She opened her door and climbed inside.

I waited until all three women, and Gianni, were in the car before nodding to Reuben and trotting down the street to get ours.

Mina

I managed a few hours of sleep, but couldn't linger in bed for long. Especially when I realised I was alone.

I pulled on a pair of track pants and a singlet, and headed downstairs.

That was where I found Reuben, sitting on the couch, facing the view. He held a cup of coffee in his hand. His eyes were glazed, lost in thought.

I didn't say anything. I just lay down and placed my head in his lap.

He went on drinking slowly while running the pad of his thumb up and down my cheek.

We stayed like that, in silence, until Damon and Gianni came down the stairs.

"Morning," Gianni said cheerfully. He wasn't showing any signs of suffering from a lack of sleep. "Is anyone else looking forward to having a little chat with our guest? I'm sure he's ready to be helpful."

"He will; he's a coward." Damon said, his phone in his hand. He still looked weary, but better than he had a few hours ago, when he was all but dead on his feet.

"That seems to be the criteria for being an asshole," I said. I would have sat up, but I was too comfortable where I was. Too secure lying here with Reuben's fingers on my face, Damon beside me, and Gianni sitting in a chair opposite.

Reuben made a sound of agreement in the back of his throat. "They usually are. Any further information on Kurt?"

"Nothing yet," Damon said. "If Mr Graves is forthcoming, we'll pin him down soon." He tossed his phone down on the table. "*When* he's forthcoming. If anyone knows where Lasalle is, it's him."

"Assuming he's still there," I said. "By now, he'd know we dealt with a lot of his minions. He may disappear."

"Then we go back to Leon. He'll tell us where to look," Gianni said. "He won't be going anywhere for a while. He's too useful."

"We will find him," Reuben said firmly. "He knows we're closing in. He'll make a mistake."

"He already did," I said. "He thought Clarissa was on his side. If she was, I wouldn't be here now."

"Yes, you would," Damon said. "No way in hell we would have let Kurt take you anywhere." He locked his gaze on me, solid, unflinching and rapidly growing darker.

I didn't move while he lowered his mouth to mine and kissed me. I wrapped my arms around him, holding him to me, while Reuben continued to stroke my face.

I slid my tongue across Damon's lips and into his mouth.

He pressed a hand to my hip and stroked my tongue with his. His touch had my body on fire. I should have been exhausted, but I was energised all over again.

After a brief hesitation, he peeled up the front of my singlet and kissed his way down my cheek, across my neck and down my chest.

My eyes on him, I pulled my singlet off the rest of the way, and raised my hips to let him pull off my track pants.

Fingers trembling slightly, I touched the front of his pants, where his erection was straining, begging to be let out.

"Damon," I said breathlessly.

"Mina." He slipped his hand between my thighs and over my pussy, lightly teasing my clit.

I rocked against his hand while one of Reuben's moved down to stroke my nipple.

Damon slid a couple of fingers inside me, hooked his hand around and stroked my G spot. The heel of his hand created the perfect friction on my clit.

I arched my back, pressing my head deeper into Reuben's lap as I came.

"Good girl," Reuben said softly. "You come apart so beautifully."

That made my orgasm last longer, reaching peaks I never knew existed.

Panting, I finally came back down to earth. Damon's hand must have been drenched from my release.

I caught my breath and undid Damon's pants. I

pushed them down far enough to free his erection. My tongue darted over my lips and I swallowed.

"I… I want you." I said tentatively.

I glanced up at Reuben as he said, "Only if you're ready."

"I'm ready," I said firmly. "I want Damon to fuck me."

Damon hurried to push his pants off the rest of the way, and tossed them aside.

"Anytime you want me to stop, I'll stop," he said. Eyes on mine, he carefully knelt between my legs and pushed the tip of his cock against my entrance. He stopped there, waiting for my reaction.

I swallowed again, but nodded. "Please." I was done being scared of being intimate with them. I wanted this. I wanted it with all of them, but him first.

I needed to know I wasn't too broken to let them in fully.

Damon nodded and pushed in further, slowly, slowly easing in until he was fully seated inside me.

"Are you okay?" he asked.

"Better than okay," I assured him. "You feel good. Amazing." He filled me up so perfectly, like we were made to fit together.

As slowly as he slid inside me, he started to move, thrusting carefully, watching me the entire time. This was no wild, frantic fucking. He was gentle, tender and holding back. Just what I needed for my first time.

"You take him so well," Reuben said. "Good girl."

I looked up at him and smiled. I could feel his erection behind my head, but he made no move to satisfy his own needs. This moment was all about me. I was the centre of their world, and I loved every minute of it.

Gianni moved over to kneel beside the couch and slip his hand between my body and Damon's. Eyes slightly wider, he circled my clit with his fingers, while the rest of his hand would have felt the slide of Damon's cock as he moved in and out of my body.

"Fucking hell," Damon whispered. "This is..." He shook his head, at a loss for words.

"Perfect," I said. The way all three of them were touching me had me closer to the edge again already.

"Come for us again," Reuben said. "I want to see you come around Damon's cock."

"Okay, boss," I said, half-teasing.

I dropped my head back, matching the rhythm Damon set, rocking my hips harder and faster until I pitched over the edge again, coming harder than the first time.

My muscles squeezed Damon's cock, drawing an orgasm out of him too.

He went still, eyes half closed in focus, an expression of bliss on his face. Finally, he let out a ragged breath and sagged forward.

"Holy hell, that was incredible," he said. He leaned down to kiss me. "Thank you. Thank you for letting me be the first."

I smiled up at him. We still had a lot to deal with,

but these three men were helping me to feel whole, for the first time in years.

Damon slowly slid out of me and rolled off, almost landing on Gianni who had to hurry to get out of the way.

"Bro," Gianni complained.

Damon smirked and snagged up his pants to throw over his shoulder. "I don't know about anyone else, but I need some sleep."

"Me too," Gianni agreed. "By the time we're awake, our guest should be too. But first, let's get Mina cleaned up. After-care is important."

They both offered me their hand to stand before we headed up the stairs, Reuben right behind.

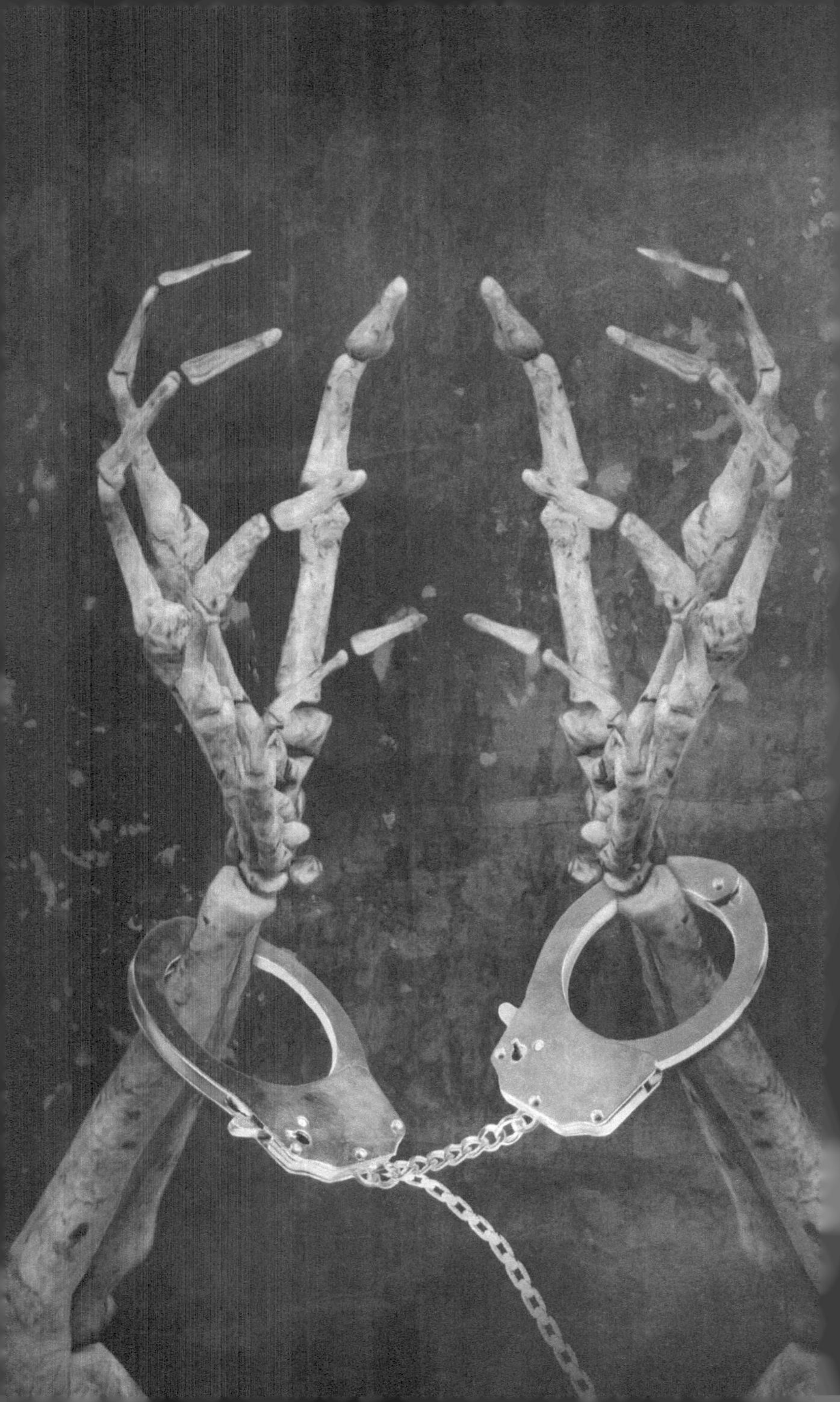

EPILOGUE

"Well, isn't this cosy?" Gianni said. He stood with his arms crossed, looking at Leon who was on the floor, his arms raised above his head. On his wrists were manacles, attached to a chain which was, in turn, attached to a ring in the ceiling.

Leon was just beginning to wake up. His head hung to the side. Finally, he roused, straightened his head and looked around himself.

"Fuck," he grunted.

"Sucks to be you," Gianni said. "Welcome to your new home away from home. All you need to do in order to get out of here is tell us exactly where Kurt is. It's that simple."

"If I tell you that, you'll kill me," he whined. He looked ready to piss his jeans.

"You might prefer that to sitting down here for days

on end," I said. "I know you have some idea what Kurt did to Mina. You were there."

Fucking piece of shit.

"You saw the conditions she was kept in. After all that time down there, all she wanted to do was die, and she's a shit ton stronger than you are. How long do you think you'll last before you beg to die? A day or two? A week? A year?"

Leon groaned. "If I tell you I don't know where he is, you won't believe me."

"That is a correct fact." Gianni pointed a finger at him. "Because we know that you know. And if you don't, we know that you know how to find him. All you have to do is tell us and this will be a lot easier on you. Personally, I don't think you deserve it, but Damon is nicer than I am."

I glanced over at him. "Since when?"

"Since I suggested I pour some acid into a bowl and place his hand into it, and you said no," Gianni said.

"I said no, put his *foot* into it," I said. "Starting with his toes. Toes are a lot more sensitive than fingers."

We hadn't had that conversation until now, but none of that mattered. The only thing that did was that Leon was listening, and his eyes were getting bigger and bigger. He had no reason to think we wouldn't follow through with everything we mentioned. Because we would, if necessary.

"Right," Gianni dragged the word out. "I guess that

means I'm nicer than you then. Hmmm, interesting. What else did you have in mind?"

"After we burn off his other foot with acid?" I asked. "Then I guess we start with his stumps. All the way up to his knees."

Leon groaned. "Please."

I leaned forward, towards him. "Please, what? Like we said, we can make this easy for you. Just tell us where Kurt is and none of this has to happen. At least..."

Leon jerked his face up towards me. "At least what?"

"I think it's only fair that we leave some of this up to Mina, wouldn't you say Gianni? She might not want to go easy on him, since apparently he didn't give a shit about what happened to her. All we can do is try to convince her that you're not a bad person. You're just a guy who got caught up in some stuff, a long time ago. What were you supposed to do? Let Kurt kill you?"

He should have done exactly that.

"Yes, yes, exactly," Leon said eagerly. "I was in the wrong place at the wrong time. I didn't want what happened to her to happen. I mean, I didn't do anything to her. I couldn't stop him, he was determined to do those things. Kurt is fucked up. He's wrong in the head. He probably should have gone to therapy or something. I mean, who locks a woman in a cage for..."

Gianni crouched down in front of him. "Five years, Leon," he said, his tone icy. "It was five fucking years. That's how long she went through all of that. That's how long Kurt did those things to her. Things I couldn't even bring myself to do to you. You're right, he is fucked in the head. But are you any better? Did you ever go to anyone and tell them she was there? Did you try?"

"Nnnn... No," Leon stammered. "But I should have. I was scared. I knew if I did, he'd... He'd know. He'd come for me. He thought of her as his property. If anyone tried to take away his property, he'd—"

Leon screamed in pain as Gianni stabbed a knife into his calf.

"Oops, I slipped," Gianni said sarcastically. "Women. Are. No one's. Fucking. Property. Especially not his. You could have come to us and told us, and we would have got her out of there. We might have even protected you. Got you a new identity and made you disappear. You could have gone off and lived your best life, instead of hiding in the shadows like a fucking coward."

Gianni gripped the hilt of the knife and twisted it.

Leon screamed again.

The sound grated on my last nerve. No wonder Reuben left stuff like this to us. The noise was painful. So much so, he'd insisted Mina sit out. To the surprise of everyone, she'd agreed and went off to have a long soak in a hot bath. That sounded like fucking heaven right now.

After this, I might even join her. If she'd let me. Fucking her was addictive. I wanted to do it again, over and over, until she was so comfortable with my cock, I could stop holding back.

Right now, I wasn't going to think too much about the spanking Gianni mentioned. That was too enticing, I needed to take time to get my head around it.

"We'll ask you again," I said calmly. "Where is Kurt Lasalle? If you don't tell us, this is going to get a whole lot worse for you."

I didn't feel too bad about that. Even if he told us everything we wanted to know, I might let Gianni continue for a while. Just for shits and giggles.

"Okay, okay," Leon pleaded. "I'll tell you everything."

I leaned against the wall and listened, my phone in my hand to record every word.

"Fucking hell," Gianni whispered when Leon was finally done.

Thank you for reading! The story continues in Corrupted. If you'd like to know what Mina and Rose talked about in Daze's house, when they went off alone, you can read that in the bonus scene here.

ABOUT THE AUTHOR

Maggie Alabaster writes reverse harem romance.

She lives in NSW, Australia with one spouse, two daughters, one dog, and countless birds.

Sign up for Maggie's newsletter! Sign Up!

Join Maggie's reader group! Join here!

Follow Maggie on Bookbub! Click here to follow me!

Check out Maggie's website- www.maggiealabaster.com

ALSO BY MAGGIE ALABASTER

Book 2 Crown of Mist and Heat

Book 3 Sword of Balm and Shadow

Book 4 Whisper of Frost and Flame

Dark Masque

Book 1 Bait

Book 2 Prey

Book 3 Trap

Saving Abbie

Book 1 Pitch

Book 2 Pound

Book 3 Session

Book 4 Muse

Book 5 Rhythm

Book 6 Encore

Novella Venomous

Saving Abbie books 1-4

Saving Abbie books 4-6 + Venomous

Ruthless Claws

Book 1 Ivory

Book 2 Crimson

Book 3 Elodie

Harmony's Magic

Book 1 Summoned by Fire

Book 2 Summoned by Fate

Book 3 Summoned by Desire

Shifter's Vault

Book 1 Discarded

Book 2 Deceived

Book 3 Disgraced

My Alien Mates

Book 1 Star Warriors

Book 2 Star Defenders

Book 3 Star Protectors

Academy of Modern Magic

Book 1 Digital Magic

Book 2 Virtual Magic

Book 3 Logical Magic

Complete Collection

Summer's Harem

Book 1: Shimmer

Book 2: Glimmer

Book 3: Flicker

Complete collection

Short reads

Taken by the Snowmen

Jingle All the Way

Also by Maggie Alabaster and Erin Yoshikawa

Caught by the Tide

Book 1–Pursued by Shadows

Book 2 Pursued by Darkness

Book 3 Pursued by Monsters